Praise for Brian Christopher Moore

Labyrinth of Dreams

"The four novels of *Labyrinth of Dreams* comprise an epic fantasy reminiscent of Charles Williams at his best. Moore's tale is beautiful and mysterious, and great fun even as it plumbs metaphysical depths. A *tour de force!"*
—Jess Lederman, award-winning novelist and founder of The Works of George MacDonald (worksofmacdonald.com)

Beneath the Silent Heavens

"Brian Moore's historical fantasy of Noe and the building of the Ark is, at times, almost more poetry than prose. Playful, profound, delirious with reality, Moore's book felt like reading 40 pages, not 250. I have to say at the start that this gem from Angelico is a must

read for all lovers of literature, regardless of their faith."
—Julian Kwasniewski, TheImaginativeConservative.org

"With melodious prose and marvelous metaphors, Brian Moore guides us through the right doors, tapping the ancient sap of our longing for Eden and probing the trials piqued by a great chain of creation that groans for redemption. He mixes high fantasy and playful comedy, traditional storytelling and novelistic philosophizing."
—Joshua Hren, founder of Wiseblood Books, author of *This Our Exile: Short Stories*

"Writing in the great Christian tradition of fantasy pioneered by Tolkien and Lewis, Moore's Beneath the Silent Heavens nevertheless leads us into new spaces of the Christian imagination, which is, as we know, inexhaustible."
—Michael Martin, author of *Transfiguration: Notes Toward a Radical Catholic Reimagination of Everything*

City in Exile

Labyrinth of Dreams, Book 2

Brian Christopher Moore

Cover art and design by Alexander von Ness, nessgraphica.com

ISBN: 978-0-9986030-6-3

Contents

Chapter One

Elnaria

Autumn

And the Elder rubbed his hands together for sheer joy at the cold arrow sharpening the air. It was the first jolt of autumn, brandishing its broom of color. It was that harbinger of death that was not cruel, but a promise of the hearth, and festival, and song. The cat, however, was not amused. She burrowed into her warm pillow and looked at him with accusation. Why had he allowed the north wind entry into the house?

"Alright," he said. "Time for a walk. I'll take the dog."

"Yes, yes," said the cat. She stretched a bit and gave a last, pleading look. She was a sweet feline. But when he left, before she forgot him until it was time for brunch, she thought "let him take that cretin dog. It likes to romp about in the muck. It brings in the odor of stories from the outer realms. I smell them when I nestle against its heaving sides, the bellows of its breath whispering of strange lands."

Malchidion

Malchidion was Guardian then. He dressed always in a dark robe, rising, like a specter that great barbaric head, his bald dome sheathed in a thick, dull skin so that no glory of light appeared to reflect back at the viewer. Indeed, darkness was his métier. His eyes were death black and set deep, dark, inscrutable wells. When Malchidion stared, the strongest would shudder.

Friends, he had few, though he had many counselors, a tribe of administrative flunkies, and lawyers who seemed to nest like spiders in the shadowed corners of buildings that he maintained. He had been Guardian so long; it was nearly forgotten who had gone before. Naturally, the clerks of Elnaria knew. The people, if they could be troubled to remember, would have, but why bother about such things?

It was whispered, because such rumors are vaguely comforting, that he kept an idiot girl as a mistress. And some said, no, but that he kept a little Chihuahua dog and fed it bonbons, but this was only a joke the clerks told as it was so perversely impossible.

The only person who dared stand up to the Guardian was Uhraine, a woman so old she seemed to have no past. Strangely, she had always been in the City, though everyone was convinced she had come from elsewhere. Some said that Uhraine was Malchidion's mother and others said Malchidion had no mother, this tavern talk, but even then, the sideward glance.

As it happens, Malchidion did have a mother, a stout, upright woman who liked early Renaissance polyphony and ancient Roman pottery. She did not, however, like her son, a fact from which can be traced Malchidion's lifelong respect and devotion to her memory.

Subterranean solidarity

The marshlands are in the south. So is the harbor, the fishermen and sailors, the loading docks and warehouse district where the chatter of a dozen tongues sought to badger and cajole a favorable commerce. The market was plenished with goods for every whim from ancient scrolls, reputedly, to cosmetics, silken cloth, oranges, plastic pez dispensers to baboons in cages. This morning, the Elder had need of a particular root that was seasonable and to be found hidden in wetland places known only to the otters, the manatee, and such as himself. When dried and crushed, it yielded a cerulean pigment of great beauty and endurance.

Leaving his residence, the Elder nearly slipped on the outer staircase and felt both foolish and awkwardly vulnerable. It was strange to age. *And I am just the same and never identical.* While crossing the long bridge, he happened upon two masters he had not seen in perhaps a decade. Their names were solidly inscribed in sleepy journals. "Great philosophers are explorers," said Péguy. "Those who are not great are those who have only thought of being solemnly accepted at the Sorbonne." Whether they remarked him or not he could not say, though they turned rather abruptly and began to whisper.

The Elder did not give a fig about these scholars. He disagreed violently with their convictions and criteria of judgment. And still, he could not forestall a certain unbidden pang of embarrassment. Such is the subterranean solidarity of humankind, that even those we abjure and disdain carry some hidden weight.

As if in token to this chapbook observation, the Elder came upon a scene both puzzling and plaintive. At the end of a long line of shops, there was a cobbled piazza that led to the ruined edifice of what was once the royal treasury. Besides this building of essentially neo-classical lines, though embroidered with a facade of baroque, if not rococo embellishment, one discovered a small villa of ancient tombs. These belonged to Guardians deceased for centuries or more. It was not conceivable that any of the interred held a significant connection to the living.

Nonetheless, a young woman with long, lustrous hair was washing one particular monument of solemn obsidian. As she did so, she sobbed and wiped the engraved name with her unbound locks. Though she invited the stares of passersby, no one was eager to seek explanation.

Further on, in the market, a mélange of gaudy sights, noises and odors competed for attention. Disputes and gregarious haggling employed familiar tactics. Near the docks, a blind beggar boy chanted: *sat-chit-ananda, sat-chit-ananda.*

The most noble color

There was an interesting quarrel between Goethe and Newton regarding color and light. Curse this machining of the cosmos. Mass, the *res extensa*, quantifiable, objective, that they grant. Color as a refracted wavelength, something that registered on a meter, yes, that they would acknowledge as well without having the slightest notion how a mechanism of electro-chemical firing of neurons in the brain produced the experience of *qualia*.

So with boneheaded hubris they did away with judgment and wisdom and the pull of the Good called forth by beauty. And blue is the most noble, most mysterious of colors.

Earlier, yes, he thought it must be earlier, though tenses, certitudes of past and futurity, well, all that was something of a pose when everything was dancing, *epektasis*. Did they know? No, of course not. How could they?

Only yesterday, the way yesterday is, he'd been talking with a fellow, a sharp man with verses in his head. The Elder and he shared a nice conversation on an astrolabe belonging to his son. Now, according to the usual calculations, the poet had been dead for centuries. Folks thought that way. They were used to their fellows dropping off, coming from the nothing and then entering into the dust, untimely, violent, sick, serene, gentle, many ways into that night.

And then they were in the habit of thinking of the untold ages that preceded them, tens of thousands of years, generations back, the bulk forgotten, utterly nameless – a long time, though not so long as the memory of the land which reached back into aeons.

The astronomers speculated so many cycles that no one could truly think that number, but you could say it, write it down times ten to an exponential. But sticking to the life, not yet accounting for the slow, soft, rooted vegetation, or the long, wooded memory of trees, or the rapid, beating metronome of a mouse's heart, thinking only of the tongued creatures who tell tales, these thought a vast, great distance between the unlettered or silenced tongues, what's the difference, in the end, when all enter the silence?

Anyway, they thought of those times as far apart, spatialized, so that oceans of time separated them. But soul stuff is strange. It might be otherwise. The lived and vital times, the time of limb and hands that touch, eyes that see and beseech, they can touch too, in scorn, pass by indifferently, love, that mystery, the touching that is love, well, say all that is the expression of a present, a present that does not dim or pass.

You don't think that way. You see the comings and the dropping off, the latter like disappearance into a void. Only the afterimage of private memory or public renown keeping the nothing at bay, that's how it seems. And then the time of forgetting gets longer and longer, that's how the past gets further and further away.

The intimacy might be deeper, the nearness something that doesn't vanish like broken perception. Rather than a spool of ever expanding thread, time might be intensity of light, unified, refracted, the scattering more like a fountain renewed from an infinite source. It might appear more a night's sleep of distance amongst all the generations, and then not even that.

A flickering creature

An idea, like a subtle fragrance, tugged at the edge of his consciousness. It teased him with close company. A flash of childhood. He remembered paper and colored wax. One begins to know not with the naked mind, not in a language of pure concepts, but in the flesh. The body, neither subject nor object, but a permeable boundary that was somehow both and neither, interwoven polarity.

The Elder sighed, unable to yet discern what was beckoning to him. The evening before at the house of Rabbi Naftali, that soft, electric shiver across the hair of one's arms had alerted him. They had been talking of the living creatures, the *nephesh hayyah*. The Living was a quality most mysterious. It can be approached only with finesse.

Naftali recalled that in the *Zohar*, there are seven types of earth. *Eretz* signifies land, for instance. *Adamah* is the ground or soil. As Adam means man, *adamah* is a kind of yearning of the dust. It was not the force of compulsion that drew the earth from the four corners of the world to the summons of *Yahweh Elohim*. It was desire. The ground quivered in ecstasy as the breath of life penetrated the human form and touched the soil.

The Elder thought of that wonderful observation of Hadley Hemingway's made poignant by the irony of time's inexorable flow and the frangible nature of the young lovers. They were charming and sincere and artful from an era that had its poseurs. The first, best wife remarked how there are many sorts of hunger and more in spring and that memory is hunger.

Memory is also the hidden depth where the mysterious particularity of the human race resides and is disclosed. While it is true that regrets and horror sear deep the house of Mnemosyn, the most humane, most sacred places in the heart preserve and protect with gentle tenderness traces of childhood wonder, moments of courage and sacrifice buried under the mundane and thus only lately understood. Recollection is the homage of living men and women set against the disaster of death, or so many thought.

A light tear came to his eye as the image of a friend from childhood's dream suddenly stood before him. She was singing, no speaking in that mocking, gentle, and daring way, how to explain her, she couldn't possibly exist? And then he heard his old papa hovering over a typewriter gathering dust, the music of the Swan Princess, he said, would heal the wounds of time.

Then Feirefiz suddenly sprang forward, the faithful dog not minding his word, but joyous, as if flouncing along, having cleared the brush after retrieving a felled woodcock.

Then he saw her, too.

It was only a blink's ration. The girl leaned with languid insolence against a pillar devoted to an ancient naval victory. It was the same dark hair, thick, shoulder length, the delicate face of an artist's model joined to the coltish indifference of a waifish tomboy. Her mocking brown eyes were sad and troubled, however.

The Elder must have shocked some with his sprint to the obelisk. His search was vain, the girl a flickering creature.

The truth is a tension

The truth is a tension. Like a walker on the high wire, one must deftly negotiate the complex art of discernment.

The Elder stepped lightly upon the wet sand, resting on a sandbar large enough to be a small island. In the distance, he saw a pair of loons. Though the strange music of their call was mute, he heard them in memory, and in memory he recalled the far stranger music that had called him from his weary slumbers, his permanent discontent and disappointment, called to him precisely when he thought he had stopped listening.

He was still vates hearkening to the call. A glistening shell caught his eye, a shiny thing he rooked to with flying, whimsical, aviary avarice. He caught it in his hand and held it in the plane of his palm.

A boy named Joe had once held such a shell and pondered its soft, regular curve. The charm of it had made him smile in his heart and think the universe a wonderful puzzle. Years later, he was killed making the landing at Normandy, a gush of crimson offal spilling like butcher's waste upon the beach.

Et a sens le mot joie
Malgré la mort
Là où creuse le vent
Ces braises claires.

And the word joy has meaning
In spite of death
There where the wind will stir
These burning embers.

  ---Yves Bonnefoy, from "There in the Hollows of the Wind"

Faruiza

Fog was the name the children gave to the old man with the pigeons. He could be seen sitting in a garden chair dragged up to the roof of the apartments, talking to his birds. Sometimes he would carry up a cello. The fella was still vigorous. He'd play a soothing, melancholy tune that would float along the horizon, cling to lines of wash, and make children stop their play and stare whilst others suddenly grew pensive and remembered lost loves.

It was near dusk. The Elder decided to wait till he saw the first star. He'd give her that long before declaring the end to his vigil. He rubbed his beard nervously and peered sharply into the sky. Then there was a flutter of wings, the favorite returned.

"Faruiza," he said with happy relief, "I am too old for scares."

He saw then with wonderment that a bright piece of paper had been tied to her leg.

"Come, come, dear one," he called to her.

He unwrapped the scroll and recognized the hand from a lifetime ago.

He had begun to forget her face

He had begun to forget her face. Incomprehensible treachery, but there it was. The arch look her brow assumed when she was playful, the nearly shocked expression, as if a child suddenly slapped by a stranger, when sad. He had begun to forget. *If I forget, you truly will be dead.*

And then one day he dreamed and did not know he was dreaming. She stood before him radiant in all her glory, naked on the beach. He was asleep in his dream, and she was pouring salt water from a conch onto his body and laughing. And he looked up and there she was. He thought nothing of it. It was not strange. They were living their life as they had always been meant to do.

Then a little breeze kicked up and sent her tangled hair whipping across her face. He sat up and rubbed the sleep from his eyes and in that moment she had crept down next to him and pressed her warmth against his. She whispered gently into his ear. Words in a language he was well familiar with, as old and comfortably his as her body. He fingered the tiny butterfly etched across her right shoulder blade and waited for the syllables of her message to come clear, but for a long time they meant nothing to him.

Like a lost child he clung to her, kissing her neck and smelling the fragrance of her. The words became one with the air, the gulls soared upon it, the sea murmured, insolent mystery, for no man could reckon with the tale.

He held her – and it was not in the sea. Closing his eyes, he held her – and it was not in the breeze. Whispering her name – silence.

Her name on his lips, he awoke to solitude.

A name for wandering

What was before was a blur she could not remember; it was a taste a name a face just on the edge of recovery a tang of sharp experience, it was *her her her* but she could not find herself wandering the City she had wandered in a new section how new she did not know but its sleek metallic overpasses crossed the horizon with unsurprised calm to be fifty feet up where pedestrians strolled and chatted amiably and looked about there was a boy carried on his father's shoulders laughing and pointing at a vendor who was selling balloons and down below them a fountain with a sculpture of black stone and steel and fluorescent, plastic lips it was bizarre with mechanical mobile parts hippos and biplanes and a long train that shot forth a plume of spray and made everyone smile it was very nice how odd artists are to think up all that and yet she kept walking because there did not seem anywhere to be or any reason to stop and all the while tearing at her sleeve like a lost sad child was the thought that she could not remember it was causing her to get a chill and she thought she might cry and everyone would look and ask her why and then she would be embarrassed and even more scared so she hurried herself and walked and walked until she came to the edge where the new part was lying next to the Old City like a puppy resting bumptiously against the old hound that was dozing in the noonday sun there was a row of shops with windows filled with fashion and gadgets and a travel agency with posters advertising adventurous venues and one in colorful inks that reminded her of Cassandre it had tall buildings and large airships like aerial cetaceans living maternal navigators that would take one across fantastic spaces and in bold script it enticed one promising a Sky Odyssey it was really too scrumptious but then her heart began to fail her again she felt a strange sobbing in her and if only her friend was there with it would have been lovely so she kept going and going and going feeling she must drop any minute but she did not nor did she abandon the canvas bag she carried and then after a while a terror began to grip her for why didn't she why not she was tired wasn't she it was odd not to be but she kept walking and walking and the rest of the City fell into darkness and night revels and then silence and many slept but she was still walking it was well what was it endlessly traipsing about with no notion who one is and where one is going and she thought yes everyone is like that only some don't know and some are too scared to say and probably thinking they are the only one and then it was very very quiet so quiet that one could hear the settling noises of old buildings and the scratches like the claws of tiny animals in the walls of silence and still she could not stop like the girl with the magic red shoes and she began to see them the eyes it was so strange the eyes coming out of a lamp post or the middle of an empty bench or sometimes the neck of an old drunkard wheezing and crumpled like a twisted rag of carpet why should they look at her like that and she felt the night grimace and stick a collective tongue out at her and then the doors started to open and haggard blind faces turned towards her they could not see they were blank blank blank lacking features altogether yet they turned with a kind of mechanical rigor so that they pointed as a flake of iron in water towards their true north each flawlessly discerning her shadow and her steps as she walked by and she ran a few steps her heart like a startled horse but she could see no path at all every step was lost and aimless and a vertigo took hold and she felt she should sink then and there in a heap upon the cobblestones except for fear that something was coming relentlessly tracking merciless to its prey and the skin on her sparked and she felt a malice like a razor that would slowly cut away all her skin and take her eyes and gloat or perhaps nothing at all just flay her and move on as if she had never been more than a vapor her very being was a cry for help and nothing came and no one saw her and silence like the blood dripping slowly from the martyrs hung upside down to slow their agonizing deaths mocked or insipidly ripped into a naked scar of pain with only cold eyes and silence and darkness and no tenderness or pity just silence and drip drip drip before an unwelcoming dark though somewhere some were thriving and throwing parties and congratulating themselves on success and no one cared and no one ever cared for it was a curse to be born don't ever be born that was the best advice and no one heard her cry and no one regarded her death and she was left skinless and blind and it was as if she never had been and perhaps it was like that all a mirage a fake it was a mistake to think one had a face but then she was at the bridge the moon casting down a great net of ghostly light upon a strikingly tall beautiful one he was dressed in a dark cloak and tunic with a belt of silver it was like a picture his hair was long and silver and he was peering down from the bridge and there was a great impossible kind of midnight tiger with ice blue eyes and every now and again he would speak to the big cat they couldn't possibly be real but she crept up slowly and before she knew it she was at the bridge and normally she might have been afraid but she wasn't and the tiger said a kind of aloof but polite in the high manner hello and then the Man looked at her and said, "You've been walking a long time" and she thought "No one has spoken to me in a long time" so she said "yes and she was getting ruddy tired" though she wasn't and that was the problem it was scaring her but she didn't say and then she walked over and stood shoulder to well somewhere in the vicinity of the abdomen he was so tall and they looked and there from the bridge they saw a mass of glowing barges and flashes of light that seemed to fall from the stars and he started talking about the Off-Worlders and she looked intently wondering if her friend was among them though she could not remember his name either only a sort of smile in her soul and he asked her again if she was tired and could he find her a place to stay and what was her name and then she could not help it but began to cry and she could tell him barely nothing and she suddenly felt very tired and she told him the first thing that popped in her fool head and so that is how it was and she had a sort of lifting and floating sensation and later she wondered if she had dreamed it all and in any event that was how she remembered it before she woke and heard the cello playing she must have told him her name and then she thought it was rather clever of her and everyone called her Sky Odyssey what a lark.

Cat amongst the pigeons

Sky Odyssey awoke from a deep, refreshing sleep to find herself on a low couch wrapped in soft bedclothes. She was certainly not at home. Confused, but not alarmed, she sat up and gazed with bemused detachment at an odd chamber of pillars and books. A brooding melody fell moodily from the rafters. She stretched and cast off linen clean, but betraying a scent of cedar and mothballs.

Following the music, Sky ascended a stairway and entered into a cluttered attic. She was momentarily startled by a headless clothes mannequin and movement that turned out to be her own image in a standing mirror. Orphan pieces of furniture, trunks marked by stickers from far-flung destinations, and numerous stacks of books were vaguely drawn by the dim light of nascent dawn that filtered through a small rounded window.

Sky discovered a box of matches in an ancient armoire and lit a hurricane lamp still carrying a swish of kerosene. This antique had come with the Takashimas, but had long since drifted up from below. Midori was ever installing recently purchased usurpers and sending the outcasts to commiserate in the attic.

She changed out of her blouse and cowgirl skirt, revealing a tall, voluptuous body full of muscle and riding bruises. Sky examined her image held in the mirror. Big-boned, they would call her, though she wasn't given to fat. She opened her canvas bag and pulled out a long linen gown for sleep. "Too late," she laughed.

Not alone, for out with the gown came an unannounced stowaway. Rising like silver breath was a face that settled first on the mirror and then on the window. Sky knew its kind. She had often seen its like when she followed a solitary path. This was some small attendant angel, the ghost of a stalagmite, perhaps. They were usually quiet, shy and slow.

The spirit looked upon Sky, its eyes compassionate, understanding, yet sad. Without words, it lamented her migration. For a long moment it bid her farewell, this surprise, this last and longing survivor unwilling to part, and then it was gone, leaving behind only a faint mineral odor redolent of caves and cool, dark spaces.

Sky briefly wondered if there had been a basin or small sink in the room with the divan. With a sigh, she rummaged through her carry-all for signs of identification. There was no clue, no helpful tag, not even a monogram. There was, however, a thick black woolen turtleneck and a long plaid skirt. "I suppose I like this," she commented.

A loft ladder led to a hatch in the roof. Sky pushed upon the hatch and emerged at the top of a brownstone. An elderly man sat with his back to her bowing a cello to the new sun. She was within a few paces when he stopped and turned to her. He was silver-haired, bearded, with dark, piercing eyes. Against the morning cold, he wore a long gray coat and a black beret.

A Persian cat, a calico of silver and pumpkin and cream, appraised the newcomer with a mixture of suspicion and curiosity. To the Elder's left was a small wooden dovecote painted white and covered in chicken wire. A half dozen pigeons cooed from within the structure.

"A long time ago, in a different world, I was someone else," he said.

This did not seem to Sky the most direct mode of introduction. "Aren't you afraid your cat will kill the pigeons?"

He gently patted the head of the calico. "Audrey is afraid of pigeons. She is only present because I am here to protect her."

Morning in Elnaria

The Elder invited Sky to break fast with him. As she suddenly realized she was as hungry as the Mongol hoards, this was not a bad idea. They retraced her steps back to the room where she had slept. He told her she was in the apartment of the Takashima's. The Elder resided two doors over. The attic had been separated off by bulkheads, though most sections possessed trap doors leading onto the roof.

Shortly afterwards, Mr. Takashima entered. He was a short, compact man with a stern face and merry eyes. He bowed to the Elder and expressed in a soft voice of broken English the hope that Sky had slept well. How precisely she had ended up in the

Takashima apartment was left unstated and unresolved. Before she could pursue the question, the Elder had delicately, but quite deliberately escorted her down three flights of stairs and onto the sidewalk outside the brownstone.

"Well, Sparrow," he began, "there is a little café not far from here that makes excellent omelets . . . and blintzes. There are also waffles with powdered sugar and a bittersweet espresso you may like."

Sky's stomach duly noted the savory promises, but she was distracted by colorful townhouses and the early energy of the morning. From one doorway an argument about packages ended in bickering rudeness. At another, a carriage stopped and deposited two young children.

Following them out of the vehicle was a creature very slim with long, graceful limbs. Although roughly humanoid in shape, there was also something vaguely suggestive of an insect in its bearing. The chest was narrow and long pointed like a thorax towards a relatively tiny abdomen that allowed for a waist beyond the ambitions of any corset. Its skin was milk white.

Whether fashion or the need for protection from the sun, the creature's outfit was designed to cover all but the neck and face. The sleeves extended fabric to include a glove for the hands which were finely shaped with long, narrow digits. The torso was covered in dark brocade, but the rest was a flamboyant crimson rendered in a cloth that was somewhat like silk, though perhaps more durable.

All this in a second, for the Elder neither altered a brisk pace, nor answered to her curiosity. They turned sharply right and followed a narrow alley that merged into a little square, one side of which was taken up by a low building with awnings of striped cinnamon and white. Round wooden tables were set up along the walk.

The sun cast the pleasant first warmth that pierces, but does not overwhelm a brisk morning chill. The Elder asked her if she would prefer to eat inside, but the prospect of watching the life of the city enticed Sky to choose an outdoor table. There was so much she wanted to say and ask, so much that she could not think where to start and ended up saying nothing.

The Elder certainly understood this. He bestowed a severe smile upon her.

"Some people like adventures and some do everything they can to avoid them."

Sky rather liked adventures, she felt certain, without being able to justify her feeling.

"But there is one adventure that no one can aver. Pushed out the door without a map, as they say." There was a slightly malicious twinkle in his eyes.

A young woman in her twenties who had been sitting at a nearby table suddenly rose and approached them. She carried a book in one hand and sported a short, careless coif.

"Benedicta!" exclaimed the Elder, evidently pleased. "May I introduce Sky Odyssey? Sky is new to Elnaria."

Benedicta glanced at her with dark intensity. "A pleasure to meet you," she said with warmth and offered a firm handshake.

When the newcomer had joined them, the Elder and Benedicta spoke briefly about mutual acquaintances. Then Benedicta turned to her and explained that there was a malady common to Off-Worlders that resulted in amnesia. It was sometimes only partial and perhaps temporary.

"But I don't remember arriving here at all," Sky declared, feeling ridiculous, angry, and woebegone all at once.

"It will come to you, by and by," said the Elder.

"But isn't it strange?"

"No more than everything else."

Sky did not know if the Elder meant reality in general or Elnaria in particular, but just then the waiter brought her banana crepes and poached eggs with sausages and tiny biscuits with a little chocolate kiss in the center. A tear fell down her cheek. She was momentarily embarrassed, but then she thought it doesn't matter and it didn't.

Servants of the Sha-Rule

On the way back to the Takashima's apartment, the Elder explained that Sky was not to worry about funds. As to where she should stay, the Elder suggested she remain with the Takashima's. He assured her they would be glad of her company and would treat her as a member of the family. Sky thought of Mr. Takashima.

"He acts very formal, but his eyes can't help laughing."

"You haven't met his wife," said the Elder.

Sky could not tell if this was a warning or a commentary on Mr. Takashima's irrepressible mirth. She would have pursued the matter further, but just then an eerie cry, deep and sustained, shook the morning air. It utterly surprised Sky.

As for the citizens of Elnaria, she noted an ambivalent response. It seemed to her that they acknowledged something terrible in the sound as one would respect nearby thunder. And yet clearly they were also used to it. A short pause, almost nothing, and they returned to their various concerns.

"The Shiriloth," declared the Elder. "They are raised by the Anshari, but when they have reached maturity, they become creatures of the Sha-Rule."

This could mean nothing to Sky and she shrugged her shoulders in unconscious irritation. The Elder gestured towards a group of pale courtiers similar to the one Sky had seen emerge from the carriage. "The Anshari are native to Elnaria. You will see what they are like."

After the caesura of the mournful skirl, there was an almost comical beep. A youth on a bright red motor scooter quickly zoomed past them. The Elder watched it with fleeting nostalgia.

"You like that sort of thing?"

"What, to be a young man with bravado and daring ignorance? To navigate deathless because not believing in one's own mortality, to soak in the elemental energies of life and believe them one's own?"

"Do you always answer questions that way?"

"Which way is that, Sky Odyssey?"

"The way that nobody ever understands you," she said, sticking her tongue out at him.

"You will understand when it is time for you to understand."

"You're doing it again," she said.

Hoolie Hoolies

For the next few weeks, she hardly saw the Elder. The Takashimas made up a room for her with a four-posted bed and thick bed curtains lustrous as the wine dark sea. Mrs. Takashima provided her with an eclectic array of vintage clothes that fit her reasonably well. There was a gray poodle skirt and a flapper's cocktail dress and a long coat that could have been army surplus from World War One.

"Fat like the sun," said Mrs. Takashima, whether in indictment or approval was hard to say.

Sky spent an inordinate amount of time looking out of the window at an establishment across from the apartment. Its signage encouraged its patrons to imbibe Townie's Brown ale, though she doubted anyone was so particular. In the evenings before dusk, the children would clamber about, unsupervised, playing at stick ball, roller skating, or dare devilling on their bikes. She half expected to see a baseball card stuck in the spokes.

Once, she saw the Elder walking home. His expression was serious and preoccupied. A few children approached him, but he kept on, oblivious, until their courage gave out. Then a few self-designated toughs snickered behind his back and called him old Fog. At this, he stopped, turned about, and glowered at the whisperers. The boys began to mumble and stare at the ground. A few girls, in on the joke, came forward then. This game they played ended with a parceling out of jawbreakers, jelly babies, and chocolates wrapped in silver foil.

On two evenings, the Elder received visitors. A number of Hasidic Jews came by dressed in dark, somber clothing and speaking Russian or Yiddish. For all that, they appeared happy among themselves and laughed when the door to the Elder's apartment was opened to them. On another evening, Benedicta showed up accompanied by a tall figure she saw only from the back. He wore a pleated white cassock, but Sky could determine nothing else before they disappeared into the Elder's place.

Sky had to admit she felt rather dropped and left out.

"Fruit bats," she said, and tried on a green gabardine jacket and soft brown leather boots to make herself feel better. Indeed, they were so lovely she felt compelled to do a walkabout if only to be seen in such a splendid outfit.

Though she had extended her range a bit, Sky was reticent to adventure too great a distance from the brownstone. She followed a familiar circuit that took her past a florist shop, a seller of Tibetan singing bowls, and a grocer with a pet mynah bird that swore in several languages. It didn't seem to matter if you laughed, were offended, or took umbrage and swore back. The bird laid down the same cards over and over.

But one day, Sky drew her face close and stared into the rude bird's eyes.

"Is that really kind?" she asked.

"I love you," said the mynah bird.

After that, they were friends. The grocer was closed, however, and the flowers were somnolent, their colorful songs muted into gray dullness. The sight of them drained her and she contemplated ending her jaunt. With a kind of dogged insistence, however, Sky attempted to push out one street over which was new territory for her.

Almost immediately, she regretted the decision. The dark cobblestone street was sunken and filled with ponds of stagnant water. A block of dirty yellow buildings with windows boarded or encased in iron lattice work exuded a mood of seedy despair.

A number of cackling old men in thin tee-shirts were throwing dice against a wall. From the darkness of an external staircase, a solitary vagrant held a bottle wrapped in a brown paper bag close to his chest. He eyed her warily whilst hovering over a nearby heat vent. She was about to turn and go when the vagrant called out to her.

"Sister, have you got a match?" This was a hopeless and not very original line.

"You're not a sailor, are you?"

"Not that I recall. Why do you ask?"

"No reason."

"A man has got to be somewhere. If he didn't have a body, he could be left alone."

"That's very profound. I'll write it down when I get home."

"Didn't anyone tell you, sister?"

"Tell me what?"

"Well, if you don't know."

"I think you better tell me, now that you brought it up."

"Ahh, it's better if you don't know."

Sky had known drunks like this before. Most likely, he had nothing to say. He would keep hinting and winking and in the end, all he wanted was a quick feel. She shrugged and started to walk away when his bibulous voice came careening after her.

"Elnaria is a prison planet. They like to pretend it isn't, but that's just what it is."

"Rather elaborate for a jail, don't you think?"

"What else have they got to do? Keeping you down is part of the fun. I don't blame them. Meanness is the only reliable pleasure in life, I say."

"You're not a very nice fella."

The drunk ignored her or took it as a compliment. "Anyway, why they take away our memories if they've nothing to hide? They got them all stored away somewheres."

"Who are they, exactly?"

He looked at her with incredulity and then suspicion. "Them. Everyone knows about them."

"I don't."

The man shuddered, then pulled his overcoat around him and curled up against the grate. He appeared to have forgotten her. Then softly, with a child's voice, he cried out into the night.

"When the Hoolie Hoolies come, they see right through you. Their eyes are fire. You become ash. Then the wind blows and scatters you to nothing."

Perchance to dream

The next morning, she knocked on the Elder's door. Her resolution was equally distributed amongst anger, confusion, and diffidence. This equation produced a sharp, though courteous rapping which the Elder answered with an exasperating serenity that all too evidently expressed his complete satisfaction and certainty that not only was it Sky Odyssey at the door, but precisely on time.

The interior of the apartment surprised her. A large circle had been cut away from an interior wall to provide entrance to a sitting room. A thin iron post with a spiked finial was placed in the center of the opening, from which a wave of delicate filigree made up of flowers and curlicues extended to the outer circumference. The remaining, unimpeded half revealed chairs low and wide, padded to surfeit in a light, embroidered fabric.

The room itself was a mixture of high, vertical lines interspersed with more fine metalwork that mimicked the curve of nature. Sky was momentarily delighted and astonished, so much so that she forgot the weight of her emotions and merely stared at the cat. Audrey, in fact, looked rather cross. "I suppose this is her room," she thought, and then, "of course, that will be true of the entire."

When she took occupancy of one of the chairs, the feline response was so unequivocal that Sky had to fight back the urge to apologize.

"I have some questions," she said.

Then Sky rambled rather breathlessly. None of it was ordered right and she gushed in the end trying to convey a feeling of unbearable sighing that was continually tearing her apart. The Elder paused, as if he were making sure Sky was entirely done.

"Time," he said, "is rather like water to a fish. The piscine professor thinks he knows all about it, because he's lived in it all his life. It's only when he's on the hook and flailing about in the boat that he suddenly looks about and gasps with his last breath, 'Ah, so *that* is water.'"

Then the Elder went over to a samovar and poured some tea into delicate little cups shaped like tulips. It was warm and soothing, with a hint of cinnamon.

"This is the place where the soul has its roots. Your whole life, with all its history, has moved secretly in this world."

Musame and the clock

Afterwards, Sky was conscripted to help Mrs. Takashima run her little errands which were mostly forms of shopping. Sky saw Benedicta picking through tables of second-hand books, but when she tried to stop and say hello, the constant refrain of "Musame, come now" kept her in tow. Later, she thought she saw the tall brown man in the white robe that had accompanied Benedicta on a visit to the Elder's. She would dearly have liked to follow him around and find out what he was up to, but "Musame, come now" would not allow it.

Finally, now encumbered with a small army of boxes and bags containing Midori's purchases, she found herself standing below the most delicious clock tower. The clock face was a beautiful and complicated mechanism that showed the hours in both Arabic and Latin numerals, along with a smaller circle with the signs of the zodiac and fixtures meant to indicate a sun and what was either a moon or Elnaria herself.

Enameled blues and golds formed a pattern of circles and half waves that evidently conveyed further information, though its arcane meaning was lost on Sky. Four allegorical figures, two on each side, guarded the clock face. On the left, there was a bright stepping youth who looked into a mirror which obscured his face from those below. Next to the vainglorious and hidden youth was a man of middle age. He carried a walking stick in one hand and a flask of some kind in the other. He peered steadfastly across the clock face, staring fixedly upon a third figure. This was death, a skeleton with a blue cloak draped over its left shoulder. The skull did not return his gaze, however, but searched with its empty sockets the busy folk below who would only notice him if they wondered about the time.

Between death and the last figure a lantern was hung. Blithely unaware or indifferent to the nearness of mortality, the fourth figure held an object Sky could not quite make out. It was either an oversized key or a musical instrument, some strange kind of lyre. If the Elder had been there, she could have asked him what it meant and he would have told her something inscrutable, but at least it would have been an answer.

When she mentioned it to Midori, all she got for her trouble was "Musame, it is clock," and an exasperated pull upon her arm that said she was a most obstinate and silly girl.

I only want to remember

Several days later, Sky was invited to visit the Elder. She knocked at the appointed time to no avail. Then she tried the door and found it open. Not quite sure what to do, Sky stuck her head in and called out. The first thing she noticed was the sound of other voices. This should not, perhaps, have been surprising. She'd already seen people coming to and fro, though so far Benedicta was the only one of the Elder's circle that she had actually been introduced to.

Thinking that she was now to become acquainted with someone new, Sky rather self-consciously followed the sound of conversation. However, when she entered the chamber from which the voices appeared to emanate, there was self-evidently no one present but the Elder.

Sky stood open-mouthed a moment, then decided she already looked fool enough, so didn't ask an obvious question. The room was a kind of portmanteau between an artist's studio and a lumber room. For his part, the Elder remained silently reading a small volume bound in green goatskin. His chair, an elaborately carved sculpted animalia cushioned with thickly woven brocade padding, looked as if it might have once served as throne to Prester John.

Long, rectangular windows allowed for copious natural light. The sun in mid-afternoon slanted luminous shafts that hurled themselves like waves against a clutter of boards and sheets of metal, stacks of books and papers interspersed with hammers, knives, paints and rough hewn rock.

Apparently, the Elder did not hear the voices or did not think them worthy of explanation. Instead, he set his book down upon a small reading table and cordially related to the girl the existence of starlings the color of iridescent blue that could be discovered around Lake Tana in Abyssinia.

"I think they call it Ethiopia now," observed Sky, surprised to find such knowledge arising from hidden memory.

"Yes," smiled the Elder, "there is a lovely umber cat with a soft golden undercoat that goes by the former name. Do you happen to recall the late emperor, Haile Selassie? He kept cheetahs for pets and claimed a lineage that went back to Solomon. Forced into exile during the war by the Italians. A questionable fellow, perhaps, but that was a brutal affair. "

"I don't believe we've met," said Sky.

Among the works haphazardly thrown together, a copy of Picasso's *Girl Before a Mirror* was set incongruously next to an icon of the Mother of God and John the Forerunner known as the *Deisis*. The Elder said that there were several versions of the icon and that this *Deisis* was written (icons are written and not painted he noted in passing) to translate for fleshly eyes the prayer at the Last Judgment for the pardoning of sinners. The Theotokos and the Angelic prince intercede that Mercy might be realized in Justice.

As such, he explained, it transgresses the distance between time and eternity. Sky was reticent to explore theology and refused to be bated into a discussion of said time and the somewhat too much eternity. Now the Elder began to tell Sky of how the writers of icons endured a long apprenticeship and of how different masters specialized in the making of various parts of the icon. For instance, some were experts in the folds of the saint's robe and others were dedicated to the gold leaf which was the light of eternity.

And then the Elder began to tell her of the artisans whose only task was the establishment of the saint's ears, but when he said this, a note of skepticism entered the countenance of the girl and the Elder could not continue without grinning and both were happy and laughed at the joke.

The Elder showed her a board of red alder wood. He eyed the grain along the *kovcheg*, and then placed the board before him, contemplating the empty space as if the icon were mystically already written.

"This is hard to explain, Sparrow, but we are porous beings, much more so than folks often believe. There are borders everywhere and in our ordinary actions, we cross realms. The way we speak and perceive are actions, forms of diplomacy and aggression, depending on the choices we make. Many people live their whole lives unaware that they act for and against kingdoms."

Sky wondered if all this was a roundabout way to acknowledge the voices, but if it was, the Elder never came out and said so. Instead, he rather pedantically insisted on saying what evidently he found important that she should hear, even if it was theology.

"The icon is not a snapshot, nor a summary judgment from a static eternity. It is, rather, a peering into the Hallow Ways, a choosing of elements that suggests an essential quality that persists and unfolds in endless novelty."

"I see," said Sky, meaning not at all, but the Elder was presently concerned with giving the lesson, presumably to be reflected upon and perhaps made helpful on that always promised occasion when everything would start to make sense.

"Not everyone can be a name-giver," he said. "Imagination is a kind of memory. In the *Cratylus*, Plato says only he who sees that each thing has by nature a unique gift is able to express the true form of things. This is the art of the vates, to be a true artificer of names."

The Elder evidently found some satisfaction in this last, adding only that it was Hermogenes, a Mumbo Junkie, who sneered and said a name is only convention.

This was too much for the girl to take in. Sky pointed at the Picasso which appeared to be a nude woman reconfigured as a cubist-surrealist jigsaw, whose mirror image was darker, death-tinged. It was not perhaps entirely clear.

"And what's her name?"she asked.

Rather than answering directly, the Elder related the opinion of a former master who held the prejudice that the Renaissance was decadent, choosing a passive, malleable surface upon which the artist painted an indulgent illustration utterly blind to form and that the moderns were even worse and more aggressively hostile.

"I suppose he'd hate the girl, then?" Somehow this made Sky sad.

"Yes, I suppose," answered the Elder in a soft, trailing voice.

"You don't agree then?"

The Elder shrugged. "I understand him. I know what appalled him, but light *is* more perplexing than he admitted." When Sky remained attentive, yet silent, he added, "The icon is meant to disappear, to become a medium for eternal light to shine. The Renaissance attended to earthly vagaries, to shadows and perspective, and all that seemed a grubby diminution, even a lie to my master. My friend thought it a kind of arrogant stealing. I think, however, that transcendence is, how shall one say? Many voiced."

And then the Elder gestured towards the Picasso. "As for the wench, I like her, too. Marie-Thérèse was his mistress when he painted her. I prefer the blue period pictures, but he saw something. They all did. The world was breaking down and they tried to sound the alarm. There's a beauty in the breakdown, like the release of unguent oils when the clay jar is smashed."

Sky looked back at him with shy sweetness. "I only want to remember," she said at last.

"Sparrow, dear little sparrow," said the Elder and his voice barely concealed lament, "You hardly know what you are asking for."

On the border

"Two months ago, when I first arrived in this township just short of the border, I resolved to guard my eyes, and I could not think of going on with this piece of writing unless I were to explain how I came by that odd expression." The Australian author of those particular words was of interest. The author explored liminal spaces introduced by questioning private memories examined at length with recurring, phenomenological intensity.

The results of such investigation, themselves more a metafiction likely to appear monotonous to a conventional reader, touch on the apparently indiscriminate manner in which memory seems capable of weaving encounters with fictive realities into the unique, perduring consciousness of the subject. This could suggest to some weakness of sensibility. Under certain circumstances, the human being is apt to lend equal credence to the factual and the purely imaginative.

Husserl's method of mental expansion from the object to its malleable possibilities was a more cautious endeavor that nonetheless recognized the role of creative repetition in coming to knowledge. One imagined the small white house before one as yellow or gray, large, stone, stucco, a mansion, a cottage, testing the range of the licit to arrive at a sufficiently capacious, though rigorously exact concept able to dexterously manage the complex uniqueness of phenomenological reality.

Yet the bolder venture might suppose that differing aspects were, in fact, thrown by the object itself, inferring that the imagination might disclose discoverable depths and not merely projected fancies.

The slender olive green book bound in Moroccan leather that the Elder now read did not contain such speculation, but there was an association that teased. The Australian author spoke of an asymptotic approach – "just short of the border." However, it was unclear if one ever crossed the border or if one did, if one would be aware of having done so.

Was there a connection between these words that express awareness of possible crossing, perhaps transgression, and the resolve to guard one's eyes?

Odd mitzvah

The Elder's book was an English translation of the gospels from the Arabic. It had been gifted to him by an Egyptian Coptic priest met while the adventurer Henry Ellwood was retracing James Bruce's route in search of the source of the Blue Nile. Bruce did not find it, though he died believing in his spurious identification. Nonetheless, in the course of his quest much else was reported that seemed merely grotesque and risible to Bruce's audience of Enlightenment Europeans.

Ovid had explored the same equivocal energies in the Augustan age. The Roman vates recognized the protean passions smoldering beneath a thin crust of rationality. Civilization itself might be ambiguous. Did it open up towards transcendence or merely seek to direct desire into governable order? Conversely, the rejection of social custom might be aspirational, seeking the hidden Source of desire or decadent incoherence, form degrading into nihilating, loveless sensation.

It was easier to accuse Bruce of outrageous fibbing than face a fundamental questioning. Secular reason still rested in the stolen comfort of revealed divine love. The complacency of Enlightened sensibility might have known better through introspection, and subsequent centuries of Western experience took away even the fig leaf of denial.

The volume of the evangel had been lost or misplaced during one of the many moves of houses and continents that beset his family life. When he came to his present house on a different world, the Elder found the volume waiting for him in the room he had designated for a study, just one of many odd *mitzvahs* from invisible hands.

When Sky walked into the room, he was tracing the words – for some reason, he never did this otherwise that he could recall. When he read this particular book, he touched the words with his finger as if it were necessary for flesh and word to meet. The Elder wondered, suddenly, as the girl was watching and waiting to tell him something, if this was how he had read as a boy.

He thought of the book he and Ewa loved. The tall house at the top of a hill high above the town entered his memory. He felt as if he had lived in that house. And the words of the gospel said "This is the disciple who testifies concerning these things and who has written these things, and we know that his testimony is true. And there are many other things that Jesus also did, which, were they written down one by one, I think the cosmos itself would not contain the books that would be written."

Most folks understood that to be a rhetorical flourish, but the Elder suspected it was meant quite seriously as ontological truth.

Waiting for the sign of the dove

In the darkness of the waters, like being bathed in night,
she could not tell near from far,
    the glimmering of light, lunar, opaque, a velvet fog,
and her body, the flesh
    sunk, struggled, fought to a surface that offered no
vision, not a glimpse of craft or island,
        there was nothing in this darkness to grasp;
    floundering, gasping, swallowing the darkness.
    In cold, briny waters, mocked by the milk vapors, lost,
so lost, surrounded by indifferent swell, gravity tugged at
heavy limbs, pulled her towards empty depths,
        unconsoled.

Yes, she'd forgotten all that. It was before, if time made any sense.

The promise

See there, the little girl dressed in her sailor suit, it was a thing
then, apparently, and she is holding his hand and swinging her
arm with happy, playful energy. It was just like how the cat would
sometimes grow so pleased with herself she would nibble on your

fingers and stretch out along the rug to be petted, looking back for soft murmurs and signs of approval.

And there were shop windows filled with toys and jewels and hats for mama. Then visits with ruffians and yellow ink scribblers – papa had a low view of journalists; then meetings with more respectable men, some portly, some thin, but each destined to be swallowed up in a veil of pipe smoke before at last she was taken to the tea room with dancing girls and waiters dressed in flowing silk with turbans on their heads.

An ornate silver lamp perfumed the air with incense said to come from southern Arabia. Now the little princess was sleepy and content with the orange sponge cake bestowed upon her. A wee old woman no larger than a doll was standing on the table and the girl wondered if she was dreaming. Her father was explaining something to a rapt audience about a living book and the weaving of many states of being along an axis or mundial tree.

She yawned, and then suddenly felt that she was falling from a great height.

The guests were startled when she cried out. Then the rough shadow of papa's beard and the little girl smelled the spiced rum aroma that emanated from the folds of his coat.

"Claire Bright, are you well?" he asked, but she could only shake her head and cling tenaciously with her child arms wrapped about his shoulders and neck.

When she had evidently calmed down, it was decided that papa was a rogue for keeping her too long past her bedtime. Still, the adults kept talking until she was swaddled in a rolling flow of language. She was really almost asleep when she heard the high, child-like voice of the forgotten old woman whispering in her ear.

"Dear one, do not fear the darkness," she said. "You shall not be abandoned, even in the abyss. This is a promise from the house of Mnemosyn."

It was you!

In the dark waters, she heard the same tiny woman speaking urgently and though there was overwhelming danger, part of her noted how the pitch and inflection of the voice was remarkably like Billie Burke's good witch Glinda in The Wizard of Oz, and the voice said, "grab on." Only there was nothing but the waters, and the gasping — and then, from nowhere it seemed, a large, barrel-chested flash of chiaroscuro, black and white, a pelt of flesh warm and churning with serene energy. Almost without knowing, she flung herself upon the wave of animal movement, and somehow found herself crying like a baby on the shore. That was before.

Before the walking, the endless walking, before Sky Odyssey.

Now in the Elder's sitting room, a giant dog was lazing with majestic repose by the fire. And then, sudden astonishment; recognition.

"It was you!" she cried out in delight and gratitude, to which the dog raised its head ever so slightly and thumped its tail.

A night out

A pair of crows picked like bored undertakers upon what was left of a mnemo seller's corpse. Some newcomers glanced up at the macabre bauble festooning the gate, only to quickly avert their eyes. Most of the crowd, however, paid little heed, the price for theft being well known. Sky, too, was oblivious, full of her own anticipations for the Elder was taking her to meet some old friends. It was the first time she had been brought out into company and she was strangely ebullient.

The night was cool at *Café de Flore*. Madame Hadot had a very intellectual face. She wore a dark knit cap over her short dark hair. The only concession made to vanity was the rather thick cravat she had fashioned from a colorful silken scarf. Nonetheless, it rested haphazardly, trying not to interfere with the mental cerebrations of its proprietor.

The Elder was speaking in the manner one does with old acquaintances. Madame Hadot was listening very carefully. Prince Raveh was middle aged, urbane, and not without wit, yet there was something about him that irresistibly evoked the sad child left behind to roam the empty rooms of a large villa whilst his parents vacation elsewhere. Sky had to beat back the irrational impulse to hug him. Where Madame Hadot was quietly intense, the prince was softly melancholy.

"Forgive me, Elder. I *have* been listening to you, but something you said a few minutes ago, I cannot remember what, set my mind

41

questing for a distant memory. It is something I read in the second best library, so it is a borrowed memory at that."

"Beorn, you are very much like your father. I used to tell him the soul will find it for you if you can leave off looking."

"That's just it, Elder. I can never discard skepticism about such things," said Prince Raveh.

"I seem to remember the sage Chryssipus was your teacher?"

"Yes, I occasionally receive a letter from him. The fellow is quite old, but still trying to knock some sense into his dim pupil. Do not mistake my views. I hate the crass and vulgar mind that can only mock. Thirsites, who cankers all authority with his jibes."

"That's from *The Iliad,* girl," added Madame Hadot. "Comedy must be philosophic or it makes the softheads arrogant and contemptuous. Is that not right, Jean-Louis?"

Sky wondered if Madame Hadot had given her a clue to the Elder's identity, for no one else could possibly be Jean-Louis, but just then Lord Raveh's soul retrieved the forgotten book.

"Ah, it was a memoir. A scholar was retelling the experience of a woman which was a deflected way of mentioning his wife. Apparently she was dull and the world was dull and she was resting her head against a window of her car when the tall trees that lined the road began to elongate. The very greenery of their leaves became streaming hair reaching into the heaven of heavens. The limbs of the trees trembled; the roots stretched and appeared to vibrate in depths beyond the earth. The entire world was momentarily unlocked and revealed to be a kingdom of august and shining song. It didn't last, of course."

"What a corker," said Sky, mainly to see the effect on Madame Hadot.

Madame Hadot frowned slightly, but deferred pronouncing judgment. The Elder began to try and tempt the prince away from his sadness, but Sky was distracted by a distant sound of marching. The table next to hers was occupied by a fellow in a camel hair jacket who pointed towards the ribbon of street below them. His companion, who had the tattooed face of a Tartar warrior, shrugged in amiable indifference.

In any event, the conversation had moved on by the time Sky resumed listening. The prince must have said something, but she missed it because the Tartar warrior had been gazing at her with unnerving intensity.

"Yes, Beorn," remarked the Elder. "The City stands ever ready to sacrifice. It is the long wisdom of its ways. The precious and unique thing is lamented, its agony beautifully mourned. What is it but temporary truce, accommodation to the encroaching chaos that waits like a great beast outside the gates?"

There was a rueful glint in the prince's eyes, but he said nothing.

"How goes the war?" asked the Elder.

Sky was shocked and wanted to say, "Wait! We're at war?" but no one else seemed to be alarmed, so she maintained a casual air and snuck a glance at the Tartar savage. The prince, evidently bemused by some private whim of his own, returned to the philosophic conversation.

"And we are back to our old question, the one my father once asked a bold artisan years ago – 'How to reconcile peace and unquenchable desire, the war that is infinity?'"

Lord Raveh smiled, looking now very much like Arco without knowing that his father had taken up residence in his sad face. A distant rumble of thunder mixed with the increased vaunt of marching men. The man in the camel hair jacket leaned over from his chair and gesticulated towards his illustrated companion.

"He says she is surrounded by sibilant shadows. He says that emissaries of the nether world follow upon her steps, and begs me to offer her the holy oil."

"Thanks, no need," answered Lord Raveh with steely charm. "We have gas lights and cognac."

Sky laughed then. Her own soul remembered lines from before, whatever before was.

"And the walrus said, 'What is this going on about my blubber?' And the whale said, 'I am not a tonnage of lamp oil. I am not a storehouse for ladies' perfume.'"

At this, Madame Hadot could not resist a sigh. "You are a most peculiar girl. Jean-Louis cannot approve of eccentricity."

This severe rebuke was modified somewhat by Sky's sudden perception of the head of a pot belly pig poking out with innocent sagacity from an opening in Madame Hadot's commodious handbag which rested in her lap. However, the joy of revelation was somewhat abated by the zealous arrival of the troopers.

The martial lines of the cohort broke through the traffic of the citizenry with haughty sharpness. The plumes of their helmets danced above them, bouncing with vainglorious aplomb as the populace turned left and right to avoid them. Their march headed towards the citadel built high in the old city; once a palace, then consecutively a museum and a jail, now domicile to the Guardian's private cudgel.

The Elder followed them with his eyes, and then looked out at the horizon and the distant outline of the city's edge. Outside the city there were farmlands and seas, forests and desert. There were bleak steppes inhabited by bandits and places long abandoned, houses grown feral and sinking into mud and dust where even the outlaws would not venture.

Lord Raveh spoke of the Chora Makra, dark lands beyond measure. The Elder explained to Sky that it was against her own desolation that Elaria stood guard. The Expanse was not constrained by natural geography, went unremarked in the atlas of any world.

"The abyss changes, arises anywhere, sleeps in the heart, an enemy within, though the *bien pensant* scoff at the madness of the folk who believe such things."

"But then they are tempted to throw salt over their own shoulders," laughed the prince.

Soon, he too grew serious. "No, they are real enough. You forget that my father and I have seen the enemy and met them on the lines."

"The City itself is Chora Makra," answered the Elder. "The siege is quite other than what everyone imagines."

I make myself small

Sky had borrowed a piece of charcoal and a sketch pad. The Elder had suggested the experiment. "Learn patience," he said, "learn to attend before you draw. Do not be passive, be receptive." As patience has no prescribed time limit and thinking about how long patience should last was decidedly not the way to achieve it, Sky decided to simply try drawing something; ineptitude being less frustrating than waiting to be receptive.

Trees seemed easy enough, but a first foray gave a stilted mash of awkward lines with no life in them at all. Trees, of course, are not at all simple. Had Sky really thought about it, she'd have had to consider that the conversation of a tree is only partly given in space, and even that is a matter of perspective. If you climb a tree, you know it with your hands and knees, the flesh communing with bark and negotiating height and weight tolerance. One bantered with a tree and then negotiated the higher you went up. You couldn't rightly climb a tree without a covenant of trust.

And then there was the angle of approach, seasons, and changing light. The same tree at night took off its public mask, spoke the ancient tongue. And yet more, there are idiosyncratic relations of singularity, for a tree was also given in historical memories, not to mention the crude carving, like graffiti, that bore testament to halcyon days of new love or the simple witness that Joan, aged nine, once rested in the crook of a benevolent, many-armed behemoth.

And while one should dissociate the living tree from those material products that no longer bear its essence, there might be some remnant aspect hidden in paper, and fruit, syrup, ships, furniture and so on. No, a tree is hardly simple, but then again, nothing is. If the essence of a tree was known in its aspects, there was no reaching the limit of its spiritual sap. The counting was forever.

However, at this stage, Sky's main insight was how awfully embarrassing not to be able to even get a tree right and now she couldn't draw and was getting ruddy hungry and this patience business was simply the Elder's idea of letting a fella know she was miles and miles yet from getting anywhere. With this thought, a drift of incense reached her nostrils.

Sky followed the olfactory trail, but the smoky bread crumbs appeared to disperse in a busy courtyard that led onto a refectory where several students were boisterous in their repast. A few enormous tuns lay on their sides. Sky could only guess at the contents; whether apples or flour or wine, they bespoke communal largesse. The smell of roses greeted her, but she could see no rose plant. The plangent undulations of litany began to mix with the friendly banter of those taking in a meal.

Aspérges me. Dómine, hyssópo, et mundábor: lavábis me, et super nivem dealbábor. Miserére mei, Deus, secúndum magnam misericórdiam tuam.

Sky looked about, but could not discover the source for this liturgical petition. Further, it did not appear to disturb or even interest the rest. Indeed, she had noticed that apart from a few notable individuals, her own presence often went unregistered.

Puzzled, Sky sank down onto an empty bench. She had the unaccountable feeling that something or someone was hiding behind one of the large barrels. Then there was a flash of light, followed by a young woman who appeared from out of the shadows.

"I make myself small," announced the young woman with a winsome smile. She pointed at the barrel. "They keep beer in that one."

An unusual tree

"So, you are here," she said, as if they had long planned a meeting.

"It seems so," said Sky, "but I can't quite work out the details."

"We've been attempting to find our way for a long time," said the girl. "You think you know what you're doing, because you think you know what you're intending, but you didn't start out from scratch. It's hard to figure, because of what came to you that you didn't think up. It's the same for those who pick up the threads you weave yourself. What you do seems like it's separate from everything else, but it's all one. If you could see it all together, you'd know where you are."

"I've heard a lot of that sort of thing since I got here. The way you tell it, I almost feel like I understand."

"Oh, I must be doing it wrong then," laughed the girl.

"I don't even know who I am," confessed Sky.

"You are the one who will carry the flower."

"Fruit bats," thought Sky.

The mid-day meal at the refectory began to break up. Scurrying groups of students passed by taking little account of Sky and the girl. They began themselves to walk, following a seemingly aimless path that led past a busy market and then brought them to a narrow street of humble buildings festooned with flower pots and lines of wash hanging overhead.

"My man used to live there," said the girl, looking up at a second story window. "You should sketch that and see if he remembers."

They spent a half hour talking, though always dancing away from direct questions. It was a shy, deliberate intimacy. When the girl had gone, Sky realized she had never gotten her name. The drawing by some good fortune was remarkably good, amazing, really, for someone who couldn't manage a stick tree not an hour before. When Sky showed it to the Elder, he was silent. She could feel him check the desire to query her.

"A remarkable demonstration of patience," he said at last.

The night train

Benedicta came by calling and suggested a walk in the park. Sky wavered. Just that morning, she had been looking at a collection of things she had accumulated in a short time. Objects always seemed to her imbued with their own unique mystery. There was a small purple glass unicorn, a diaphanous scarf she discovered in the attic wardrobe, a pen case covered in Japanese Meiji cloisonne, a piece of pyrite that had been ensconced in the flower beds outside the brownstone, and a little cactus she bought from a vendor because he vaguely reminded her of an oversized otter.

These personal items would enter into her thoughts or whisper vaguely of secrets. When such a mood was upon her, Sky could not bear other people. She looked out the window at the sun flowing down in a soft light that is perfectly inviting and she imagined the carriages with young women in pretty dresses and older gentleman with walking sticks and she refused them all because they were uninterested in a piece of fool's gold.

But then the Elder was handing her a parasol and Benedicta was laughing at her rapid, almost absent-minded surrender.

The park was filled with long, serene greens almost too beautiful to walk upon. There were avenues lined with poplars and round-abouts encircling marble sculptures. The people strolled in little packs of three or four. They were almost all dressed in their finest clothes and even the poor had done their best to beat out the dust and to make the most of threadbare cloth.

Benedicta, the Elder, and Sky formed their own moving tribe. Sky was gazing upon a placid lake and the pleasant little benches spaced so that people could rest and commune without becoming fatigued when her attention was caught by an Ansharu who came at them from the opposite direction. The Ansharu had two children in his charge. Sky imagined he was their tutor or some elevated servant. While the children, a boy and a girl, were immaculately dressed and quietly obedient, there was something unsettling about them. They appeared almost somnolent, their pretty faces passively frozen in a mask of polite rectitude.

Sky was sure she caught a brief moment of wry acknowledgement in Benedicta as they crossed paths, but then it was gone and Benedicta was pointing at a small island of thickly wooded area that was evidently regarded as an excursus for more adventurous hikers.

By the time they skirted the edge of the forest, they were quite alone. The Elder stepped out in front of them to lead the way. Whatever path he discerned, it was not well marked; not at all so far as Sky could tell. They pushed their way through a thicket of trees. Brambles and branches scratched and stung the skin until Sky began to feel like one of those self-loathing enthusiasts who flagellate themselves. She was surrounded by a sudden ambush of trees that were certainly not in her path a moment before and then everything went very wrong.

The sky darkened to nearly ebony. There was a repetitive, metallic mussitation. The ground heaved and the air compressed into a fetid thickness. Indeed, she felt enclosed, oppressively so. An odor of stale urine and sick wafted over her. Nausea was quickly followed by terror. Faces compressed and blanched with fear stared back at her wondering gaze. They were mostly women and children with a few old men. Some were praying and others rocked back and forth. Many cried.

Despair vied with visceral bodily anguish. For a long moment, bodies pressed so tightly against her that breath was painful and her head began to go swoon black. Sky tripped or fell forward and someone caught her and steadied her by a soft embrace. Then she was standing at arm's length from a middle-aged woman in a dark coat with a gold star sewn onto it.

"It's alright," said the woman, who then turned and spoke to a woman of similar age that Sky could not properly see. "She's alright, Rosa."

The next thing Sky remembered she was sitting on a large rock with the Elder and Benedicta looking down at her. The Elder was rather ridiculously waving his beret above her in a vain gesture at resuscitation.

"I think she's alright," said Benedicta.

Sky frowned. "I seem to have lost my parasol. I must have left it on the train," she said.

The Elder and Benedicta helped her along the path back to the wide greens of the park. No one said anything for a while. Something in Sky made her unable to broach the episode. She felt degraded and ashamed and in need of a bath.

A trace of memory

Sky heard it first from a seller of roasted peanuts who took pity on her glum face. Then she asked about at the pub across the way. Many gave her a cold shoulder, preferring to ignore her inquiries. Really, it was too rude. Frank, who was a counting house man in his prior years, was somewhat dubious.

"It is likely an old wives' tale," he told her, "but they're a mysterious bunch. Like gypsies, they are." And he drew a rough map on a napkin. "You'll have to ask when you get there. Someone will point out the right place."

Later, a garrulous blue hair who sat in the empty space of a stairwell, reeking of cigarettes, booze, and cheap perfume, added the final piece.

"You have to bring a gift, dearie. Something personal, though it don't have to be rich."

Sky could see at once that the Reception Room was built for occasional use. It was less a chamber than a narrow hanger with a wide open space opposite the closed end where the Anshari woman sat quietly in a high backed chair. A sprinkling of small gifts, flowers and jewelry, tin boxes and tiny satchels of incense lay at the foot of the Anshara who studiously attended to long needles from which a tiny fabric of flashing orange ribbon could be seen.

Sky was surprised to see her dark, lank hair uncovered. Her dress and appearance was nothing like the extravagance of Anshari men. The woman did not once look up from her work, yet Sky knew she was attended to. A wash of embarrassment began to gnaw at her resolve and she felt the heavy beat of her heart as she approached the woman. She quickly whispered some incoherent drivel about her lost past whilst adding the small cactus to the offerings at the Anshara's feet.

Then she stepped back and stood just outside the room, waiting with naïve anticipation. The naked wooden rafters formed a mild peak. Towards the open end and seemingly out of place was a wide arch cut into the wall. And yet there was something right in its seemingly useless aesthetic though Sky would be hard pressed to justify it.

The Anshara began to hum, and then chanted softly. *All the Pleasure of Life, all Worlds allured him to make them. All Angels and Men, all Beauties and perfections all Delights and Treasures, all Joys and Honors allured him to make them.* Something like a golden tracery of smoke gathered in the rafters. Imperceptibly, it narrowed into a thin line that entered into the folds of the Anshara's robe and attached itself to the long needles.

Twin ribbons of fabric began to lengthen so that two streamers suddenly emerged, stretched out and reached towards where Sky breathlessly stood. They came so close that she could feel the sweep of air as they neared her cheek. At the last moment the fire stream swerved upwards towards the stars.

Two sharp swaying lines of ribbon jutted out and produced long, loose strands with tiny, claw-like hands. They joined and the rough likeness of a body appeared. Then a bud of a neck flowered into a perfectly formed human face with flowing red locks. It was a sort of kite with a Botticelli face. The face looked down then upon Sky, a tiny child-like smile etched in its visage. An explosion of images, too much to parcel out assaulted the supplicant.

Then the rush of colors and smells and sounds thinned out to a single image. When Sky was a girl, she used to dream so vividly, she often could not tell whether she was awake or asleep – or perhaps they were not dreams at all. She'd ride out across the wild, seemingly endless prairie, speaking in whispers and little chirrups to her roan, Madison, and let her eyes sweep across the land and up into the horizon low enough to kiss.

Sometimes, a creature as long and serpentine as a dragon, but with the head of a porpoise and deep, lambent eyes would come in a soft, whispery motion, flying just above the low, scrubby grass. It would come right up to them, floating at the level of Madison's withers, but the horse never riled. The creature would nudge at Sky and then fly off, circling higher and higher into the cloudless air until no one could possibly see it and Sky would wonder if she'd imagined the whole thing.

Anamnesis

The mistake that everyone made was that they thought when Plato talked of *anamnesis*, of the knowledge that was recollection, they thought they understood what memory was, and they thought they understood memory because they believed, everyone did, that they were thoroughly familiar with forgetting.

Forgetting was possession that one failed to recognize. Forgetting was temporary or permanent. It might be lost without trace, senility robbing one of years, of the slow-wrought identity, good or bad. It might be like that, or more amiable, slightly awkward, almost endearing, an absent-minded fumbling. Yet all agreed that forgetting was second.

First, there was event, the happening, the thing that was there in order to be forgot. It was a strange way to put it, but there it was.

The forgotten was the shadow of a past presence. This is what all agreed must have been meant.

Except, that was not what was intended. Forgetting was first.

Forgetting was not forgotten if the forgetting was not also forgotten. The other forgetting was something of an ape, already tied to the something, anything, grasping after the determinate. It was not forgetting.

Original forgetting was gift, plenitude, forgetting was to come from nothing, but the nothing was also unthinkable. Memory is not tied to the past. It comes, strange as it may seem, from the future.

But that is also not what it appears to be.

A runner

Arched passageways. Old stone echoing, time trodden, immemorial. The dessicated, old flesh mouthing familiar phrases. Shining and cherubic, dense and bored, young flesh waited for just the right time to slap Harry when the master turnbacked to the relentless sea of blank faces. Always new and familiar, empty of slowly accumulated knowledge, built of the dead, experience transformed into inky marks, tabulated, a skeleton, like a coral reef.

Master Quinton paced, his slender wraith of a body wheeling on bony ankles which rattled when he turned, breath smelling of garlic and leeks, waiting for the break so he could light a fag, waiting while the chant drill sang its grammiliar cycle. *Hic haec hoc. Huius huius huius. Huic huic huic. Hunc hanc hoc.*

Martin, a bright boy, with thick luxuriant locks cut short in lenten rebuke over his pensive skull, yawned while pondering the details of his book by candlelight, a sanguinary history of the Cathars. The master, swift as fate, let fall the rule and the boys near the offending party blinked in quick wincing empathy, whilst others chortle half silent.

The clock tower chimed the quarter hour. A slight breeze rustled the chain of climbing ivy, the bursar and the dean settled into plush leather chairs. The dean called for coffee while a young scholar made a desultory play of stirring the embers in the hearth. A long way off, full of tremulant morosity, a hound cried, its howl eerie, following the mortared path of the academy.

Quinton froze, arrested by a pricking in the marrow of his gaunt pedagogic bones. There was something in it. The boys all leapt in spirit, wakening at the pause as it grew and grew until it was momentous, filled with the vaporous, melancholy canine keening. But it did not make them sad or worried. Too young, they only felt delicious surprise, silent anticipation. A little longer and they began to whisper.

"It's a runner, a runner!" they cried.

Quinton remained silent, trying to appear oblivious of them.

"It's nothing. Nothing," he said at last, his voice soft and distracted. "Let us look at the rule for third declension I-stem nouns."

The master cleared his throat and by the magic of that expectoration, normalcy was imposed. The tired heads resumed their sluggish, donkey ways. They noisily turned their pages.

Sky saw him darting out from behind the alley where the bakery made those delicate pastries of light, fragile crust with a dusting of sugar. The youth might have been an older sibling to the usual pair that were constant wards of the Anshari. He managed a powerfully compact impudence in the glance he bestowed upon her, then ran along an arcade and ducked down a staircase leading to a waterway.

What became of him after that, she did not know, but a posse of Ansharu flooded the streets. They were unusually animated. She sensed expectancy. It was a hunt, singing in joyous bloodlust.

The voices of the Ansharu rang out: "We shall hit you. We shall strike you with sticks and glaves and frying pans!"

Then they roared and Anshara danced about and watched with pleasant, holiday faces.

"It's Magramentia!" declared a jovial Anshara and a newly arrived grouping of Ansharu shouted back, "We shall hit you. We shall strike you with sticks and glaves and frying pans!"

And the Anshara answered antiphonally: "Until you burst!"

A nesting doll

Midori Takashima was a nesting doll. At the outermost layer, she was a rounded, respectable pear-shaped mama that wore comfortable sweaters and tortoise shell glasses whilst cultivating an interest in lamps with unusual shades or coffee tables made from driftwood. She purveyed estate sales like an omnivorous shark patrolling shallow waters at night.

The haul from her forays into antique shops, flea markets, and the rummage of other people's houses maintained a steady gravity towards the Takashima apartment, creating a constant eddy that flowed into the attic. Indeed, Sky rather suspected Midori had passageways between the bulkheads, so that the entire upper space of the building could accommodate her displaced discoveries.

Mrs. Takashima was delighted to acquire her new daughter, for this meant someone besides Mr. Takashima could appreciate her powers, for it had to be admitted Mr. T was often rather Stoic about her findings. Beneath this layer, however, were others. The second doll was a counterweight to the first, avid for old traditions and a stickler for the way one should drink tea or pour sake.

Sky quickly discerned this sober matron that merely tolerated the outer shell as a form of protective disguise, though it was unclear what motivated the necessity of misdirection. Even so, there was yet a third Mrs. Takashima. Sky had been attempting to draw Mr. Takashima's attention to the finer points of an end table made from a spool of steel cable when she was astonished to find herself the subject of an acid glare from Midori, followed by a vituperative dismissal of the now discredited table.

It was only later that Sky's cheeks burned with ridiculous humiliation. She recognized the heat of jealousy. Somehow, Midori had taken her enthusiastic encomium for repurposed industrial products as an attempt to attract Mr. Takashima. From this maladroit incident, a host of other examples involving neighbors, strangers shopping at the corner grocers, pedestrians casually glancing upon them with polite indifference took on a preposterous hue.

The third nesting Midori was positively convinced of the undeniable allure of sweet, unassuming, quiet Mr. Takashima. The little tuft of graying hair that stood out like a hirsute island from his receding hairline waved with invincible virility upon the feminine heart. It was axiomatic for Midori that Mr. Takashima invited the swooning admiration of an adoring womankind.

Sky pondered the Elder who wished to discover unity which was somehow an eternal glory. And she thought, yes, that is a part of my longing. But she had to admit that she, too, was a nesting doll.

Data collection

The moody, half light of the gloaming snuck up upon the city, inducing the gas lit lanterns perched on lampposts to come alive like incandescent lemon drops. The pitch of voices, the very nature of sound took on a new quality. The night had its own code, its own selling of goods and bartering and justice. An express restaurant selling calamari and squid and egg drop soup sprang to life. Boisterous youths could be heard within a tavern whose entrance was decorated as a gaudy hellmouth. The lamplight at the corner of a block of stores illuminated the glass storefront of a ladies' haberdasher. In its reflected light, a diminutive, solitary man stood with an attitude of vigilant dishabille. He gave off the air of a disgraced soldier selling contraband on the black market.

The gray man has a way of seeping into the human clutter. He infiltrates and does nothing, nothing you can see. He attends, watches, takes careful notes. What he sees may only be a narrow band. It's possible he mistakes a radical narrowing for expansion of vision, but none of that bothers him. This collector of data has a kind of indifference. He makes no judgment as to particulars; that is someone else's job, to judge.

He is only there to spy unobtrusively, to mark down acquisitive habits and the random, stray action. What the specimen does is a matter for tabulation, calculation, spread sheets, and the like. There are accountants who stipulate the value and state of the citizen subject of review.

However, sometimes the gray man finds it useful to remind the citizen of surveillance. He might provoke a confrontation, strictly against policy, show them an array of chronotopes, and let them see what they are about. The ensuing panic is often most revealing.

The short man spoke in a soft, high voice, his cadence both ingratiating and vaguely sinister. "Mädchen, may I interest you in a watch?"

His sleepy, somewhat protuberant eyes looked out with ennui from beneath heavy lids. The fella opened his overcoat to reveal a satin lining set as backdrop for perhaps a dozen timepieces of diverse age and quality. One little clock was kept in an ornate cage. Another appeared a sturdy, well-used pocket watch that might have belonged to a civil engineer. Each glinted with flashes of lantern light.

"There is a watch for every person, for every person a watch," continued the man. "But the springs differ. Everyone knows, but everyone tries to forget."

"I'm really not sure," said Sky, politely trying to extricate herself.

"Perhaps you do not see one to your liking. I have many more," continued the seller of time.

Then he shook out his jacket and the fabric lengthened and spread, growing into a fantastic tableau of satin interspersed with hundreds upon hundreds of clocks and watches, there was even a sun dial and a water clock, so that the entire block must be covered in chronometers. Sky gulped and held back her amazement.

"Thank you, not tonight," she whispered in barely suppressed terror.

A surrender

In a blink, the overcoat was closed and Sky was left wondering if she had hallucinated the entire episode. The short man stared back at her in malignant silence. In order to compensate for her unease, Sky rushed into the nearest lighted shop, which turned out to be a specialty boutique run by Anshara. The shop sold paper and ribbons and spools of thread. The wares were sorted by color so that one might match a silver thread with silver paper.

Little cards of identification were labeled in a simple hand script. Olive, lavender, wine, and boysenberry were easy enough. An earthy pumpkin orange was marked "Harvest," which was somewhat metaphoric. But how one was to observe such obscurities as "dryad tears" – emerald with veins of periwinkle, "warlock's song" – a turgid gray overlaid with splashes of russet and black, or the oddly pearlescent mauve of "Uhraine's secret" could only be a matter for speculation.

A beaded curtain separated these wares from a table of inks and pens suitable for calligraphy. Sky thought to herself, "how lovely," and to her surprise, one of the pens startled into the air, then dropped its nib in a well of violet ink before limning by an invisible hand "how lovely" in a flowing, ornate script.

This was all preamble to her night of wonders. Next to the pens was a table of mirrors framed in various textures and materials. Sky stood before one bordered in bamboo with thin wire ivy of platinum and jewels of opal, beryl, carnelian, emerald and amethyst interspersed as flower and fruit. When Sky looked into the mirror, a feeling of tranquility washed over her, gently soothing her nerves. In this reflection, she sensed her most beautiful, ideal self.

In another frame of ironwood held fast with strips of leather binding her visage was subtly altered. It matched her expressions well enough, but Sky felt the mirror judged her or revealed some normally invisible truth. She stared in uneasy fascination, unsettled by the enigma.

A third object appeared to be no mirror at all, but a kind of shallow dish made of unadorned pewter. As she was puzzling over this apparent anomaly in the collection, an Anshara joined her. Wordless, the attendant poured water into the dish, then took from the folds of her dress a tiny flask of cut crystal. The Anshara pulled the glass stopper and allowed two small drops of an extract redolent of pomegranates to mix with the water. Then she smiled and put a finger to her lips before withdrawing.

For a long moment, nothing seemed to happen. Sky could not clearly see herself in the liquid, nor did any particular feeling accompany her attempt at observation. The intervention of the Anshara seemed too pointed for such an anti-climactic result. Then, without a flicker of warning, a face vividly appeared. It was the face of the young girl she had seen at the refectory, her eyes fierce, yet compassionate. Whether she saw Sky was unclear and left uncertain. A rough commotion in the forefront of the store drew her attention away.

There were gasps and cries, then the curtain was wildly swinging as a youth came awkwardly crashing through. He sprung forward with a bolt and Sky thrust her arms before her fearing violence. But no harm came to her. The youth carried the visceral anxiety of flight, but mastered its energy. With unexpected delicacy, he knelt before her, and lifted his face in quiet, beseeching gentleness. In a rush of instant recognition, Sky knew him for the hunted prey of the Anshari.

The store quickly became a gathering of native Elnarians. There were words of expostulation in an unknown tongue and tones of rising anger followed by counter-blasts from other Anshari. The runner was kicked and made to rise, whereupon his hands were roughly bound behind his back. Horror and a strange, unfocused shame took residence in Sky's heart.

The Anshari continued to whisper and dispute among themselves. They were pointing at her and arguing. Sky wanted very much to leave. She ran towards the store front, but was held fast by two Ansharu, as much a captive as the unfortunate who had so mysteriously chosen her as the object of his surrender.

The prisoner, Rut

Further discussion in the Elnarian tongue offered no more clarification of her situation, but their actions were less than consoling. The Anshari blindfolded Sky and her mouth was silenced with a gag. Yet their behavior towards her was otherwise formal, and even respectful after a fashion. Their words were courteous, if enigmatic. They directed her movement, firmly, but also with a degree of gentleness that seemed at odds with their evidently hostile attitude towards the escaped fugitive.

Sky was brought out into the night air. Her captors became quiet. The ritual halloo of the chase took on the mood of the clandestine. They walked carefully, and then Sky found herself guided down stone steps. She could hear the lapping waters of a canal. Then she was maneuvered into the seat of a gondola. The journey was relatively brief, and soon she entered a covered walkway of some sort and was escorted into a new building.

Next, they were removing the cloth binding that held her blind and mute. The Ansharu guards kept staring at her with perplexity and wonder. Then an Anshara matron who evidently held their respect arrived and preemptively commanded Sky to follow her. All this time, Sky was trying to steal glances about her in hopes of some clue to what was happening. The walls were of dolomite and pale limestone, so she must be in the old city. There were even places where the flooring was interspersed with mosaic, but she could not stop to ponder any of this.

At last, Sky came to a door before which an armed Ansharu stood with solemn mien. The Anshara directed him to stand aside. The door was opened, and Sky found herself pushed within a small holding room. Sky gasped. The insolent fugitive sat before her upon a thin mat of reeds. All traces of his previous demeanor were lost. His fashionable clothes had been discarded in favor of a rough hewn garment that might have been cobbled from burlap sacks. When she spoke to him in commiseration or attempted to discover the reason behind his imprisonment, he remained in placid repose despite the welts and cuts that decorated the exposed skin of his face and body.

After considerable prodding, the best she could get out of him was the monosyllabic grunt, "Rut." Whether this was intended as information, explanation, imperative command, it was certainly a surd to Sky. An Anshara entered with a bowl of vinegar and water and a small sponge. As she ran the sponge over the face and arms of the prisoner, she cooed softly to him, "Shaa, shaa."

Though she was ignorant of the goings on, Sky could not help remonstrating with the girl, who was perhaps herself not much above twelve years of age. The girl looked back at her with dull wariness; then said words that meant nothing to her, though in her mind she heard "*he is nearly ready. The dawning must be prepared.*"

Rut, as Sky decided to call him, was led from the holding room into a large open arena. Its massive walls were tall and crenellated. In the center, an equally imposing marble column stood. To her amazement, Rut was bound in chains to this singularly ominous stake. The Attendants Several routinely ignored her further queries and exhibitions of moral outrage. These Anshari had an unmistakable air of condescension. She was tolerated despite her obvious stupidity. When a small cot with a blanket was brought forth, it became clear to her that she was meant to continue her vigil beneath the naked heavens.

Then the attendants withdrew. Sky yelled rather wildly at Rut's captors, and then tried to cajole signs of intelligence from the unhappy youth. Her sedulous efforts were unable to engender more than sporadic effusions of familiar monotony. He was docile, showing no pity for himself or recrimination for those who had beat him and constrained him to such a strange confinement.

When evening dropped into the fullness of night, the air became chill. Sky wrapped herself in the blanket and stared into the canopy of stars. She had intended not to sleep, but she must have dozed. She dreamed and in her dream, Rut suffered one of those unaccountable oneiric transformations. He was still tethered in iron chains to the column, but his body had grown immensely, his features coarsened and molded to that of an earthen giant.

In this state, a new poignancy emerged. When she talked to him, he lowered his great head like an obedient dog so that she could pat him with soothing affection. The slightly sour anger of his flight had been replaced with such gentle submission, she could hardly help from crying.

"Oh, Rut, what are we going to do?"

The giant blinked and murmured softly as if she were the one in need of mercy.

Dawning

At dawnlight, the creature that was Rut began to alter still further. His chest deepened, his torso widened and expanded. His height and length threatened to burst the limits of his confinement. The pallor of his skin took on a silver sheen as the flesh shimmered in gargantuan musculature. Rut's arms bowed out, the palms of the hands acquiring a thick pad. Whether he possessed a tail or was roughed off at the rump like a Manx was left for Sky to conjecture.

Indeed, he had become too large to contemplate in toto from her current station. She had a glimpse of aureate wings that rose like massive shields from the shoulder blades. These were as yet still pressed close to his body. But all this she assimilated at the margins of perception, for her gaze was concentrated on the great face of the creature.

He seemed to look out upon her from a silence deeper than mourning, his very being rising from silence. The eyes were large and limpid, somehow suggesting both great age and child-like innocence. They were not merry, a touch sad, but not resigned or timid or tragic.

"O, Rut, dear Rut," she babbled, not knowing what she was speaking.

The face, she decided, was almost numinous and princely and she must be getting dim for he was clearly familiar. His face rose before her, became as wide as the horizon. He did not seem to fade; instead she had a sense of a rush of compact, vibrant energy, too radiant for a mere biological form. Then she stood alone in the enclosure.

The Attendants Several approached her with glad smiles and tears in their eyes. She was made the center of a dancing circle. An elegant cycle was accompanied by a sinuous chant. Then the young Anshara that had spoken to her in the waiting room solemnly placed a silver ring with a white stone upon her left hand.

Sky laughed and cried. "I guess I'm something like his godmother," she thought. If there was more explanation, it was too rapid for Sky to assimilate. Soon, she was lead onto a narrow bypath which opened into a boulevard with trees placed just so and she was free as the day. There was a bridge and a lovely waterway. Two barges were tethered side by side, the still surface of the water wrapped in morning quietude. The few on-lookers must have thought her addled to see her remonstrating with herself.

"That magnificent head! Why he's rather like the Sphinx, you goose!"

See what we can do

Sky was swimming. Another girl swam with her. It was not the mysterious friend, but flesh familiar. Her sister was with her beneath the surface of the water. The water was warm and mildly brackish. It was like floating in amniotic fluid, in a sleepy maternal sea. Her eyes were closed; some luminescence lit her face, her lips full with a blush of peach pink. The air she must have engulfed pouted her cheeks slightly.

Sky was wearing a thin camisole and her thick auburn hair was spread out in long, luxuriant waves. It was very Pre-Raphaelite. Her younger sister was beside her and somewhat below. She already wore her dark hair in a short bob. Amanda was always quick to find the edge of a new fashion. One arm must have been wrapped around her and the other reached forward and held her own hand.

Sky recognized the blouse with the long, chiffon sleeves. It was a drowning picture, but neither she nor her sister had fear in their limbs. They swam in languid, intimate serenity, a single white feather floating above their clasped hands.

And then there was a strange winged creature flying at night through a rounded gallery of alabaster columns. A rabbi appeared as if amidst the books of his study. He looked at her with profound care and spoke. "What is the Sabbath? Spirit in the form of time."

Next, she was floating in a translucent bubble. She saw the grocer standing before a birdcage. There was an expectant expression on his face. He had a treat for the mynah bird in his hand. Sky had delicate gloves on and a pill box hat. She was like a beautiful genie, but the grocer gave her no mind at all. She was mildly perturbed at this. It was not that the grocer could be so obtuse to a large sphere with a beautiful girl; or rather, the chief thing was she was looking so splendid and wasn't it rude not to admire her?

Then her bubble was outdoors and it must have been a cool morning, because the children were dressed snugly in woolen coats and scarves. A waiter was arranging chairs about the round tables of his establishment. A boy was sitting idly on his bike, whilst an older gentleman was standing with his hands in his pockets with that long suffering look men begin to acquire when the fires of ambition have died into grumbling resignation. Again, no one remarked her, but by this time she expected it. There was still a bit of haughtiness in her smile, but it was mainly bemused.

A man in the crowd suddenly looked up at her. He had an impish twinkle in his eyes, and perhaps in the manner of his speech, but his words were somewhat chastising. "They only want to order something from a waiter," he began. "When a person is confronted by the need to speak, however, he no longer sees speech as a tool by which he can make himself understood . . . he is seized by speech because things demand to be understood by him."

Night returned. The spectral tiger that had waited at the bridge along with the impossible man was crouched in lush, tall grass, her eyes glowing like twin stars. And then a painted monk appeared before her. He held a book in his left hand and though he was clearly an image, this did not stop him from raising his right hand, his fingers before his lips invoking silence.

Now she was walking along a lonely beach. The sky was umbrous and gray, dotted with low, docile clouds. She was wearing a dark dress. It must have been near noon because despite a long, billowing fabric, her shadow was a miniscule mound beneath her dancing step. She held the parasol she had lost in the park. A man appeared walking from the opposite direction. At first she thought it was the Elder, but when he got closer, he was younger, though the same face.

"The gift is first," he said. "It is only when the answer is revealed, that we understand the question."

Soon, the morning light was fighting through the thick curtains of her bedchamber. She was surprised to find that once again she had misplaced the umbrella. The ring given to her by the Anshari winked slyly. The white stone reminded her of the bubble that had carried her.

"See what we can do," it seemed to say.

The orb ring

Of course, she told them what had happened to her. She didn't know what to expect, but it wasn't the rapid dropping of the subject. It was as if she had broached a topic unfit for polite society. Sky had expected they would give her some explanation or congratulate her or perhaps remonstrate with her for causing them worry. Certainly anything but the strange silence that only exacerbated the hidden alarm bells all through her body.

Somewhere, sometime, she had known just this acute sense of shame and loneliness. Something had happened and no one had talked. It was not vicious, not even a conspiracy, but dangerous. She was smoldering for a week before she realized she wasn't really angry at the Elder and Benedicta, but at the nameless others who had contrived a smothering wall of tacit silence.

Benedicta joined her at table in the Takashima's kitchen.

"I knew a fellow, brilliant, but exasperating, named Scheler," she said. "He was a strange character. Had a way of talking, little phrases, you know? He would say, 'pure *Washeit*,' that is 'whatness.' They were like religious prayers by which he attached himself to hidden worlds. But he was completely useless in ordinary situations. You would find him in a restaurant staring at a hat rack. He was waiting for his wife to tell him which hat was his."

For some unaccountable reason, this reminisce introduced a gush of emotion in Sky and she felt herself fighting back tears. Benedicta grabbed her hand and held it lightly. The ring the Anshari had granted her presented a noble simplicity.

"It's lovely."

"Yes."

"The Anshari call it an orb ring. It is a rare gift."

"The first night I wore it, I had a string of very strange dreams."

Benedicta straightened in her chair. "Would you like to tell me about them?"

Sky shook her head. "It was all very random."

The sun peeked in through the kitchen window. Benedicta smiled slightly and bowed to the reticence of her new friend. "You must tell me if anything appears more than random."

"Will it? I mean, should I expect that?"

"I think you should, to be honest."

For weeks afterwards, Sky was looking for something more than random, which meant, unsurprisingly, that nothing particularly seemed to happen.

At the agora

In the evening, if you look across to the smolder heaps of Gehenna, you will see fire glints staring back. These belong to the eyes of feral hounds that wander in packs and take possession of certain byways and alleys. Territory that during the day formed an isthmus to civilization is reclaimed in the darkness.

The floating boundaries shift again with the day. Then men once again walk in the places porous to desolation. The garbage carts, with their slow, grinding wheels have large canvas bags attached to hooks on the back. These are for the dead dogs left over from the night.

Seemingly far from ashes and strangled hopes, the agora near the Lion's Gate formed a marketplace for commodities dealers. There, amongst the wide, tall pillars, the marble steps and broad spaces for traders and large houses to bargain, one also finds clerks and beggars, pickpockets and artists. The latter bunch dispersed by police making rounds, reform with admirable speed in their absence.

Here, Sky ambled as her fancy took her, gleaning snippets of speech and chance spectacle. The Elder would say, "Tell me who speaks to you and I shall know who you are." But sometimes the voices were a blur, it was too much, and yet thin gruel.

The clock tower chimed the mid-day hour. The merchants were beginning to stop for lunch and scatter into smaller groups when there was a slowly moving hush. Sky followed it until her eyes came to rest on a solitary crone dressed in somber rags walking freely amidst the traders. At first, Sky thought her an especially bold mendicant, but she never stopped to beg alms.

Indeed, there was an imperious quality to her gait. Onlookers stepped back from her presence with a combination of appalled fascination and awe. Her face was a grotesque origami of folds and wrinkles shrinking from her sallow skull, yet the eyes maintained a patrician resolve.

When her glance fell upon Sky, the girl felt a sharp intake of breath like a knife. There was something more in those eyes. They were old, old, but neither dim, nor decrepit.

Later, after the ancient one left, Sky heard the gossiping waves of her name whispered about. Uhraine, Uhraine, Uhraine.

A rather magnificent merchant with the beard of an Assyrian king dyed to magenta was holding court, unflustered by the appearance of Uhraine. "Deco is like his mother. Everything is a floor too low. His brains are in his heart and his heart resides —"

"No wonder she fell for you, Flavius George."

After a round of laughter, one of the younger traders asked after Flavius George's daughters.

"You mean the Fates? Aurora has discovered astronomy. She has commandeered a telescope and chatters on about galaxy clusters and binary stars and many other ridiculous things. Diana is obedient, quiet, and respectful, which means she is planning my assassination.

And Narina, lovely Narina, is in love with a chicken. I gave her a rooster for nativity day and now I am going to have a grandson named Chanticleer. I will be the only man in Elnaria with grandchildren that cluck and fly about."

Child of hope

Out of the corner of her eyes, in a sinking moment, Sky would see him, the squat mercenary who had offered her a watch before she slipped into the Anshari shop. He'd be hiding in a blink just at the edge of her vision or herds of contrary moving pedestrians would clear and he would be standing against a lamppost, a sardonic, gnashing smile smeared across his face. Sky began to wonder if she were imagining him; he was like a malicious sprite with a gargoyle sense of humor.

And then he began to appear in her dreams. He would be walking towards her in his shabby overcoat and tired collar, with an ominous watch chain trailing into a pocket. He was always peering downwards so that his gray fedora shaded his eyes from her. There was usually the stub of a cigarette in his right hand. No matter how frequent his appearance, Sky was always startled and apprehensive.

Sometimes in her dreams she did not know him at first, but as he came nearer the certainty dawned that it was indeed the gray man. Then she would be running, running, but as is the way with dreams, her motion was ineffective. No matter where she ran, the gray man would appear. But also as in dreams, just before he could arrive to confront her, the scene would shift – the desire to escape altering the landscape.

Once, when this happened she found herself in a field of golden heather beneath a brisk, Hibernian sky of cold beauty. Her heart was suddenly as serene as it had been panicked. Sky was alone, but she did not feel lonely. A patch of whirling light sparked with aureate, vegetal energy drew her. The heather took on the specter of dancing peacocks and within the spiral of their movement, she discerned a pearlescent glow.

Then Sky was floating and soon she had entered the cosmic darkness and it was as if she was staring into the heart of a white dwarf sun. Next, she discerned the tendril limbs of roots woven like capillaries into the skin of the earth. The light was a sphere, though she could not tell if she was staring up or down into its splendor. A soft glow of warm innocence radiated out towards her. A certainty came upon Sky that all this was the orb ring itself.

An unborn child was nestled within its transparent surface. Her heart thrilled with wonder and a yearning to protect and also something quiet, yet shattering, a mysterious hope.

The vates Herakleitos speaks into the wind, "Aeon is a child, childishly playing at moving about counters; the kingdom is a child's!"

Wheels within wheels

The Elder listened carefully to Benedicta and then to Sky. Then he went for a walk. When he returned, he sent for her. He informed Sky with laconic economy that she was to meet with an ancient seer. "Though how much he can or shall tell you I cannot command. It is a gift of the Spirit," he concluded.

A few of the Elder's select company of friends were recruited to facilitate the audience. Terrence Bunn, as it turned out, was both a rangy Maasai and a priest, the figure in the white robe who had so captured Sky's curiosity. She waited with the Elder in a little bistro on Metz Street, a charming residential area of four-story buildings with tall, narrow, rectangular windows, small iron patios three stories up, walls of golden patina and brown shuttered bays decorated with red flowering begonias.

The priest joined them and chatted in that nervous fashion of new acquaintance. Sky was surprised by the way this introduced a penchant for occasional school boy flippancy into the priest's perfect Oxford English. Father Bunn related a brief family history which began with the information that the Elder had known Father Bunn's uncle, a fellow with the delectable name of Toby Jaguar and ended with his chagrin that he had never killed a lion.

At length, the Elder suggested that they start out without the fourth of their party. Bunn was apologetic whilst admitting that most likely Ratcatcher had forgotten all about them. They would have to bring the mountain to Mohammed, as it were. However, when they had all stood up and begun to walk in a certain direction, it became clear that the Elder would not be joining the adventure.

"You're the mountain," said the Elder. "This path is yours, Sparrow. I shall pray for a good word."

Though this last was added to soften the blow of her surprise, Sky could not dissemble her unease. Indeed, she was suddenly afraid that there might be embarrassing waterworks. Once the Elder's figure had retreated from view, Father Bunn explained.

"You know, he can't bear to see Brother Timothy. They were good friends in the old days."

And with that enigmatic, darkly melancholic note, the priest led her on a variegated path through the Crescent Quarter. Though some miles away, the pungent tang of salt sea spiced the air. Blotches of green and brown fungi stained the steps and reached like a slow, covetous animal over the blue paint that covered the lower sections of the white pitched walls. Father Bunn paused at one point to stare at a sign marked in Arabic.

"Café Baba," he said. "Wonderful coffee."

"You a coffee fiend?" asked Sky.

"We really must rush," he said in a regretful tone.

"I mean, if your friend truly has forgot, he probably isn't waiting. Unless, of course, the timetable is terribly strict."

Sky gave a slight nod in the direction of the establishment. Somehow, they found it necessary to stop just for a short while to examine a little porcelain cup. Sky was required to throw a veil over her head to accommodate the proprietor, but the coffee — very rich and slightly bitter, just right.

"They call it a dark angel," said Father Bunn without any semblance of superstitious omen.

Sky recognized the shy kindness of the priest, that the entire episode was intended as a diversion from her new fears and sadness. Then, remembering their mission, he hurried her out and past a tangle of cluttered side streets and back alleys until they came to an iron gate that barred the opening to a storm relief sewer.

This seemed a rather deflating end to their effort, but soon a hard-bitten, unshaven fellow appeared on the other side of the gate to let them in. Father Bunn slipped a "coin for Charon" across the interval.

"You're not kidnapping me, are you?" asked Sky as archly as she could manage. "Because if you are, this is a rather elaborate mousetrap way to go about it, don't you think or do you?"

The unshaven fellow gave her a contemptuous smirk and pulled out a cheroot which he quickly lit.

As they passed through the gate, Father Bunn answered her with light patter. "Nothing like that, Miss Odyssey. It's just that the City is wheels within wheels. There's much more to the old girl than you might think."

"I see," said Sky, who plainly did not.

Ratcatcher

Stone steps led down to rounded brick walls, the last arrows of light from above accentuating the shadowed darkness below. An iris portal served a corridor dimly lit by opaque globes that came to life as soon as one came near and just as quickly blinked into dormancy once passed. The gatekeeper left them at the portal. For some time afterwards, Sky attempted to memorize the route, but soon became hopelessly muddled.

"I shall starve if you should suddenly drop dead," she announced at last. "They'll find our skeletons and make up ghastly stories about our bones."

"Not to worry," said the priest in his carefree English even as he pressed heavily against a large circular grill which he pushed aside to reveal a more expansive realm beneath the City. "The wild dogs should take care of us well before that."

Sky felt unable to tell if this were a joke or not. A thin line of wire was stretched to allow a string of weakly incandescent bulbs exposing a bricolage of masonry, rough hewn stone, and natural mineral formations. Father Bunn casually removed a dirk from his belt whilst handing Sky a small dagger with a silver guard and hilt of bone.

"The path we are taking, well, most likely they won't be needed."

Sky was so surprised she forgot to wonder at the incongruity of a priest with an arsenal of weapons hidden inside his robes.

As they progressed through a series of interconnected tunnels abundant evidence of underground existence met them in a variety of echoes: muffled conversation, whispers, occasional shouts, and even singing could be heard. The last had the unmistakable swaying camaraderie of a drinking song.

Shortly afterwards, they encountered a smattering of solitary travelers. The imposing height of Father Bunn was an advantage. Sky found it amusing to see how some would puff themselves out like a small beast of prey deterring violence by trying to appear larger than they were, whilst others would crawl into shadows, risk a darting glance filled with a mixture of groveling and hatred.

Later, when they came upon packs it was another matter. Even the timid rested on their dignity with the insouciance of numbers. Then the Maasai priest would lightly flash the steel of his blade. The restive would mumble into silence. Those hardier or inebriate might snarl, part riposte and part greeting of sorts. This social parade lasted for some minutes until they came to what was ostensibly a shallow alcove, but in reality an opening deceptively masked.

The new passage leveled out into less enclosed spaces and a sprinkling of regular chambers. One had the impression that an ancient city street had been imperceptibly transported by time to this covert site. Apparently at home in this ghostly neighborhood, Father Bunn rapped perfunctorily upon a sturdy wooden door unremarkable from all the rest, then produced a key and ushered Sky into a most unusual abode.

The entire domicile was a single room constructed of ribbed arches so that it was like living in a barrel turned on its side. The floor of fired bricks shifted from vertical to horizontal patterns like two streams at perpendicular. A dark wooden table for dining complete with a hanging chandelier was located near a deep set brazier made from the same brick that covered the walls and floor.

The warm glow of its fire set forth the arcana of the alchemist. Sky could only guess at the elaborate system of flews that would allow for a hearth at these depths. Several rounded ovens were also in use, one of which was heating an immense iron pot. A plethora of flasks, most shaped like eggs or gourds rested on tables or little shelves. A thin tree limb hung from short iron chains anchored to the arc of the ceiling. This impromptu beam served as support for burlap sacks of various sizes.

Yet Sky's attention was focused elsewhere. The Ansharu called Ratcatcher was carefully decanting some dark liquid from an alembic. The extreme concentration on his face and the technical skill of his motion were somewhat offset by the titmouse that peeped out from the folds of his cloak and also by the tiny wren balanced upon the worn derby hat propped precariously upon his head of wildly askew hair.

When Ratcatcher had finished the procedure, he sighed. It was unclear if this meant that he was satisfied or not. Then he glanced at Sky and spoke in a polyglot as patchwork as his appearance.

"Scusa, Dwy insula mädchen the cries of the umbra gather in cor gimna. Czy masz yacki april?"

Father Bunn translated: "Ratcatcher considers you the girl from the island of St. David apparently. He begs your pardon to inform you that the tears of shadows gather in cold hearts. He also wishes to know if you would like to imbibe the wine of an early spring."

"Does he always talk like that?"

"Oh, no, usually he is quite cryptic."

The Valley of Dry Bones

Back in the open air, Sky had a brief span of disorientation, like a sailor still on sea legs. Topsiders, as the denizens of the Underground called them, blithely gossiped, bought falafel from a man at the kiosk, sold bonds, read newspapers or some other activity that let them walk briskly in their hats and wear earnest expressions, oblivious to an entire social structure known mainly to students, bohemians, and dangerous sorts.

This was all too easily romanticized, yet it pleased Sky to contemplate life as a Gothic diptych. As a kind of coda to her reflections, a portly red-faced man cursed with admirable zeal and inventiveness as he chased errant apples and geese, escapees from an upended farmer's cart. There is a pleasure in feeling one's horizon expand and a quick pride in seeing others as obtuse or enclosed in comfortable ignorance.

Sky did not reflect on the immensity of her own ignorance or even the jejune quality of her new knowledge. As she waited along the pier with Ratcatcher at her side, Father Bunn negotiated with the captain of a long, sleek boat with sails the color of tobacco leaf.

Ratcatcher offered judicious commentary. "Teran the fluted thigh still whistles in the deep," was his considered opinion.

"Quite," said Sky, and the Ansharu nodded at her evident good sense.

Soon, they had passed through the canal near Utbridge and were gliding effortlessly down the river Wyvern, which is also called Darkwitch by the folk. The wind was with them and they quickly overtook the small junks and barges that carried goods. The fishermen looked up from their work as if the craft were itself a living creature swimming out to seas too distant for their concern.

The closely knotted buildings of neighborhoods began to thin until the river bank was increasingly given over to thickets of ripe vegetation broken by an occasional structure slowly falling back into primeval abandon. The captain proved a taciturn fellow, having expended the bulk of his word hoard talking to the priest. Once, however, he pointed starboard and spat.

"Yeadran they go fer, them whileys take an arm quickspittle," he said.

Sky pulled back from ship side when she saw the general import of his meaning conveyed by the rapid splash of creatures with the muscular burst of eels and massive, carnivorous jaws armed with a double row of serrated teeth.

When it seemed they must be headed for nothing but a boondocks, Father Bunn explained that they were faring towards an ancient monastic fortress that was now chiefly a sanitarium and some time retreat for the brethren of his order. The zenith of the day was well past when they rounded a bend in the river and were met by the hulking stone walls of Casa Balthasar. There was still sun enough to dapple the land which ended in a dark green line where the surrounding forest nudged up against the thick skin of the edifice.

While they were yet outside the shadows of the fortress walls, Ratcatcher grabbed the priest's shoulder and pointed at a spur of wild grass at the water's edge. Sky could see nothing to explain his interest. Father Bunn whispered softly to his comrade, then more loudly.

"Crouching low by the river. Look now or you will miss her."

There was indeed a dark, shadow creature, a young girl, nearly naked, with sable locks crossing into her eyes and reaching down into the lustrous water. Her face held such a strange, ambiguous expression: wild and prepared to shrink away into deep woods, yet her shining, alien eyes seemed equally melancholy and waiting, for what who could say? Something in Sky cried out at the sight of her.

"It is a Nocturne," said the priest. "They are hard to see and many prefer not to. The kindly brothers and Anshara matrons of the sanitarium leave them baskets of food in nearby meadows. Some of them find their way to the city."

Their craft was approaching a sprawling double arch stone bridge. Only now did Sky begin to feel self-conscious, and to wonder what was in store. After they had floated past, a monk spied them and began to shout. Soon after, the river boat was lightly tethered and the passengers disembarked. After not a few steps up towards the main gate, a hooded porter descended from the barbican to meet them. His solemn eyes bid them wary welcome.

The lean smile of the porter held unasked questions. Something in the nature of his visitors bothered him. Few came to the Casa anymore; few knew the lore of the Nazarene. Though the monks did not answer to the Guardian, the order occasionally found it necessary to safeguard an inconvenient person who had recently developed an ailment requiring solitude. Ostensibly, the newcomers had come to visit the sick. The Ansharu claimed to know one of the matrons of the ward. It was plausible, but almost certainly a subterfuge.

The porter barely bothered to hide his disbelief. Sky's guides were themselves not quite certain of their mission. The Elder did not tell them everything. All they knew was that he wanted his old friend to see the girl. In the times called past, the friend had often been able to discover lost things.

A young novice was summoned to lead them through a series of extended corridors. It must have taken an army of brothers to beat back the dust. His awkward manner made Sky blush. It seemed a long time since she had felt really pretty. This tolerable hiatus from her fate was brief enough. Soon, the novice left them at the threshold to a capacious room of arches and columns that had once served as both library and Scriptorium.

The architectural space was softly lit with the waning evening light that entered by narrow, thickly glazed windows. Rows of beds had been set up where the monks once labored to preserve the long learning. A unique pungency melded from pine boards and beeswax and the ghosts of vellum manuscripts perfumed the air.

The Anshara that approached them blankly acknowledged their presence. The matron wore a head-covering and garb of pure white. Her eyes were the palest shade of gray. She was truly quite stunning, though no one in the ward betrayed interest. When Ratcatcher spoke to her, the matron lifted the veil of her serenity ever so slightly. The corner of her mouth twitched, but soon resumed its placid equipoise.

"They're cousins," said the priest in a whisper.

The Anshara called then for an assistant to take the watch and disappeared. While she was gone, Father Bunn drew Sky's attention to a text that stood on a single bookstand. It was a lovely calligraphic hand sprinkled with marginalia of beasts, trees, and a pair of eager paramours. The priest read aloud:

> *I have arrived in my garden, O my sister, my spouse.*
> *I have harvested my myrrh, with my aromatic oils.*
> *I have eaten the honeycomb with my honey.*
> *I have drunk my wine with my milk.*

"It's from the Song of Songs, a canticle well pondered by celibate religious."

Again, Sky could not tell if puckish humor were intended, though she was starting to think the priest one of those rare souls who combines kindness and wit as naturally as breathing. Meanwhile, Ratcatcher was busy demonstrating the innumerable benefits of hiding a ferret under one's hat. A thin-faced youth who had lain as one of the dead raised up in his bed; clapped his hands like the boy he had been just a few short years ago.

Then the matron returned. There was need for efficiency. The captain had refused to anchor his boat for the night. They would have to journey back with lanterns attached to the mizzen. The Anshara directed them to a narrow passage hidden near the back wall of a cupboard. Then they were left to discern the path alone. Vacant cells coldly echoed their steps. Father Bunn raised a solitary torch that tickled the walls with a feeble luminescence which mutely determined the entrance to a crypt. Quickly, they proceeded past the bone archives.

A regular light beckoned to their frail torch. The source proved to come from what was more a rough alcove than cell. A board placed upon a ledge of rock evidently served for both bed and table. A silver oil lamp kept a steady flame beneath an icon of Christ Pantocrator. A slight figure knelt silently before it. How it should have mattered was a mystery. When the monk nimbly raised himself and turned, it was evident that he was blind. Nevertheless, he sensed their presence.

"Ah, so we have made the pilgrimage and all that. Such a long way to see a rag of flesh. What? Toby? I don't need the ledgers. Not for a long time, old friend."

"We've brought someone new, brother," answered the priest with admirable forbearance.

"Yes, yes, I know. The flibbertigibbet. Where did you find it?" The monk shook his head. "Don't tell me. What does it matter?

He's always casting his net. Never tires of it. Personally, I'd throw it back."

"No you wouldn't," said Ratcatcher – and Sky was so taken aback she forgot to be angry with the old monk.

The monk shrugged. "The Anshari always know better, don't they Toby? And the sad thing is, he's right. Well, girl, come near. I have to read in Braille nowadays."

Sky stepped forward gingerly. The monk ran his fingers lightly over her face. His breath had the faint smell of sour wine. Then he stepped back and closed his blind eyes.

"She is sitting in the jungle, a chalk girl with her hands on her ears and a frown on her face. There is a flame memory. It rises from the ground. It forms an arc that crosses behind her, lying in state. And there too, a hulking viridian shadow apes her posture, its ancient and mischievous eyes peek out from miser's lids; it smiles."

The monk was quiet then. On the whole, and basically altogether, Sky found it rather less than pleasing. But at least it was over. She began to retreat, feeling rather numb. And then the monk coughed. It turned out there was more. This time, the voice of the monk was strong and sustained, lilting with energy from who knows where.

"It is well-known in the ancient cultures, that is, the ones so remote that they have been thoroughly forgotten — it is thought that it makes no difference whether they had ever been, so thoroughly have they been lost — yet in the wisdom of those long erased from conscious recall, it is certainly understood that it is a perilous thing, if one should be summoned, and it is a request, though also something of a polite demand.

If one should be asked, what honor, what trepidation, the war between primordial curiosity and the certitude of death. Indeed, it is terrible to be asked to present oneself, alone, bare, and unprotected, the heart racing at the threshold. One is not quite oneself, buried like a seed of trembling in the heart where the ecstasy of secrets is revealed in doom, the body bereft of hope as it enters the chamber of the worm.

This one unweaves in the night what is woven in the day. Demeter's child, Pandora's twin, let her look now to the office of the Cup Bearer. She be the one chosen from before ages."

The Waves

The wind was listless or against them the journey back. The captain muttered and cursed and yelled at the mate for lack of anything else to do. The priest and the Ansharu hovered nearby Sky, protective, but afraid to speak.

Sky wasn't much in a hurry to speak either. She couldn't stop thinking about the strange words of the Elder's friend – and about the Nocturne.

They arrived at last in the city at dawn. The people were shaking off their dreams and readying for the day. Sky did not want to sleep. She stood waiting in front of the Elder's door, wondering if it was too early to knock. After five minutes, he opened it himself.

Sky pushed past him and made straight for the beautiful parlor room. Then she was sitting in one of the lovely chairs and Audrey had evidently forgiven her so completely as to have crawled into her lap. For a long time, Sky just sat there and absently pet the cat who purred contentment. Then, at the end of a line of unspoken thought, she asked, "How many?"

The Elder could not say why, but he felt it was right to bring her to this place. The answer was here, where he did not wish to go. How often had he sensed a desire to return, but had not, unwilling to walk those sands alone. And yet for days now, the urge to find the place, to look with older eyes, had been pressing up against him. So when the girl said, "How many?" he packed a day bag with flasks of water, some cheese, and a long baguette.

They left while many were still asleep. The breeze was gentle. The sun blinked into the horizon, softly bidding the day. But it was a long hike and likely to become laborious. When the mountains came into view, he said "memories put on flesh" in a tone of wistful ache.

The further they progressed, the more it became clear that he was reading the path for signs of a previous passage, of steps taken with another. He would question the very stones to see if they remembered. He looked at Sky, startled, recalling his present task. Then the Elder scanned the horizon and gathered himself. He walked like a man condemned. By mid-day, she knew the summit he was leading her towards.

"When you fall in love," he said, "you don't simply yearn for the beloved. The body does not merely desire to embrace and be embraced. Everything, what she loved and touched, the places you were together, the way she sang in the morning . . . the body of the beloved becomes a whole world."

He did not look at her when he said these words. The voice she heard was not bitter, or nostalgic. It was nearly a young man's voice, full of wonder.

Then the climb became steep, every breath reserved for the ascent. When it leveled off, they were looking down at the flank of the mountain. The Elder was questioning it, trying to find an old wound. Then they followed an ancient path that could only be discovered from above. When he found the fissure, the crack led within to the cavernous heart.

Though some light filtered down from an opening higher up, he had a lantern ready. Already, when they first entered, she heard an echo resounding in the vast emptiness. Sky could not help but contrast this journey with the one of the day before. Here, too, descent into depths, yet she was not prepared for the great aqueous mirror of the lake. A soft, dreaming light revealed the arched shoulders of the mountain. The limpid surface of the water reflected back stalactites reaching down from above. At the center of the lake, a small island was located, upon which a marble bier had been erected. On this bed, one could not tell if it were made from stone or was astonishing reality, the recumbent form of a sleeping giant.

"It is Artorius," said the Elder without further explanation.

And they walked still further, each alone with their thoughts, communing in silence.

"What you asked for is a number known only to the Father whose cloak is Night," he said, breaking their companionable quiet. "We are timid and broken. None of us are whole. No life is complete. The longest fails to reach what it obscurely hoped for. We hardly know what we hope for. Some, like the young of certain turtles, are gobbled up by vipers, barely having registered life. We are scattered, confused, lost in the dark and pretending to know the rules of the game. A forked creature bargaining with the void, we harbor monsters in the deep.

But still, there is beauty that enchants and somehow love remains, in spite of us much of the time."

Rather than retrace their way back, they followed a narrow trail upwards and across to a different opening in the mountain that led onto a path several hundred feet above the sea. Time inside the mountain had passed rapidly. Evening had come. Moonlight illumined natural outcroppings of rock breaking the severe surface of the precipice.

Odd, humorous creatures, marsupial in appearance, adorned many of these ledges. The Elder called them snow rays. Their faces were covered in a dark fur that grayed around the edges of their amber eyes. They chattered amongst themselves and pointed at the newcomers with thin arms that appeared to emerge from a diaphanous cloak that covered their bodies with the exception of a whip-like tail.

Abruptly, one of their numbers leapt into the void, opening out its arms as it did so. The cloak unfurled, a light, silver-white gliding wing. It carried the creature in lazy arcs to a rocky shelf far below. This departure initiated a scramble of hasty imitation. The creatures fell, headlong, hundreds of feet below without remorse or fear. At the last moment before destruction, they would pull up, quite unharmed, the gossamer wings of the snow rays bearing them aloft.

After this outburst of activity, they would settle in new groupings upon a further series of ledges that fell in terraced steps to the base of the mountain. There, they resumed their noisy commentary, grooming themselves and looking back at the intruders with ambivalent curiosity.

Lacking such natural protections against doom, the Elder and Sky were unwilling to risk further descent in the darkness. They remained on that high level gazing up at the cloudless night sky until the vista of stars had slowly turned into dawn.

In the passing of the night, despite two days and nights of continuous adventure, Sky found it difficult to sleep. She listened to the suspirious waters of the deep running to ground. The countless waves cast themselves with profligate abandon upon the shore. Billions upon billions of endless cries that flooded shallow pools, traced out thin rivulets, then vanished, hopeless into the cold sand.

Chapter Two

How Amanda Became Miss Ellwood

How to begin a story

The retired race car driver turned and looked at Claire. He'd noticed her when they had walked into the ballroom. There was something in the way she sat peering at the guests as they passed by. She observed, her long body poised, yet relaxed. The girl was nothing like a siren, yet she emitted an undeniable, cool attraction. He caught at a slight, barely discernible smile. Had she been listening? The conversation was dull enough. Perhaps it was some private reverie, a memory sweet and incommunicable that bowed her lips.

"I don't suppose *you* know how to begin a story?" he asked with an impulse of bravado too rapid for deliberation to check his tongue.

"I should begin with a girl going out for a walk," answered Claire as casually as if they had been practically old friends. She did not look at him, but followed with her eyes a man who had been pushing his way forward through the crowd of elegantly dressed, middle-aged people. The women were laughing too loudly at strained efforts at wit. The men fancied themselves droll.

No one seemed to notice the man who oafishly found his way to the bar, though he stood out in his drab gray trench coat with an umbrella held awkwardly under his arm. His face paunchy and vaguely jaundiced, like a fat and slightly overripe pumpkin, was oddly solemn.

"Isn't that rather prosaic?" asked the woman in pajamas. There was just a hint of annoyance in her voice.

"You should always start with prosaic," said Claire, still not looking at them. "Is it raining by any chance?"

"Dry as a bone. What next?" said the speed enthusiast.

"Oh, anything. Have the girl walk until she suddenly finds herself in an unfamiliar neighborhood."

"What kind of neighborhood? Here's the crisis —." The driver grinned at his companion, but she refused to be assuaged.

"Well," Claire turned to them now, her limpid blue eyes taking them in with a kind of icy playfulness. "I would have her recognize the neighborhood as something she had seen before, maybe in an old photograph. Then I should have her ask a young child for directions. The child begins to answer her when she has a wild thought. She has not only seen this neighborhood, she has seen this girl. 'What is your name?' she asks, her throat tightening in disbelief and unaccountable terror. The girl answers. It is her mother or perhaps her grandmother. There, that is a start."

"Hey, that's not half bad."

"Tolerable," admitted the woman.

A spice

Sandrine wore her silk pajamas during the day, smoked cheroots, talked in a way that was matter-of-fact, one-of-the-boys, but at the same time, pure sex. She'd dabbled at playing a journalist when she was twenty, married well at twenty-five to a man three decades her elder. At forty she was a widow who wore silk pajamas and served as the star of her very own self-styled salon, a retinue of crooks, artists, and bored rich.

The first time she saw Joss Wherryweather, she looked him up and down like a horse buyer contemplating a purchase. He almost expected her to ask him to show her his teeth, but all she said was, "Well, you're not a crook, not yet, and you're not rich. That must make you an actor, a novelist, or a painter."

"At this point, I am only an observer of the human condition, actually."

"Close enough. Much money in observing, is there?"

"Not if you tell the truth," he said. Looking around at the mix of her society, all of whom, in the first shock of meeting, seemed awash in the same jaded fog, a decadent, wry smile waiting for the *bon mot* of their queen, he added, "If anyone here still believes in truth."

"Oh, don't mind them." Sandrine took a step closer and flashed a warm smile that was unexpectedly powerful. She put a soft hand on his elbow and turned him away from the crowd and towards the balcony. Then, in a low voice, "they don't even believe in themselves."

Sandrine, of course, meant nothing by it. She wasn't actually interested in words, except as props in a performance. The boy was charming in an awkward, quaint manner, the way he was insecure and half-despising them all mixed in with priggishness and envy.

Less charming was the way he kept looking at the Ellwood girl with puppy eyes rather revoltingly sincere. There had been a scandal. She could not quite recollect. Something about the girl's father. Madness in the family, an affair, no? Well, whatever it was their poor mama had needed to find a lifeboat with two young daughters. It was lucky she still had her looks.

Margaret frowns

"Do be kind to Margaret, poor thing."

"Oh, why?"

"Haven't you heard?"

"Not a thing. No one tells me anything."

"Well, if no one is saying."

"Archie!"

"Yes. Archie."

"Well, I suppose. In the interests of charity, that sort of thing."

"Do be charitable, Archie."

"I like to be kind. I'm that sort of chap."

"Sure, Archie."

"Not that I'm one to gossip. I simply abhor cheap talk."

"You always have a good reason, Archie."

"Archie Crumpet always has his reasons, that's what I say."

"Come off it, Archie. We offer you plenary absolution, now let's have it."

"Thanks. Anyone have a cigarette? Nasty things. I suddenly have an irresistible desire for a smoke."

"Archie!"

"Oh, alright. Forget the smoke. You know that boy Margaret has been carting around for the last two weeks?"

"The one that used to go about with Amanda?"

"The sculptor."

"No, that was the last one. I don't believe he has declared a profession."

"Why bother, really?"

"Yes, yes. Well, imagine, all this time Margaret has been playing hard to get —"

"She must be some actress."

"Now, now. We did say charitable, didn't we?"

"So what's the scoop?"

"You don't see the undeclared fellow, do you?"

"Actually, there he is. Over there by that awful painting of Sandrine's late husband frowning down at everyone."

"Ah, but you don't see him with Margaret, do you?"

"No. Let's see. No. She's standing next to Martin Last frowning at everyone."

"An awful lot of frowns."

"Turns out, you see, that Margaret's friend is —"

"No!"

"Alas, no. Such a good looking boy, too. No, my dears, he is a conscientious objector. Some sort of religious thing, I dare say, though it can't be that. In any event, he just won't and there is poor Margaret. All this time, she thought he was playing the game. Now it seems he wasn't playing at all."

"Oh, what a lark."

"It isn't any fun playing at virtue if you've actually got to be virtuous."

"I dare say."

The Dodo

"You haven't seen my *Raphus cucullatus*, have you?" Joss's nonplussed helplessness only bemused Tim. "A fowl about the size of a turkey, blue snood, large beak, useless wings and large yellow feet that plod about like your grandmother's galoshes."

"Ah, you mean the dodo. You know I had thought . . ."

Tim gestured him ever so casually, yet emphatically into the sitting room. Claire Ellwood offered a cordial smile. Joss took her hand and bowed slightly, amazed that the thump of his heart wasn't audible across the room.

"You know that dodo is a corruption of the Portuguese – *duodo* meaning silly and stupid," continued Tim with studied avoidance of Wherryweather's obvious crush.

"Terribly unfair, poor things," said Claire. "I wish that I could give them flight."

"One day, perhaps you *shall*," said Tim gallantly.

A conversation

"So there we were having an entirely sensible conversation about cravats and the interesting topic of whether orchid was a responsible color. Basil's opinion, well, you know he was raised by Oratorians, so one must make allowances, is that any shade of purple is suitable for lent. I said to the poor boy that one was getting slightly recherché to match one's cravat to the priest's stole, but he's like that."

"How very fascinating," said Amanda, bravely suppressing a yawn.

"Oh, but then this towering, uncouth fellow from West Virginia planted himself in the doorway and refused to budge. His head was shaped like a bullet or a malformed yam, very little cranial space, but this did not stop him from initiating a monologue of quite Shakespearean proportion. It was a soliloquy devoted to the dubious practice of what he kept calling chaw.

Poor Basil and I looked at one another in sheer wonderment. At first, I thought he was talking about some instrument in Native American medicine, some element in shamanic practice — which is quite possible, now that I think of it. Anyway, the Yankee kept recurring to chaw, chaw, chaw until it cleared in a flash. The damnable fellow was examining the niceties of tobacco chewing amongst ladies of the antebellum South."

"Archie, you said you were going to say about Claire."

"Oh, she was there. And looking quite lovely, but you know the girl. She always seems as if she'd rather be somewhere else. Basil said the fellow was having one over on us. Thankfully, another damnable fellow barged right past the American and stopped him flat or doubtless we should have been treated to a history of the spittoon. This one had that harried, savage appearance so he was either a journalist or a hobo, so difficult to tell them apart. Wanted to know if we had a copy of Bradshaw's handy."

"And Claire was with no one special?"

"There was that one. He used to come about with you, I should think. Or perhaps not. I will say he was that type. Did I tell you Sandrine would make a ghost look flabby? She's going to be one of those knotty old ladies you could fit in a drainpipe."

The perfect criminal

On the way out that evening, Claire stumbled upon the crasher. The man in the trench coat was stuffing his face with éclairs and tossing down glasses of champagne. He looked back at the girl with guilty surprise.

"They just can't see you, I imagine," said Claire. "Father always said the perfect criminal is someone who couldn't possibly exist."

"Oh, I don't know," said the brazen fellow. "Some folks go in for a bit of mayhem. It might be useful so long as you keep it off the books."

The most spiritual eyes

"He has the most spiritual eyes," remarked the girl in fluttering awe.

Joss looked around for the source of adoration. A faded poster of the renegade Osama bin Laden, so faded it had been nearly forgotten, adorned the side of a rough utilitarian edifice designed to provide minimal protection from the rain for commuters on the transit. He remarked, rather sternly, upon the proper nature of retributive justice in the case of her idol.

"There's no proof, whatsoever, that capital punishment acts as a deterrent to crime," she shouted rather more loudly than she intended.

Joss shrugged and answered in an annoyingly calm voice. "In China, in the twenties of the previous century, there was a crack-down on crime. The government put up billboards upon which were attached the severed heads of condemned criminals. Rather effective advertising, I should think."

The girl said nothing. To her rough way of thinking, the 1920s were so long ago, what had happened then was hardly true anymore. Then, after an awkward pause, she brought forth the killing riposte. "The only thing you care about is money." This was the most devastating charge she could think to throw at him.

"Money's rather important," he said soberly. "Turn around."

"What?" She was mystified and stared at him with blank incomprehension.

"Turn around,' he said in a commanding voice and strange to say, the girl turned. With delicate care, he shoved the tag of her shirt down below the hem of the neckline.

"Sticking up," he said. "Someone should have told you."

"I was in a hurry," said the girl.

"Yes, well moral severity is rather ridiculous when joined to accidental unkemptness, don't you think? You may resume, if you like."

"No, no," she answered, suddenly shy and thrown off. He was a good-looking bigot. "You obviously just don't get it."

"Yes, badly educated, I'm afraid. It's a fault of my upbringing."

As she was raised to believe that social conditions were, indeed, responsible for most problems afflicting the world, she had no ready rejoinder for this confession. The city bus came and they sat resolutely apart from one another.

A beautiful friendship

Exasperation had latched onto Joss Wherryweather with the vengeful tenacity of an irate tick. The material universe had entered into the conspiracy. Milk was sure to be sour, the phone rang at precisely the most inopportune moment, the tin of biscuits destined to scatter upon the floor. At the cafe, the woman with the battered Rabelais and the mocha beamed at them. It was clear she found them quite beautiful boys. When they had walked a distance away, Joss nudged TimPig in the shoulder.

"That woman undoubtedly thinks that we are a couple of fruits. Someone ought to set her straight."

Tim laughed, then checked Joss, who was about to turn back. "Oh, don't disabuse her. How exceedingly rare in this life are any of us granted a charming moment. Right now, she has the exhilarating feeling of being spiritually large, her superior tolerance joined with what she conceives as the quaintly picturesque."

"Picturesque?"

"Well, yes. I, so slight and dressed in my tailored clothes. You, a rugby sort in tattered, bohemian deshabille. We're a picture, don't you see? You wouldn't take that away from her, would you?"

Joss stared at his feet as they walked, imagining that every fair maiden was looking at them precisely the same way. Then, sulkily, "only she's wrong."

Tim was half-enjoying his friend's despondency. It was so ridiculous, if only he would see it.

"I am wrong half a dozen times a day. Rarely does it allow me the pleasure of benevolent generosity towards my fellow man. I assure you, she is not going to tattle to anyone of consequence. Those who know us will only find it funny. Tell it to your girl yourself. She'll tease you, think you sweet beyond words, make gorgeous, ravenous love with you into the night."

Joss, still sulking, "I haven't got a girl."

At this, Tim waxed even more enthusiastic. "Even better. You ought to go pay that woman to noise it about. The girls will flock to you. First, they'll feel safe around you. Then, they'll want to show you the error of your ways. You won't be able to beat them off with a stick."

At last, Joss rewarded his friend with a wry smile. "You have a unique approach."

What he didn't say – that sometimes his yearning for woman, so intimate and painful, would seem to him only an echo of a deeper need. Joss had the feeling that his desire and his unhappiness were too strong; that the woman he longed for with such aching tenacity, her voice, regard, soft touch and smile should prove inevitably unequal to the pain. He would find her, this elusive she, and love her — and still be unhappy.

He wanted something from life that life cannot give. *I want to get inside . . . push past to the page after the last.* He spotted someone waving at them from a crowd, a young man dressed casually, surrounded by children eating ices and listening to mammas, nannies, and whatnot. He had an expression of acute discomfort.

"Look, there is your friend, Adam," said Tim.

A niece called Wanda

"Wherryweather, come here," commanded Cyrus Peabody.

Pym Smalley was standing as close as he dared, salivating at the thought that something unpleasant was about to happen. At that moment, Joss recalled a kitten that had been discovered by passing boaters three miles out in the Gulf of Mexico paddling for all it was worth. He abhorred cruelty and was deeply pleased the young cat had been rescued, but a sincere urge to similarly dump Pym Smalley into the Bermuda Triangle struck him as entirely commendable.

The young woman from the bus stop was unaccountably standing next to Peabody. Recognition and increased bemusement slowly migrated across the face of the girl.

"Wherryweather, this is my niece, Wanda. You've been working on some of her scribblings, I dare say."

A step up

The editor's office was two floors above. It was nearly its own separate apartment where Cyrus Peabody kept a watchful eye on the minions below Olympus. The entire operation, of course, was wholly a subject of individual largesse. If it were not for the independence and, what is more to the point, the barrenness of a number of well-placed maiden aunts – judiciously spoken to before fitfully giving up their last breaths – the journal would long since have gone the way of all flesh.

Peabody was particularly known for snuffling out recluses with money, sad, lonely souls with large bank accounts and no one and nothing to remember them by. Peabody's grand ascendancy to the editor's chair had been settled by the placing of what he called a page of "eternal donors" just after the table of contents, where the likes of Margaret Withers and Augustus Ninney were acknowledged, as with the Chinese, as ancient and venerable deities responsible for the general well-being of the enterprise.

Joss wondered as he ascended the stairs to the editor's "chamber of decision" – that was another of Peabody's pretentious phrases – if the Victorian photos nailed rather judiciously to the wall of the staircase presented a number of the departed patrons. They were not, though Peabody sometimes said that they were. He also sometimes claimed that they were eminent worthies of his own family, but, in fact, they were a hodge-podge of forgotten souls picked up at various estate sales over the years. One particular stern old lady, her eyes acute and grave, attracted Joss's attention. He paused a moment, listening to the heavy silence of the nearby office, hoping for some wisdom to be mystically conveyed. Alas, the solemn ghost refused comment.

Peabody sat in his large, leather chair, his heavy visage sinking into flab, though not without a touch of erstwhile regality. He appeared suddenly to Joss as an escapee from the land of children's fantasy, a toad somewhat successfully masquerading as human, a raj amphibian larking as the head of an obscure art and polish journal. For a long, uncomfortable half minute, Peabody said nothing. Indeed, he did not appear to have taken cognizance of Joss at all, though Wherryweather had introduced himself upon first entering the precinct of decision. Then, as if coming out of a prolonged reverie, Peabody suddenly erupted into speech.

"I am sorry to say that Bradley Unger has left us."

Joss was momentarily baffled. In the eighteen months that he had worked at the journal, he had never once met or even heard mention of such a person.

Wherryweather did the best he could. "He got a better offer, sir?"

"Rather a command performance. He deceased last Thursday whilst visiting his son, the undertaker. One cannot help but admire the economic irony of Providence. I only just heard. The religion writer, you understand?"

"I didn't realize we had such," confessed Joss.

"Well, priorities, lad. It wasn't unusual for Bradley to skip six or seven issues between pieces."

"It's a loss, sir," said Joss, wondering why Peabody was making such a production of it and when he might begin to cross examine him on the matter of his nieces' article which was a truly mad bit of hysteria about the fascist tendencies in nature or as Joss liked to put it, accusing the sea horse of patriarchal appropriation in seeing to the nurture of young fish foals. The founder editor continued with no interest in Joss' discomfiture.

"Though we at *Ulysses Attic* are broad, too broad, some say, we shall not turn coward before criticism. The journal has always had someone to keep an eye on religion and Cyrus Peabody is not going to be the one to drop vigilance."

"That's very commendable, sir, but I don't quite see —"

"The problem is that Susan has her hands full with society, Peter politics. Richard is already pulling double duty with food and novels. Dan does the talkies, Bertie Theater. We're all stretched rather thin." It was part of Peabody's annoying predilection for the fake that he insisted on referring to cinema as the talkies as if Al Jolsen had stunned everyone with *The Jazz Singer* in recent memory.

"But as you say, sir, if it's only once every year and a half." Ulysses Attic was a quarterly.

Peabody sighed and bit down moodily on his unlit cigar. "Wherryweather, I'll be honest with you. Nobody here is terribly up on God."

"You could invite the odd free-lance writer."

Peabody looked at him now with an expression of ancient sorrow. "I'd prefer to keep it in

house."

At this moment, a dawning dismay fell upon Joss. "Sir, I'm only a proof reader, after all."

"It's a step up, lad. Don't revile it just because it's rather quaint. A foot in the door, it is."

"But I'm an atheist, sir."

"Of course you are, my boy. If you weren't educated, we wouldn't have hired you. Old Bradley never prayed a day in his life."

Pym Smalley rather glowed when he heard the news. Religion writer was considered in all but technical terms a step down from proof reader, though, of course, Joss was to continue in his present duties. In fact, for a long time, nothing happened. So long as Wherryweather held the position of religion writer, Peabody saw no need to push so far as an actual article.

Aunt Imogen

Aunt Imogen was actually his second cousin and not an aunt, but family usage had designated her as an aunt for reasons rather nebulous. Most probably, it was her seniority by some fifteen years. Probably some thought when he was very young that it would be too difficult to explain the slight removal of relations constituting second cousinship. In any event, Aunt Imogen was in the kitchen pouring a teaspoon of kahlúa into her coffee and looking very smart.

Joss always liked her because she was handsome and didn't talk down to him – she'd explained right off when he first met her at the age of six that she was his cousin and not his aunt, but everyone just kept calling her aunt so there it was.

"Aunt Imogen," said Joss, "I am unhappy."

She stopped stirring her coffee for precisely .575 of a second, then smiled and resumed her occupation. "That's not so unusual, Joss. It's very difficult to be happy. Almost anyone, however, can fall into unhappiness."

Joss wondered then if Imogen was unhappy. She seemed so self-assured, yet if she wasn't unhappy, her laugh would not be so deep and wonderful. He decided that she was superficially unhappy, but not so in her depths.

"They've made me religion writer at the mag. Susan Bainbridge congratulated me and offered as a suggestion for a first article that I interview Jesus Christ as he is reportedly alive and well."

When Aunt Imogen smiled, little crinkles erupted around her eyes. *The smile of her eyes* is what Joss thought when he saw them.

A regular gaucho

Amanda admitted to herself that envy was an ugly emotion. It was especially invidious, because Claire was an entirely vulnerable, sweet-natured young woman. Though Amanda was nearly two years her junior, in many ways she was the elder sister. Claire was misty, lacking in rudimentary calculation, and perfect on a horse.

It was simply assumed among their set that girls loved horses. No one would imagine that a girl might shudder to be near them and expect the offer of an apple to result in a crunching of valuable fingers. A certain casual aptitude was similarly expected. When they had lived in Argentina, Claire would ride off into the lonely pampas like a regular gaucho. In England, she effortlessly took part in dressage and steeplechase and any other equestrian exercise that was suggested.

Amanda suspected that Claire was happier on a horse than among people. Now she was trotting up on her frightful beast to commiserate.

"Amanda, it was such a lovely ride. So sad you're feeling unwell."

"Yes, unlucky."

I'm not very good at anything

"Imogen, I've got to make money, lots of it. I suppose it was a mistake pursuing that degree in French medieval poetry."

"There's much more to life than money. You know that."

"Yes, well, no one sees the point in devoting five years of your life to the poetry of Villon."

"Why don't you explain it to them?"

"Oh, I don't see the point either."

"Don't you love Villon's poetry?"

"Not five years worth."

"I see. How's your love life?"

Joss frowned. He'd forgotten, no, he'd remembered, but he'd forgotten that liking Imogen coexisted with her impertinence. When she wasn't around, he imagined her impertinence as charming and part of what he liked.

"I am —" he paused, looking for the right word, "I am *disinclined* to love, just now. I am fond of a girl, it's true, but I do not want to be in love."

"Why ever not? Doesn't she like you? I'm sure she does, Joss."

"It doesn't matter. Love is not going to happen. I have refused permission."

"You have eccentric ideas. Why *lots* of money?"

"Well, enough to pay off my student loans and the money I owe family – and enough to have an adventure or two . . . hell, lots, Imogen, so I can cast off the dust from my feet and, and go somewhere where I'll be happy."

"You know, of course, that wherever you go, you'll have to be there."

A bitter, half breath of a laugh was all Joss could manage in response. Then, "yes, it's a problem. I can't solve it, so let's put it aside for the moment. How do I make money? I'm not very good at anything, I'm afraid."

Not very Jane

"I should like it," said Joss Wherryweather, rolling his eyes – he'd begun rolling his eyes when his parents named him Josiah – "if we could all live in a Jane Austen novel, but the sad truth is we none of us can, we none of us could, probably not even dear Jane."

"We could try," said Amanda. "You could begin by calling me Miss Ellwood."

"Ah, but you couldn't be Miss Ellwood," said charming Adam. "Your sister Claire would be Miss Ellwood. You would have to pray and pray that some dope would marry her so that you could be Miss Ellwood."

"See, it already isn't any fun," complained Claire. "I'm afraid I'm planning on being an old, unwanted spinster, Amanda. I'm going to spy on the neighbors and own about a hundred and fifty cats."

"It's just like you," chided Amanda. "I think I can already see the old prune of your face itching to come through the mask of your beauty."

"You put that very poetically."

Amanda smiled at Adam. "I'm a natural born poet," she said.

"There are numerous problems in our plan to live in a Jane novel," remarked Joss, bringing them back to himself.

"I don't remember any such plan," stated Claire.

"It isn't even possible. It *cannot* happen," declared Amanda in haughty tones.

Joss gave her a killing look and went on with his oration. "First off, we no longer live in a society that respects and prizes class distinctions and identifies good breeding with the ownership of ancestral land."

"Is that right?" interrupted Adam. "I should have thought that the main theme of Austen's novels is a kind of ethical and aesthetic compatibility. The kind of blue blood snobbery you advert to is precisely what is satirically condemned in *Persuasion*, for instance."

"Naturally, that's true, Adam, but if Darcy doesn't own an estate, the romance of the fairy tale is considerably lessened. I did not say, in any event, that Jane agreed with snobbery, but that respect for class was an inescapable backdrop to her art."

"But I do believe we still respect money," commented Amanda, suddenly serious.

"Yes, people are cowards before wealth, but class is more than simply having a lot of dough. You could be an impoverished aristocrat. It was more than simply blood, too. Or rather, blood was supposed to signify a whole tradition of manners and refined taste."

"Well, Jane may not have been a snob, but you certainly are, Joss."

Joss ignored Amanda. She was always trying to bait him into losing his temper. She did not entirely approve of him. He continued, though suddenly dissatisfied with himself. "Second, the peculiarity and elasticity of our morals —"

"I don't quite gather what you mean," interrupted Claire. "Are you admitting to some perversity?"

"I am not."

"I see. Pray, do go on."

"Second, the near complete barbarism of our times does not allow for a stable moral code. Without a stable moral code, you cannot have a gentleman, and without a gentleman, the Jane plot cannot exist."

"Ah ha!" shouted Amanda. "So you *are* a scoundrel."

"Of course," said Joss. "Scoundrels are what our society produces today."

"That's a lie," said Wanda, who had been quietly fuming at the lot of them. "We are much more enlightened than the past. Everything you say is smug and vicious. Besides, the whole notion of binary genders is fascist."

"Yes, well, a society that cannot recognize basic realties like male and female is undoubtedly on the way to rapid dissolution," said Joss. "It's quite possible the ancients knew more than us and that all our science is largely a history of forgetting or perhaps a slow remembering that is only first a forgetting."

"Don't anyone encourage him," teased Amanda.

Joss remained undaunted. "For example, in ancient Peru there were a people who wove exquisite cords of many colors called *quipos* bound together by a complex system of threads and knots. Modern scholars suppose these cords were perhaps employed as a kind of abacus for counting, but that is rationalizing dullness. The truth is they possessed a most refined language perfected to express profound and subtle insight, yet had no written language. All their poetry was captured in the weaver's art."

"You read that in Guénon," said Adam in a tone still flippant with Amanda's mocking, but serious beneath.

"Well, then," said Joss, "here is something you will not find there. Homer also understood this. The entire tale of Penelope and her weaving is a dark symbol meant only for the wise. The poem itself is what is intended, an oral tale undone in the night of unconscious and rewoven every day. The importunate suitors, bold and uncouth fools, grow impatient and think the bard nothing but a beggar who sells cheap entertainment." Joss cast a glance at Amanda.

"He read all that in a different book," she said.

Wanda shrugged and barely suppressed a yawn.

Joss, unfazed, continued. "Homer's Odysseus is not the cunning sophist of the Tragedians. He is the bearer of solar energies, Athena's counterpart. The reason he must seek out his true wife and could not stay on Ogygia with beautiful Calypso is because the goddess could only offer a stultifying idyll of static beauty. The hidden irony is that Penelope is the true goddess. She is the beloved who enacts the sacred marriage where the flux of time weaves ever and again an eternal wisdom constant, but ever new."

"That's lovely," said Claire with innocent appreciation.

"Homer, Shakespeare, the Bible. Dead white males," said Wanda with righteous certitude that she had delivered a killing indictment.

Joss briefly considered asking if Wanda intended to convey that the Hebrew divinity were a deceased Anglo-Saxon, but did not.

"The other day, I happened upon some puff piece on an *artiste de jure*. I've no idea who he was. It doesn't matter. He'll be replaced in six months by some other gyrating barbarian. What I found chiefly interesting was the manner in which he introduced himself to the camera. He emitted what can only be described as an orgasmic groan, mouthed a few barely articulate syllables, and then let forth another eroticized scream. He concluded with an absurdity that escaped his professionally dim interviewer with the words, 'that's what I'm talking about.'"

"Don't you think that sort of primitivism sometimes effective? As a form of communication, I mean?" Wanda looked around at them. As it was impossible to tell if she were attempting to provoke them or was quite in earnest, no one answered her and Joss went on with his anecdote.

"What fascinated me was the unexceptional, even blasé response he elicited. There was the usual breathlessness secured to the possessor of momentary, recent celebrity. He was lauded as 'the new thing' and therefore worthy of emulation, one supposes. Certainly, the intended audience of barely pubescent teens shall experiment with conversation preceded by and intermittently punctuated with banshee-like howls of sexual peaking."

"Not very Jane," commented Amanda.

"Not fifty years ago, even the most abandoned hedonists would have looked at him funny and perhaps suggested that the poor boy seek professional help."

"If only you had been there," exclaimed Wanda. "He might even today be kindly ministered to by a therapist."

"I shouldn't doubt he *has* a therapist who probably encourages him to express himself," answered Claire, arching her brow at Wanda. It was one thing for she and her sister to tease Joss. To allow Wanda to do so would be to admit another into their intimate set and Claire did not wish this in Wanda's case.

As if taking her words for his own thoughts, Joss went seamlessly on, finishing his useless moral protests against the age. "A hideous word, authenticity. What it means is one can be a savage and a slut without anyone caring enough about you to tell you to stop."

A category mistake

"You're clever. You could write," said Aunt Imogen.

"So what should I write?"

"Relationship books, books on sex, books on how to make money quickly and easily, trash on the afterlife or aliens, better yet, a book on the afterlife and aliens. Then, there's always vanity. Write on how to defeat aging or propose a diet where all one eats is chocolate."

"Do you read any of those kinds of books?"

"No, dear boy, but lots of people do. People who think of life as a series of problems desperately in need of a solution."

"Isn't life a series of problems?"

"It's a category mistake. Life isn't really like that."

"What is it, then?"

"Oh, don't ask, Joss. You'll only spoil it that way."

The girl with sex

Joss did not actually believe he was a scoundrel. Stashed away in a locked briefcase (he'd mislaid the key several apartments ago), Josh kept an article carefully honed whereby he purported to demonstrate the correlated decline in civilization with the waning sales of pajamas. He had merely said it because it seemed to be the appropriate next line. Amanda had a way of bringing out careless words that he was bound to repent.

There had been a time when there was almost an understanding between them. It might still, perhaps, be resuscitated. He would not call it love. Yet they had both backed away for reasons that were clear to no one, least of all themselves. That was why Amanda began to hate him and pester him, because of Claire. His lugubrious brooding was distracted by Adam who attempted to tease Amanda by talking about a sexpot known to their circle.

"Daphne is hardly bearable even with sex," said Joss.

"One is compelled to admit," said Adam, "that Miss Hudson, lovely as she is, on a good day struggles to outdistance the IQ of a head of lettuce."

Claire was suddenly cross. She wanted to ask Joss how well, then, he could bear Daphne, but instead she merely growled and remarked that Daphne Hudson was the kind of girl who would get stupid drunk at a party, commit all sorts of acts she would later regret if she happened to remember them, all the while managing to chew the same piece of gum that she had started the evening with.

"Gum chewing, especially at a social gathering, is a serious breach," admitted Adam, "but you have to give her points for frugality."

"That's not the point!" Claire almost shouted, astounding them all.

"What is the point?" asked Adam with a quizzical expression.

She looked away. Her eyes were welling up and she was embarrassed. She did not know the point, except that the world was no longer enchanting, that her childhood had disappeared and though she desperately wanted to find it again, she could not.

"The point is that a woman needs honor for love to mean anything," she said at last, feeling as if she herself had broken etiquette by speaking in an arcane and foreign tongue.

The angels in the museum

It was a small exhibit in a rather obscure museum that Claire liked to visit because of the park surrounding it. The paths snaked their way through the impressionist farrago of an English garden. When she had satisfied her zeal for nature, she would step inside and see what the artists were up to. On this day, she happened upon various works devoted to the representation of angels. She was studying William Blake's impressive watercolor depicting a cherubim when Joss appeared at her side.

Claire was not unpleased for his company, but part of her felt chagrin, as if an inner sanctum had been breached. Joss sensed her ambivalence, but it was too late to withdraw. He was immediately sorry, however, and his burst of pleasure at seeing her tainted into a moping dissatisfaction. He covered this, as best he could, with some rather stuffy observations on romanticism.

Claire, too, felt awkward. She had quickly repented of her selfish and rather ridiculous desire to keep the museum to herself. Thrown off-balance, she did something she rarely permitted. She spoke about her father.

"My father had a friend who was a monk."

"This was in Argentina?

"Yes, but the holy man was from Italy, a Franciscan, I think."

"It's funny," said Joss, returning to Blake, "how mesomorphic his angels are. His depictions of divine creatures in general appear quite beefy. Whereas, strictly in terms of metaphysics, angels are entirely intellectual in nature. I suppose abstract painting might better capture their essence."

"I know someone, brilliant, but fussy who thinks Blake uncomfortably close to an illustrator of comics," said Claire. "But I was going to tell you about what the monk told my father, I mean."

"I'm sorry. I'm stepping all over it today. I ought to go home and pull up the covers."

"I'm really quite glad to see you."

"And I am terribly keen to learn about the angels from an Italian monk in Buenos Aries." He babbled this quickly, hardly knowing what he was saying.

"My father could tell stories in the most charming manner. I can only give the crib notes."

"Most of Aristotle is crib notes, they say. Anyway, I shall enjoy hearing it from you."

Miss Ellwood led him to a bench. "The monk," she said, "claimed that the beasts in the Garden of Eden were actually their angels. So when the serpent spoke, it was not so shocking. But the main thing I remember is how the monk said that each species of animal had its own angel and that if the sparrow's mother died, the young sparrow would persist, but if the angel of the sparrow were to disappear, every bird would perish."

"You know, you talk quite differently when we're alone."

"It can't be helped. I'm just like that."

"No, it's good, I mean."

"Oh, well, that's alright then."

A night vigil

Claire, his beautiful long-haired daughter, sat waiting for him at the bottom steps of the stairs. She was yawney and snuggling to her blanket, tore from her bed to warm her wait. Yet at the footfall of his step, her beseeching eyes alit, ready for his face.

"Why don't you tell them, papa?" she asked, wanting him to explain why he would not stop their whispers, their stolen winks and half nods that the great man had gone balmy in his exile.

"I will tell them when they have ears to hear," said Henry, sweeping Claire up in his arms and gently leading her to the door of her room. "Now take care, Claire Bright, that you do not wake your sister."

She walked half-way within the threshold, and then turned softly, spoke the words of her heart. "Why don't you tell me?" But already his heavy footfall had retreated into forbidden realms of solitude and thoughts too dangerous for speech.

The unfortunate Hooboo

Joss had the feeling that he was drifting. His was an autumnal spirit, though his entire generation was mournful, which is why their laughter was so lacking in mirth and tinged with hysteria. Jackson Frawley had hung himself two days earlier. In school, Frawley had enjoyed smoky jazz clubs and the odd game of chess, but he had a strange penchant for being the sort of fellow one knew, but could not name. He also had the eccentricity of wearing tall, calfskin boots. When folks tried to think of his name, all they could recall was the boots, so he acquired the nickname of "Hooboo," a shortened version of "whose boots?"

Since Frawley was patrician class and Joss a scholar, they had little enough to do with one another. Joss had seen him infrequently since graduating and now he would never do so. Death being sometimes a known catalyst, a conversation outside the Bodleian was dredged up from murky depths.

Joss had been trying on a vague, but insistent theory. He did not wish to imply that people were mere puppets of forces estranged from them. It was all too easy for reckless sloth to take refuge in such notions. Nonetheless, Joss had a persistent emotion imbued with intelligence. The idea lived as a metaphor which took the form of an image he could not shake. He would see a vast ocean or a world made up of seas. On the surface of the water, creatures imagined themselves to be walking about in cities, founding institutions, marrying, giving birth, and dying. But all the while, they were maritime beings constantly at swim.

The connection between the image and the thought was hardly schematic. Yet for Joss, the ocean was language. Men were speaking all the time, making plans, following directions, conspiring, and dishing dirt, the usual business. The gestalt would suddenly shift, however. It was actually the sea that was speaking. Men lived in language. It was almost as if society was the tool of language. There was too much passivity in the metaphor and that is not really what Joss meant. Still, there was something raw and impersonal in the way language could get away from individual intentions.

Anyway, some version of all that he had told to Frawley and Frawley had taken it all in as if gentlemen could hardly be surprised.

"Civilization is built on liturgy, Wherryweather," he'd remarked. "Language is purified in ritual or it degrades into the whispers of demons."

Hooboo had been found swinging from a rather famous ancestral tree on his family's property. Joss could not help but wonder if he was wearing his boots.

A party

Miss Luddle sat upon the divan which had been reupholstered, but could not hide that it was a platform for chattering fools from as far back as the time of Napoleon. Miss Luddle, herself, was neither chattering, nor reupholstered. She looked through a mauve tinted eye glass. The mechanism of the toy allowed one to easily alter the color of the shade. Miss Luddle had started with green glasses, then periwinkle, chartreuse, and now tried that mongrel shade often employed by cosmetics.

It passed the time, but did not greatly increase the interest of the congregating youth who stood off in bunches of threes and fours acting like damn fools. Not a one of them had anything clever to speak of, though this did not prevent the high pitched squeaks and braying guffaws that punctuated the nebulous talk taken for conversation.

Constance Hoop came and sat down beside her. Mrs. Hoop was a widow who had known Miss Luddle in her youth, which was not so far back as 1815, but receded enough that she often found the time of her most cherished memories a blank to nearly everyone else. Mrs. Hoop was scandalized by this discovery. She had not known they were precious until no one understood them.

"Constance, these children are tremendously stupid."

"Yes, Miss Luddle." Constance never called her Isabel, even when they were schoolfellows.

"I cannot make out a single one of them who is not proof of the retarding effects of pesticides on the food supply."

"Yes, Miss Luddle."

"And who is this Emily Scribble they are all talking about?"

"I don't know, Miss Luddle. She is supposed to be some kind of bright thing, but I haven't seen her."

"And how would you recognize her if you had?" asked Miss Luddle.

"They say she always wears black. It's her trademark, but I haven't seen but six or seven girls all in black and none of them looked at all clever."

"Here, take a number," ordered a massive figure, a local basketball behemoth who had been hired to dress like Poseidon and command the guests.

"I've got three. What have you got, Lola?"

"Sixteen. Looks like we're split."

"Oh, too unpleasant. Make a trade, why don't you?"

"No trades," barked Poseidon.

Joss surveyed the maritime motif and wondered if water would be piped in. Perhaps they would be asked to fight one another like ships in a Roman spectacle. The one positive effect of the drama, he surmised, was that no one would be asked to dance.

"Watch out," warned the gossip journalist, who was writing in a small notebook the details he had just heard about poor HooBoo. "If you try to change accommodations, the sharks will get you. Then it's out you go!"

"What do you mean?"

"See those girls?"

"Those one's with the funny caps?"

"That's the ones. They're meant to be fins. The tip of the jaws, so to speak. You can try for a better boat, but if they catch you, Poseidon there escorts you from the premises. Puts a bit of risk in it."

"Might be worth it," said Joss. He scouted the other lifeboats restlessly, but could not discover an adorable face anywhere.

"I know what you mean. Ten more minutes and I'll have about all one can expect from these things. I'll have to color it up a bit for the readers, of course."

"Naturally," said Joss. "By the way, if I do anything untoward, my name's Eustace Pym Smalley and I work for *Ulysses Attic*."

"You're not planning anything, are you?"

"No, but I have a habit of public flatulence. Usually they make me carry a whistle, sort of like a leper with a bell. You could write that if you wish. I won't mind."

Joss grabbed a scotch from the tray of a passing merman. He was considering whether to wait for his doom or to aim for another craft when a girl with a foam fin stuck to a swim cap tagged him on the shoulder.

"There now, your salad days are over and you sleep with Davey Jones," she said.

He immediately recognized her voice and turned to face her. It was Claire in a flapper dress.

"Claire, you look ridiculous."

"Joss! Funny I didn't see you before."

"Yes, well I – I didn't see you either."

The briefest blush played across her features, which were both big-boned and lovely. He waited, uncertain of himself. Just that morning he had passed her house and searched for the window he presumed looked out from her room. And here she was.

"I suppose you wanted to get thrown out or don't you?"

"I seem to find everyone quite dull. I am dull, myself."

"Well, I can go get Poseidon to show you out. He's rather full of himself. I think he's starting to believe he *is* the god of the sea."

"Of course, I didn't know — it's awfully good to see you, Claire."

"Is it?"

"Yes, awfully."

"That's alright then. You can go to Hades."

"I guess I can't blame you."

"No, Joss. Hades is another part of the mansion where we sharks can send our victims. Amanda and I will be around in another hour or so. I suppose it would be dull to wait."

"Oh, not so bad."

"Are you sure?"

"Tremble, mortal creature! You are cast out from the happiness of men." It was Poseidon closing in on them.

"It's okay, George. He's a friend. I'm sending him to Hades."

George stared askance at them and shook his head, grumbling. It wasn't much fun being Poseidon when the sharks kept sending the guests to hell.

A manifesto

Adam was already in Hades when Joss arrived. "It's not so bad," he said. "From all the propaganda, I really expected worse."

"Oh, this is just the holding cell," quipped Joss. "It's once you sign the unbreakable lease that the fun really starts."

When the Ellwood sisters came by in something short of an hour, Joss could hardly keep his eyes from Claire. She'd removed the silly shark cap. The wave of her auburn hair set against her handsome face was undeniably alluring. Claire stole a quick glance in Joss' direction. The boy was suitably shaken by her beauty. Joss momentarily looked away, suddenly shy and feeling a great coward.

Quickly regaining his composure, he sought her eyes, but she had turned from him. In a kind of panic, he began to speak, not quite knowing what he was going to say.

"May I propose a new project?" he said.

"Another Josiah scheme?"

"Amanda, I do not scheme, I ponder. The idea came to me this morning, as a matter of fact. And it's nothing really, just a little bank robbery."

"Why don't you practice on a corner store first?"

"Thanks, sweet girl. I just said that for effect, though I intended something on the order of a heist, which, for your further education is no ordinary thuggish theft, but an action marked by intelligence, planning, and style. We don't glamorize the heist because of the theft, but because of the art."

"Joss clears up the fine points of crime. When is it beastly and when must one appreciate?" remarked Adam, crossing his arms and staring up at the ceiling.

"Actually," said Joss, ignoring his friend, "I had in mind something in the way of a protest."

Amanda could barely control a sudden fit of giggles. "You're not going to march on Downing Street, are you?" she blurted between snorting laughter.

"Or in front of the grocer's? Tell everyone to boycott fish because they are as amiable as cats and dogs?" chimed Adam.

"No, no, nothing so crude or annoying, but perhaps as senseless." Joss's tone was unusually sad and quiet. The room became attentive. "I suppose what I'd like is to steal back dignity that has been taken from us. I thought we might make a sort of pledge to each other. Nothing grand, no parades, but maybe we would write up a kind of creed, some part of Jane's world that could be maintained or held onto as a candle against the night."

There was, of course, something patently absurd about making a speech of this kind whilst in Hades surrounded by the foam-finned, but inspiration waits for no man.

"What do you mean, Joss?" asked Claire, feeling exposed because tears were welling up in her eyes again.

"Well, I thought we might promise not to speak in vulgarities, to avoid much television and social media, to proscribe easy congress with people who exhibit grossness of habit and savagery of mind, further to defend and try to live out the virtues of courtship and chastity."

There was a long pause before it became evident that Joss was utterly serious.

"I think, dear fellow," said Adam, "that you have just asked us to join you in a monastery."

"Yes, yes, you're right," conceded Joss. "Forget about the manifesto, then. It was just an amusement, anyway."

"No, comrade. You're not getting off that easy. You remember Cyril? Or is it Basil? It's something in the ill family, the Czech fellow, you know?"

"He's Hungarian, Adam," corrected Amanda.

"Oh, I see," said Adam. "He's a Hungarian me."

"You are an unbearable goof," prodded Amanda, very pleased with him.

"He's writing a children's book. You'll like this, Joss. He's titled it, *It doesn't matter if you're good or bad, you're still going to end up dead.*"

"No," said Joss seriously. "You shouldn't tell children that."

Adam collapsed into a huddle of laughter and the Ellwoods soon followed.

"What is it?" said Joss.

"N-nothing, old chap," answered Adam, clapping a friendly hand on Joss's shoulder. "You are too pure. I knew you should say that, is all. I predicted it before you came by."

"Your mum is here."

Mrs. Dollinger popped her head into the room, a half-apologetic smile on her round, pleasant face.

"I'm sorry Adam. I forgot about your Aunt Fish. She's coming by today and I promised you'd be around to chat. She wants to give you something, I imagine."

Since *something* last time was preferred shares in Womble and Dumpling, worth five thousand and secure at that, Adam pulled himself from the allure of the girl not quite Miss Ellwood and bid his adieus from Hades.

To see what he saw

Claire had been riding and so she was disposed to look gently upon the world. She was genial with the old Scotsman who evidently considered perpetual dour a moral accomplishment. She refused to allow misgiving to enter her countenance when she crossed the path of the frightful hag, the wealthy woman who threw parties in order to mock everyone who came. She was amiable with the fellas who dressed the grounds, walking briskly past the fountain and the topiary and directly into the house without losing her kindly mood.

But really, an unaccountable something had been flashing in her nerves, so when she saw her mother pacing in the parlor, the maternal eyes wretched pools of tortured unease, she was less alarmed than might be expected. Claire asked, ever so carefully, what could be the trouble. The answer was a sort of bleating hiccup, followed by the flourishing of a rather crumpled piece of fine stationary which then led to a slowly building siren wail that threatened to explode into banshee abandon.

Moneybags, of course, was nowhere to be seen. Progressing with the serene madness of a ghost into the inner chambers, Claire discovered Amanda sitting on the floor of the study. All about her, black and white prints lay as if in the aftermath of a cyclone. Claire absently chose one of dozens. The portrait of a boy wrapped in a winding sheath of pale fabric like a young Lazarus released from the tomb. Only his eyes and the top of his nose were uncovered. The eyes were enough to perplex Solomon. The expression was wounded, intense, beseeching, malice all at once. Claire dropped the photo like poison. Where had father found him? She was sure it was one of the late ones, when everything was changing and no one could say anything.

"Mama got a letter," said Amanda. "Just a little place where hardly anyone goes. They were thinking of putting on an exhibit of papa's and wanted to know if we could lend them some examples of what he was working on in South America."

"She's taking it rather well," said Claire.

"I don't suppose we have to go along with it, but I can't help feeling —"

Claire took a peek at the crumpled paper retrieved from mama. There was a small gasp when she recognized the address. It was an inquiry from *her* museum. When she spoke it was with a firmness that surprised her sister.

"Yes, I want him to be vindicated. I want them to see what he saw."

Amanda picked up another print. Most of the paper displayed a smoky atmospheric of various grays and bursts of cloud white, the entire print riven by pure lines of vertical light that gave the appearance of cosmic rain. The bottom left fourth of the photograph was a black silhouette of a young girl in a robe, but this too was etched by the linear spatter of light. Though one could not see any facial features, the very music of the body elicited a brooding contemplation; sitting forward and peering down – into what?

Empty hands, a book hidden in the folds of the robe, a letter? Any number of possibilities could be accommodated. Then, if you looked closely, there might be small, horizontal lines of light crossing against the grain suggesting the wings of a dove. The rain might be sharp slivers of sunlight breaking past the dark pillars of an ancient forest.

"What did he see, Claire?"

She thought of something Joss had told her. A wise fella once said that waking with new eyes was almost the same thing as waking into a new world. Sighing, she could only offer her sister the unsatisfying consolation of shared uncertainty.

"I don't know, Amanda. But I get the feeling we're missing a lot."

Thinking nothing

Claire was wearing an ivory colored blouse and a long plaid skirt with boots because she'd been riding. That was the day he knew. Probably others knew already, but he was dim that way. There she was with that little half smile of mischief and suddenly he felt his heart thumping and he felt for once that he was alive.

"So, you're here," she said.

"Yes," he answered. "It can't be helped. I was summoned."

"I think it may rain," she said, failing to show interest in who had commanded his presence.

Silence ensued. He was out of practice in the dance of courtship, though hardly anybody bothered with it any more. Joss began to focus on the lonely pendulum of an ancient grandfather's clock, a sense of desperate humiliation pulling him into a sullen state. Then he felt her grasp his hand. "You really didn't have to come," she said with a sweet sincerity that belied the gentle mockery in her eyes.

"I did, you know," he said.

"Oh, that's alright then," she answered. "It's just that, with my papa's show upcoming, it got me to thinking. He has this kind of collection. It started with grandfather. Notes and things, I don't know. I've never been able to make out what it all means. It's probably nothing."

"They say nothing comes from nothing, though if *creatio ex nihilo* is correct, that might not be strictly true."

Claire passed on the metaphysics of creation. Instead, she said "It's hard to think nothing. I know. I've tried."

Joss shrugged. "Lots of folks think nothing all the time."

"Yes, but that's not what I mean. He used to call it the Ark of the Covenant. Like in the movie, you know?"

The native guide had been found, miles from the nearest outpost of recognized civilization, his clothes tattered and vaguely smelling of burnt almonds. He could not tell the search party that discovered him what had happened to the boat or to her father. Though he gawked at them and shook his head at times as if he were indicating strong agreement or dissent to various questions, his time was out of kilter. Long, inappropriate pauses would intersperse attempted communication which was complicated by the further difficulty that the guide no longer spoke a language known to them.

At first, it was thought he was in a state of shock. He was taken by a small plane to the hospital. After a while, all their pharmaceuticals having proved helpless, he was released to the care of an asylum. Later they received a letter informing them that the guide had escaped and disappeared back into the Amazon from whence the source of his madness presumably came. So then there was nothing.

"It's a strange thing," said Claire. "When there's no body, it's as if death isn't quite real. I find myself hoping and sometimes dreaming that papa is there, in some world of the lost, waiting for a chance to get back to us."

"What a sad story," said Joss.

"I know, but that's not the whole of it. The other part, I can't help it, I'm very angry. I blame him, you see. I don't know what happened, but its papa's fault that he isn't with us."

"You mean he shouldn't have gone into the wilds and put himself at risk? It's natural to feel that way, I should think."

"He was always very clever and very brave. I am sure he felt he was up to anything."

"No, that can't be right," said Joss. "He wasn't stupid — and if he was brave, that means he had a clear sense of risk. Imbeciles who go charging into danger aren't courageous, they're ignorant."

"I'm sure you're right. It's easy to be dispassionate when you're not involved."

"I didn't mean it like that, Claire."

She turned her back to him so that he could not see her face.

"He had to go. I know that. Papa would not have been himself if he had —"

"Put safety first?"

"Put *us* first," is what she'd been thinking. "I would have gone with him," she said.

"You were just a little girl."

"He left us all the same," she said, facing him now, her words marred by savage reproach.

The Expanse

Exactly how the Expanse functions is still an open question. For years, Henry Ellwood had gathered his notes. Where he could, he made exploration, though it became increasingly clear to him that the most important horizons were interior. For those only able to think infinity as the measureless quantity of an exterior space, this inevitably was interpreted as a regrettable retreat into mystical idiosyncrasy. Nonetheless, he persisted in his attempts to explain, because even if the crowd jeers, a few may listen and discern, be surprised by discovery.

He used the language of symbol, though for his contemporaries this often suggested a literary convenience or psychic projection when he intended precisely an alterity very much the opposite: an object of undeniable difference neither commanded, nor anticipated.

Ordinary folks recognized things "out there" in the so-called objective world. They'd learned to think they were most objective when things were catalogued, weighed, measured, made docile through experimental method, though that was propaganda and ruse.

What they did not consider were the innumerable essences bearing a breadth and uncountable depth that resided within, realities presumably "outside the self as normally construed" that might only in the slightest manner rise into the waking light of quotidian objectivity.

The small beast

Claire met him in the coffee shop with an apologetic smile and a ready confession as greeting.

"Darling Joss, I've done something rather foolish."

Joss smiled his thin, toothless smile and ran his hand nervously through his hair. It was his tell by which Claire knew that he was prepared to believe her, though he answered in his usual tone of casual bemusement.

"What have you done, joined a nunnery or something?"

"Worse. I bought this."

With that, Claire reached down and produced a tiny creature from a box at her feet that turned out to be a small terrier.

"It's a Norwich," she said flatly, even as her eyes danced with glee at the prospect of the diminutive fluff dancing playfully in her arms.

"It looks like, what were those creatures in Star Wars, an ewok or something? But what's so bad about a dog?"

"Joss, one can't go around buying living things as if one were purchasing a new pair of shoes. Mother's allergic for one. For another, I can't become one of those women who carry their pets around in a handbag. Amanda shall never stop teasing. Third, I'm so tall. If I have to have a dog, it ought to be a borzoi or an Irish wolfhound. What do you think?"

"Can you give it back?"

The ashen pallor in her face told him this was the wrong thing.

"I can't just bring her home," sighed Claire. "You know the Ellwoods. We must have a family meeting and moneybags shall write out a list of pros and cons and mother will explain to me how I am an unthinking, flighty girl who imposes on her poor, put upon nerves."

Stirring his coffee, Josiah was able to come to the proper understanding. He rather felt stretched by the responsibility of caring for a houseplant, but there was obviously only one answer for the situation. "Would it help if I kept her for a while?"

"Would you, Joss? It would only be for a day or two."

"I suppose I can lay down papers in the kitchen. I take it she isn't?"

"Not yet, I'm afraid, but how bad can it be, she's such a little thing?"

"I bet she's an enormous crapper," he said with a half-hearted grin. "Does the little thing have a name?"

"Yes, it's Julian. And you're not to confuse her by calling her Piddles or the like."

Claire wagged a mocking finger in his face, her skin flushed and happy. A brief, unsettled feeling overtook Joss as he took temporary custody of his charge. He felt as if he had unconsciously signed on to more than the housing of a small beast. Had he declared himself without realizing it?

A moment later he was laughing at his punctilios. Surely he was neurotic and engaged in that ready pastime of scrupulosity, such an old-fashioned vice. It was on the way home that he got the joke about the name. He had to fight back a wave of admiration for Miss Ellwood and stooped so far as to call and assure her of the safe arrival and domesticity of her dog.

Like someone out of a picture

A soft breeze kissed against their faces bringing a fragrance of butterscotch and early chill, mint and burning leaves. A few deeply colored tatters of elm and oak drifted across the brook like lazy day boaters on their way to a picnic. Neither spoke, each unwilling to break the spell of time caught in an idyll. Joss glanced at Claire in her white blouse, long skirt, and straw hat. She seemed like someone out of a picture and his heart leapt. I shall never forget this, he thought. On my dying day, my soul shall return to this memory, this moment. He was so happy, he almost longed for death.

Claire smiled. Her cheek lightly blushed, but she turned away and looked again at the water reflecting back the sky and the hanging willows, its long, slow stretching a perfect lyric of sad and ancient dreams. Her mouth was delicious just then. The spice of danger he did not quite believe in added to her allure. He was still young enough to think of making an eternal declaration, the power of the moment thrilling with heady inebriation, though he felt an utter fool.

"Yip, yip," interrupted Julian, popping up from her bag like a jack-in-the-box.

"Oh, Jewels," laughed Claire. They were both embarrassed and relieved.

The gamp

Once, it must have been a long time ago, for she was only a child, Claire found herself looking out of a window. It was very tall and rounded at the top, with a lintel of arched stone. Because she was a little girl, the window appeared to be almost a door that one might easily pass through. When she peered out, she saw far below a country of rolling hills and emerald plains, a long, winding river and the faint blur of wild horses running free.

Though she was very far away, she felt herself at one with the horses, with the sunlight glinting on their powerful backs, the wind hearkening to them with the scent of clover. Her heart leapt to see that land and she longed to go there and to play and sing. And yet she was also afraid, for she was an agony of distance from that place and when she looked down directly from the window, she discovered that she was in a high chamber. A sheer cliff of barren stone was below her, broken only by a few gnarled limbs of ancient trees.

Then she felt trapped and sorrowful. It was impossible to go to the beautiful land. A sinking dejection buried itself in her heart. She wanted to cry and to sleep, to forget what she had seen. If she had never looked upon the far country, perhaps she would have been content. But now that she had seen it, she did not believe in any such peace. Such a peace would be false, stupid. It was bitter not to go to the land, but somehow ignoble to pretend it did not exist or to wish to have never seen it.

And I have always seen it. Were I born blind, I would still see it, for it is there, prior to sight, prior to powers, I know it in my bones. When she had thought this thought, Claire felt within her a kind of triumph. She felt with the simple justice of a child that she had done well.

Ah, but that is all empty pie. You're forgetting the dust, the hungering, the gnaw, and the gamp of it. Aye, you're all born liars, every last whelp of you. Don't I know it all these long years?

It is a frightful thing to believe oneself alone and safe in privacy, but not. Worse, to stare at the familiar room, the bare, architectural nook, shadow suddenly appearing without changing at all, as filled with a presence. Now like a tattered, dusty gown, now the folded wings of a bat, now a small, very old man with a shrunken head, that is at the same time a very large crow.

Are you going to blubber? As soon as you sleep, I am going to peck your eyes out.

Extravagant naiveté

One day, near the end, but not the last, the last was hurried and hushed and mama had been crying and there was a quarrel and then quiet and more crying, but softer, resigned, maybe forgiving, maybe not. But this before, not far, but before, he was in the study reading the letter, the one that said there was something unexplained, some magical archive, in the middle of unexplored Peru of all places.

It was so obviously fantastic, how could he not have known the extravagant naiveté in its request for credulity? And why did he give it?

When he saw how attentively she was watching him, Henry Ellwood smiled. Papa smiled for her more than anyone, and then he said, "Claire Bright. My sweet Claire. Everything is a mystery. We are each of us symbols and bear within everything that is, everything that ever was or will be. If only we could learn to read the hieroglyphs that lie hidden in the parchment of the soul."

He had that way of speaking aloud his dreams to her, as if she understood. He never spoke that way to any other. She'd waited up. She'd ridiculously gotten dressed, as if he'd take her along. Only he never came. Or she waited so long she fell asleep. A little girl. When she awoke there was a card and a little glass unicorn. And that was it.

Venetian glass

That whole night, they were especially careful with one another, as if they were observing a delicate and precarious truce, though neither understood what was behind it. It began to rain. Claire sighed, and fingered a little silver box.

"I wanted to show you this," she said at last. "I'm not sure why."

Then she opened the box and unwrapped swaddling gauze before revealing an extraordinarily fine translucent glass figure of a unicorn.

"This came from an island in Venice," she said. "It was the last gift he gave me, my papa, before he disappeared."

Mother of the earth

Amanda tapped softly at the door to Claire's boudoir. As there was no answer, she opened the door a trifle and then a bit more until she stood in the doorway. Claire was sitting, half naked, apparently oblivious to her presence, brushing her hair with a pensive, dreamy slowness that defied conclusion.

"What are you doing? Why aren't you dressed?" interrupted Amanda, conscious of the regrettable echo of her mother's scold in her voice.

Claire did not turn, but spoke to her sister's reflection in the mirror. "Archie went to march against war and Wanda is taking her expert on yellow to a speech on recycling or perhaps on how plastic causes cancer. Something, I forget."

"Are you feeling alright?"

"Joss called to beg off. He didn't explain. I decided to beg off, too."

Claire turned then and smiled apologetically. "I should have told you ahead of time. I didn't think it was so late."

"That's okay. Get dressed. We should go, you and I."

Claire sighed and stared back into the mirror. "Why do we do it, Amanda?"

"Do what?"

"Oh, anything. Anything at all." Before Amanda could respond, she was confronted with another demand. "And look at these." Claire held her breasts up as if she were offering ripe melons for inspection. "What on earth is the use of them? I feel like a big moo cow made to chew its cud and whelp a few calves."

"Half the women in America would pay a fortune for those," laughed Amanda. She unconsciously examined her own endowment with which she was reasonably satisfied.

"Men, of course, are drawn to them like iron filings to the north pole. Nine conversations out of ten, I have to lean back and bend my head to the side just to get a glimpse of their eyes."

Amanda could hardly argue. Men were carnal and irreducibly visual. She understood that women secretly relished the power this gave them and the supposed superiority of their own appetites. In comparison, these could be presented as more spiritual, though she and all honest women knew this pose to be mainly fraudulent. Her reverie upon sexual difference had captured her thoughts. Meanwhile, Claire had moved on to more metaphysical applications regarding her bosom.

"I sometimes feel as if all the earth is coming towards me. Foxes and rabbits, gazelles, elephants. Even the fish of the sea and the whales seek me out. They're all saying, 'feed us, feed us. Give us milk that we may live and spawn and die, that the cycle of life may go on and on as it ever has.' Today, I heard the beginnings of the chant when I passed by the remains of a squashed squirrel in the road and the whole thing seemed so awful I could hardly breathe."

"You need a drink."

"But where am I wrong, Amanda? That's what everyone believes. It's like nature is this idiotic yap that goes on screaming and desiring, it can't help itself, while at the end there's nothing but the dark and the cold. They all think it, yet they keep marching and going to chats and fighting for the perfect society which is imaginary and just what Joss says. No one can agree on what is good and death stands at the finish line to end all willing."

"Hell, I need a drink," said Amanda.

Claire began to pat her face with foundation, signaling a shift away from morbid cogitations. Amanda breathed a sigh of relief and wondered if she should resume her suggestion that they visit the exhibit together. Claire bent down and searched through a drawer, pulling out at length a brassiere she nicknamed Wonder Woman as its sturdy, almost pugnacious construction suggested Amazonian scorn. Her thoughts, however, were tender and puzzled.

"Why doesn't Joss believe in love?"

"Uggh. I should have known!" Amanda placed her hands softly around Claire's neck and squeezed ever so slightly. "What is the fascination of Joss Wherryweather? I'm sure it takes him ten minutes to tie his shoelaces."

"He's good to talk to. He listens. He's not gay."

"I admit, that's not always the easiest combination to find, but he's a dreamer, Claire. He'll never amount to anything. You can't live on dreams, you know."

"You can't live without them, either." Claire nearly blushed for shyness. "He looks into my eyes when we talk."

"Oh, hell," said Amanda.

"What about Adam? He'll be happy to go with you."

"The hell with Adam."

"You're a good sister, but you don't mean that."

"I suddenly don't care," said Amanda truthfully, "but it doesn't matter. He's met a girl named Eve."

"That can't possibly end well."

"Oh, the frightful thing is she's very pretty and incredibly decent."

"Fruit bats."

"Double fruit bats with apples."

At the museum

The director of the museum was quite effusive in his praise. Amanda could not help a momentary thrill at the encomium of words for the absent father, even if the fustian praise was peppered with the vapid catchphrases of current academic fashion. She felt, too, sadness that Claire had not yet arrived and so would not hear Henry Ellwood lauded. Mama, it had to be said, had recovered marvelously. None of the guests would have guessed that the suave, elegant woman laughing and effortlessly engaged in convivial bad-inage had only recently been the mad woman in the attic.

Amanda even had a moment of kindness for moneybags, stand-ing like a well-dressed mannequin at mama's side with such ev-ident pride and affection. It was like Pinocchio indulging in the vicarious fantasy that he was a real boy. Later, when the crowd had dispersed into little groups hovering over particular works in the exhibit, cocktails in hand, pattering on in that flowing babble unmistakably associated with the imbecile class, mama found her and ushered her into a corner to ask with quick exasperation about the whereabouts of the eldest daughter.

"You know Claire, mama. She's nursing a hurricane in her heart. She wouldn't say, but I think she was hoping for Joss. I know him, though. He won't come, because he's afraid. I'm sure she'll show once she figures it out."

A wrong turn

Claire did not think one could hold so many emotions at one time. She felt foolish for believing he would come after all and sad and angry all at once. That wasn't so much, but then there were the usual nerves she always felt before the prospect of a gathering of humans. It was odd to find oneself so often alienated from one's own kind, or was it? Also, a kind of reverence and hope and tingling expectation had gathered in her, a mixture which was the surface of a deeper longing for the father.

She'd dressed in a hurry and followed the usual route, only something had gone wrong. It was ridiculous and only added to her exasperation, but somewhere along the way, she must have taken a wrong turn. She did not recognize the road and then the buildings were strange. There were rows of townhouses with a quaint old patina and iron work everywhere, a tiny arm holding out a gas lamp, filigree ornamented bars over the windows. No voices could be heard behind the walls, not a single sign of life.

Then she was making her way through a narrow path between two buildings. The path intersected a thin street bounded by an extended low stone wall that guarded against a precipitous drop. There was the faint smell of a distant sea and closer by a mélange of mundane odors: the sappy residue of plants, the compost of garbage, the vaguely bitter burning of motor oil, the musk of alley cats, the wafting of bleached wash and tobacco smoke.

Claire peered down from the wall into a maze of buildings with newly lit windows blinking in the emerging dusk. There is nothing like this in the neighborhood, she thought, more surprised than fearful. The quiet moment ended with a sudden rush of wind. She hearkened to a guttural sound in it, unpleasant and accompanied by a clinging sulfurous odor.

"Who do you think you are?" it seemed to say.

Panic grew in her. Claire could not speak, could not name her fear.

"Who do you think you are? Who do you think you are?"

The voice was stronger, clarified, as if gathering strength from her sorrow. She sensed what cannot be seen, what was barely there, could not be, but was. It was not a body, not even a shadow, but a sort of wraith, the shadow of a shadow, hanging mid-air before her. If it had arms, they would be angry and pointed in accusation. The wraith was about her height. Soon, it was joined by two others that formed a circle about her.

"Who do you think you are? Who do you think you are?" they said in insipid repetition.

Undulating vulgarly, even without bodies, they were unspeakably obscene. Tears came to her eyes. She felt violated. Having no weight, the shadows could only act through the power of suggestion. Clearly, though, she could hear their suggestion.

"If you want to get away from us, throw yourself over," they said.

Don't forget the whip

For a moment, she actually felt herself being pulled towards the wall, whether through some perverse auto-suggestion, dancing wraiths or vertigo, it didn't seem to matter as she veered in the direction of the sheer drop. Her flight was interrupted by the smacking report of a lash striking innocent cobblestone. Claire turned and wondered if it was Fat Tuesday. A young woman with shocking gold-white hair dressed in an outrageous costume part pirate, part dominatrix drove a sullen youth before her. The coarse face of the boy grimaced with rebellious intent.

"Don't you give trouble, lout," shouted the pirate girl.

"I'm not an oaf, you miserable wench."

The girl looked over at Claire. "He is. He is a complete and perfect oaf. He is the genetic ideal oaf."

"I'll grab your whip. I'll give you what for, wench. I'll blemish your white arse."

"Such a fine tongue in front of a lady. What did I tell you?"

"I'm sorry. I seem to be lost. Can you tell me where this is?"

"This is the place where the knee cap meets the shin bone. Where else would it be?" said the oaf.

"I don't understand that at all, I'm afraid."

At this, the boy began to scream and cry. "I said it right," he shouted. "I told her right and look how she treats me?" With a rush of aggrieved pain, the boy ran off.

The young vixen turned to her with reproach on her face. "He thinks you're teasing him. A young man like that is fragile. Can't you see?"

Claire's eyes followed the path taken by the oaf. Some kind of dark birds, ravens perhaps, flew in a fluttering, ungainly way, until they settled not far off, shortly serene, as if nothing bad had ever happened. "He'll forget," she answered, almost absent-mindedly.

"He won't," said the flaxen-haired girl, her arms akimbo. "It will stick in his craw and maybe, one day, he'll lash out and hit some poor girl because deep down he's thinking about you."

Claire scanned the roofs and the balconies with their potted plants and the washing hung out to dry. There was no sign of the lout.

"There's nothing I can do, in any event," she stated with a shrug that belied a dusting of unsettled guilt.

"I'll tell him you said you were sorry," offered the girl. There was a certain sauciness in her manner that was enigmatic. Claire could not tell if it meant contempt or playfulness.

"Okay," she said softly, suddenly docile and unsure of herself.

The vixen began to laugh, twirling her whip as she walked away from Claire.

"He's probably watching everything just now. His father's a peeping Tom."

Claire could only gape in confusion, wondering if she had stumbled into a city taken over by the madhouse.

"I'd need a lock of your hair to prove it," whispered the girl, who had returned to Claire's side with unnerving silence. "But your hair's too fine. I'll box him on the ears if he tries anything on me, I will. I'll tell him to look you up."

"I'll box you if you do anything of the sort," said Claire.

At this, her companion gave a yelp of delight, stole a kiss from Claire, and then went skipping into the nearest lane until she was lost to the shadows.

Empathy

Julian was staring at him with such intensity and depth of feeling that Joss could not help but laugh. It was true. What had they argued over? Nothing.

"Alright, Jewels," he said. "I'll call her in the morning and make it all up. All shall be well and all manner of thing shall be well."

How Amanda became Miss Ellwood

Claire had been missing for thirty six hours. Everyone was on edge and a mess. The telephone rang and Adam's mother ran to answer it. There was something in the way her body tensed that made Adam pause.

"They found Claire," cried Mrs. Dollinger. "She's in a park near the museum. She's been strangled."

And that is how Amanda became Miss Ellwood.

Chapter Three

The Great Work

The scream

T hey have grown so dim, they think what happens to each other has no bearing on their own destiny. Though indeed, it often seems that way – the torturer binding or cutting or burning, perhaps pulling out the eyes of the victim, that sort of thing. Flesh is so eminently vulnerable. The perpetrators of these third person schemes hearken for the secrets of our nature stretched out upon the rack. Often under cover of abstraction and utility, they surreptitiously bend a cold ear hoping for ardent whispers, the intimate cry of the unique.

Believing themselves immune, separate from the victim, they alone will capture and possess that sacred name, the gift that hides. Desire to master, devour, to ascend in power, unharmed, unseen, unheard, the ring of Gyges. And yet, despite centuries of diligent attempts and momentary illusions of accomplishment, the grand efforts of the torturer have never satisfied, for the scream is universal, unable to tell the name, for we do not know it, none of us.

Will no one save us from this body of pain?

At Rabbi Naftali's

Sky Odyssey sat on the front steps of the yeshiva warming herself in the sun. Someone had set up a feeding station from which a hummingbird dipped its slender beak into nectar. A child came wandering by. There were so many children in the City, far too many for each to have home or family. "What is this place?" she asked herself for the thousandth time.

The chanteuse, Billie Holliday, was singing in vinyl. She languidly informed her lover that he'd changed, a lifetime of sorrow and whiskey and disappointment etched into her smoky voice. Naftali leaned back, his hands folded before him in sustained concentration.

"Well, my friend, you know what Rabbi Akiva said?"

The Elder shrugged, and Naftali poured a drink for the Elder and one for Billie.

"He said, 'What you leave out of the story is part of the story, too.'"

The Elder took a sip of very good Kentucky bourbon. "You've been holding out. I think that saying is from a different rabbi."

"The great fear of death is known to all men. What is less known, except to the mystics, is that the fear of death is nothing but a prelude, miniscule in comparison to the fear the soul feels when it begins to rise into angelic precincts. We know little of this; quite rightly, or we should spend our entire lives in trepidation. Besides, it is the human way to encounter the eternal in the prosaic and particular details of our earthly lives. It pleases the Divine to coax us, however unwilling, from our many hiding places."

Not to be outdone, the Elder rose to the challenge. "Our notions of time are deceptive," he began. "You think eternity is waiting as a coda to life, but it is not so. Eternity runs perpendicular. Everything is created as a whole which for the present is veiled into fragments dispersed along time's arrow. But the moment will come when flight will be done with its wandering and the target reached. Then all shall be taken up into the eternal swiftness of Unnameable life."

Rabbi Naftali nodded his appreciation. "Yet most men do not experience time opening up into a mysterious infinity. They feel it as a doom and the mark of reality that cannot be evaded. 'Time is a river which sweeps me along, but I am the river; it is a tiger which destroys me, but I am the tiger; it is a fire which consumes me, but I am the fire. The world, unfortunately, is real. I, unfortunately, am Borges.'"

The Elder smiled at his friend. "Time and doom are often synonymous, yet Creation is above all an act of love. It cannot be measured by reason or justice. Or rather, reason is already an ecstasy that reaches out beyond calculation. What is it the wise man said? One may place all the 'moaning of universal suffering that is not silent by day or night' onto one side of the scale. Rage against the injustice of the Creator, the path of revolt and despair is incomprehension that seeks out the absolute in oblivion. Love alone understands love."

Sky walked in with silky mirth. "And what are you old men talking about?"

But this was an easy return for the rabbi. "About young women, whatever else?"

This is no time for games

The city of crenellated walls, of ordered domes, of little rivers springing from deep underground and watering with melodious song a gentle willow bank. The sages floated above the streets, their long white beards tickling the cobblestones, like a wink beneath their levitating feet.

Then, there were the jade girls, their faces painted pale with sharp black brows and adventure in their eyes. They hid in caves with the bears and behind random shelves in the library and waited like ghosts to come upon the sages. They'd arch an eyebrow and ask, *"And what is wrong with the earth?"*

The high tower of the second-best house, in the long room Beorn waits and rubs his stubbled chin. Shadrael. Shadrael. Flowing black tresses, a waterfall down. Gypsy queen, creature from another realm. Bronze skin, emerald eyes. Sing to the princes, sing to the thieves. Tell them, tell them. Make them learn and see.

He sent for her. In her own good time, she has always come. Laughing with drunken abandon, she would laugh in a monastery, at a wake, at the quaking of the earth. But she has the gift, the third eye. There is no reason in the gods, only cruelty. And then she will come, baring a breast or revealing a gem pierced into her tongue, she will look at you with a sudden, acute serenity, calm beyond measure and dare you to blink.

"A lion will come in lamb's guise, bleeding; a lance in his side, blood blooming from a kiss."

Poets live in tenements or castles, but the great ones, often, come from merchants and burghers, had a tanner for a father. Crackin, the old miser, stale breath like dead beetles, his eyes dart out, fearful, lest some claim be made upon him, some coin endangered. Killed by a hansom cab charging like a barracuda, dispersing boys and wild monkeys. He was bent over in the mirror of a small piece of copper, exile from some wishing well. Round, flat, worthless discovery, half deaf old Crackin never heard his doom, died with a smile on his face.

"Ants dream of anarchy."

Looking out from his tower, wrapped in his black cloak, he saw them at first as obscure shadows, a trick of light, eyes grown hooded like the captured hawk. Days would go by and nothing. He forgot, spoke to the ministers, they always smiled indulgently, the rubbery benevolence of those venomous keepers of the public trust — safe in their official secrets, smiling at him as if he were an amiable dunce.

Once, when one of their gray numbers was speaking with recondite zeal and presenting an equation for determining happiness, complete with grids and charts, he suddenly looked out his forlorn window and saw, again, unmistakable. The minister followed his gaze. Surely he would see too, say something. But nothing. Nothing. Beorn flew into an unaccountable rage, the municipal servant scrambling to preserve his graphs, to escape the terrible storm of the mad prince.

The old scholar worrying about science, loyal to God, praying in his tears. What did he write to his niece? *"Learn to see the jewel in the toad's eyes."*

She came. Her face scrubbed clean, as plain and pink as any Quaker could like. A large gray sweatshirt shrouded her curves. She walked straight up to him, solicitous with utmost sobriety.

"What is it, Beorn?"

"What game is this?"

"This is no time for games, my prince. Don't you know I have always been your friend?"

The shop of lost dreams

All through the long vaulted tunnel into Prior Street, Digby had kept a hand in his pocket, fingering the velvet pouch. They'd have to cut his hand off to get his treasure. It was sure to bring a nice price. *If he sold it.* He desperately needed money, but Digby found himself wondering if he could actually part with the stone. Rather, the surface of his ego needed to preserve the thought that he was still free and might pull back from the gravity of hard necessity.

The tunnel was dark and crowded, full of mid-morning traffic. Buttleburr had said to be there at ten sharp, though he was late. Digby would be late to his own funeral, as they say. He walked in his shuffling gate, eyeing every passerby with suspicion, his uncertain gaze drawing to him unwanted attention. His heart began to pound as he followed a wagon laden with barrels of pickled cucumbers and crates of chickens that squabbled noisily, leaving a down of snowy feathers in its wake. The dull carter was barely awake enough to steer the mules. When at last he was free of the rush, Digby paused a moment to breathe the open air as a man condemned to be hanged might linger over the sight of trees and houses innocent of malice.

A clock tower chimed to remind him he was tardy. Like a school boy fearing censure, Digby quickly made for Glaze's Feed and Supply. That particular concern had been defunct for decades, the sign left as ghostly witness to prior industry. Mince and Kheen's was on the second floor, reached from the outside by a rickety iron staircase. They had taken over the ground floor devoted to agrarian labor years ago and used it for storage. Why they preferred to keep the less convenient entrance was one of those enduring mysteries that locals of the neighborhood occasionally pondered without ever bothering to inquire.

Buttleburr fumed upon the second-floor landing. He dropped a long ash from his cigar onto the ground below. "Here, finally," he declared in his gravelly, bullhorn voice.

Mince was a creature of legend. Some said he was a hundred and fifty if he was a day. It was further asserted that though he was six foot in his prime, the proprietor had shrunk and was now well below four feet in his boots. Digby had only once been to Mince and Kheen's and that when he was a boy. His father had come to retrieve some family silver and he'd taken Digby to learn the lesson never to sell cheap what one would have to buy back dear. Little had changed. If anything, Mince had shrunk beyond the speculative claims of gossip.

The premises were stuffed with jewelry, music boxes, bolts of cloth and disparate pieces of furniture, once proud, now dusty with age and out-of-fashion. Below ("gone to seed" was a little joke on the past use of the establishment), shelves of boxes were cataloged, each bearing some sentimental object sacrificed for various designs: drink, a crust of bread, the solace of purchased embrace, or the hope of a play at the ponies. Whenever a carriage roared across the cobblestones the grime fogged windows rattled.

As for the nebulous partner, Kheen, he was never encountered and some believed he was a pure invention. Mince, however, always spoke of him with tones of veneration bordering on awe. The visible half of the business habitually resided in the mysterious back rooms where, as he put it, "lost dreams were stored."

When Digby entered with Buttleburr, Mince appeared at the counter dressed in a long gold satin jacket. Mince's face was the color of a brown, tea-stained parchment. He had a few sparse hairs, more like quills, reaching from his brow to his neck. They had been gray, but recently had turned black. His customers tittered to think that he was dying them, but they had actually altered of their own accord. Several new teeth had also begun to push through his gums, making it uncomfortable to chew.

"Good day to you, gentleman," said Mince. The line of his mouth made a thin smile that receded into the jowls of his face.

"We've come about the business I mentioned," said Buttleburr.

"Yes, yes."

Mince neither approved, nor disapproved. He encouraged, but not without a pretense of self-effacing disinterest.

"It was hard to get," said Buttleburr.

"I've no doubt," answered Mince, discovering a magnifying lens and peering through it at Digby which made the anxious fellow jump. Digby was in a dither, fumbling with the contents of the deep pockets of his great coat. Digby was fond of the coat. It was military surplus and sometimes in his adventures, a yokel would refer to him as Captain or even General.

"Let's have it then, Captain Digby," yelled Buttleburr.

After heroic efforts and some false starts in which Digby brought forth bent pipe cleaners, the wrappers from two watermelon flavored Thomas' hard candy, and a small tin snuff box adorned with a painted rustic scene, a modest velvet pouch was deposited on the counter. With trembling hands, Digby loosened the binding chord and slid away the fabric to reveal a pearlescent stone all of a piece shaped into a rounded ancient chalice.

Mince scrutinized the vessel as if he were looking at a piece of jewelry, examining the object for any discernible cracks or signs of artful manipulation. After making many small, speculative grunts, the proprietor stopped and simply stared as if in a daze. Buttleburr had to ostentatiously clear his throat to return attention to the sellers.

"Oh, and this —," said the bullhorn as Digby opened the snuff box to reveal a lock of lustrous dark green hair.

"This is hers, then?"

"You got it. There's the proof for you," confirmed Buttleburr.

"It represents only the most tenuous claim. It could be anyone's, could it not? One could have a mismatched pair."

Though Buttleburr stared back with the steely aplomb of an experienced poker player, Digby was a puddle of blank incomprehension that anyone could cynically question the relic.

"All the same, I'll need both so I'd only be interested in the whole lot, you understand?"

"For the right price, it's yours, old Mince."

Digby suddenly yelped like a stung dog. He stuttered unintelligibly, collected himself, and then blurted with a quick concision that attempted a light tone. "I'd like, really, just to keep this bit."

"Awe, he's gone soft," uttered Buttleburr.

"I'm afraid that isn't possible, Mr . . . ?"

"Digby," said Digby miserably.

"The value in an item like this is in its uniqueness. Can't have it parceled up like pieces of the true Cross."

"Naturally, good business," barked Buttleburr.

"But it's such a tiny thing, hardly a keepsake, really."

"Quite," agreed Mince, shoveling the lock of hair into a box. "Hardly worth keeping."

Message in a basket

The messenger boy came and dropped the letter in the usual basket. The clerk was drowsy with overwork and the ordinary boredom. The return address was from a district in the old city; a hospital used to house the aged and infirm, the poor and the mad. A vague alarm roused the functionary from his stupor. He had a distinct recollection that this particular source of information was of interest to the Guardian.

The standing instructions were not to open missives from this hospital. They were to be conveyed directly and at any hour. When he handed the envelope to the Guardian, Malchidion betrayed no special interest. The hand was steady with bored efficiency that unsealed the message from Dr. Thorenson. It read simply: "The old blind men report visions. They say the light is coming. Prepare."

Prince Raveh's complaint

No longer is this a time for princes. We are leaving the stage. The briefcase and the clipboard will replace the sword. Poison rings and tyranny will go underground, the spider's malice will seep into them and they will call it pity. Why are you so drab today? Why do you look at me like a mother willing her sick child back to health? There is nothing wrong with me that death cannot cure.

She nestled her head on his shoulder. A chill wind blew in from the open window like a prophecy of frost upon his short-cropped hair. Odd. When he was a child, he remembered just this moment. Only then, he was a child rabbit and a hare without a watch snuggled close and told him it didn't matter what time it was. Unlike rabbits, hares are born with their eyes open.

"I have begun to see things, Shadrael."

"Yes," she said softly.

"I don't even know what it is I'm seeing. I can't put a word to it. No one else sees it."

She looked at him with tenderness. Oh, the woman could allure. "Like a lone she-goat dotted against the cliff, a glimpse in the heights . . . or a small hand hidden in the clouds . . . more like thunder hidden in a hummingbird. And now, it knows no day or night. A familiar stranger, it will come and read my book over my shoulder, tread softly before my tea. It glares and gargoylelates its non-existent face when I am busy with some diplomatic business, my poor visitor puzzling at my inattention. Say nothing yet!"

She smiled softly and said nothing. "And now, of recent, there is another. Something like wings, something like a torrent of running water. A sound. Just a sound — and my feet hurt!"

"They are the same," she said.

Pennyfeather

Leatherhead was already snoring when Chalksong entered through the open window in his usual condition of anarthria due to drink. He collapsed into a low chair and stared meaningfully at a laundry list left by Dunewit. Pennyfeather was sitting at his desk, wondering if the fellow was going to recover from stupefied muteness. It was dreadful when he sang.

Chalksong, for his part, was what they call comfortably numb. It was as close to nirvana as he was likely to get. In the half light of the lamp by which Pennyfeather was reading, he looked vaguely, though blissfully imbecilic.

Pennyfeather was a low ranking clerk in one of the Archives secondary registers, dealing generally with vagrants, undocumented off-worlders, feral children, hobos, and the like. His work was not highly prized, though occasionally the tides of academe swung his way. The voice of the marginalized, the keeper of suppressed voices – it was exciting for a brief moment, but he was rather glad when the season turned to some other brilliant phase. He was not perhaps content, but acclimated to anonymity akin to that of his charges.

Pennyfeather had a prodigious memory. He had always been quick that way, but he was not imaginative. The uses made of information eluded him. Yes, this is what his fellow clerks said of him and for all he knew, it was quite true. The inebriant dozed for the better part of an hour. Pennyfeather was thinking of retiring himself, when Chalksong abruptly stood up and stared about him in astonishment.

"You're home. Came in around one. It is now near two. You have been drinking."

Chalksong raised his hand in weary admission of the facts and stumbled over towards Pennyfeather like a disconsolate dog. "You're right. Too right. It's just like that," said Chalksong.

"I am a profound and just judge."

Chalksong began to wobble and glanced at the floor with a dubious gaze. He was feeling sick. It was so dull to be sick. "I might be sick," he declared.

Pennyfeather hastened to fetch a bowl. Afterwards, Chalksong discovered a more expansive mood. "There's a girl," he began, winking meaningfully. "Up for anything." There followed several minutes of dubious description. It was doubtless true of somewhere and an amalgamate experience of various someones, though it would have taken a particularly adventurous and limber gymnast of superior stamina to accomplish all that Chalksong declaimed.

"You are certainly a connoisseur of the Willow world," observed Pennyfeather.

"Yes, I see you don't believe me."

"Not at all. I think it's wonderful that there are women like that."

"Now you are adding scorn to disbelief."

"Don't sulk. It will make your hangover ever so much worse."

"You sound as if you are shouting from the bottom of a well."

"The echo would be reduced if your noggin was less empty."

"Touché. I admit defeat. Ah, almost forgot. There is a letter for you. I opened it, I'm afraid."

"Accident?"

"Frightful curiosity. It's from Malchidion. I would have sealed it properly so no one would know I peeked, but then the boys came round for a crawl, and the girl happened."

"Half the crime is forgiven in confession," quipped Pennyfeather, though his heart was beating with ponderous gravity.

"I'm sure it's nothing, old bean. I told you it was bad to be clever. Gets one noticed."

Presently, Leatherhead awoke from his sleepy abyss. Carefully, he opened a single eye and gawked. "What, Chalksong! Got any crackers?"

"No crackers. Go back to sleep."

"Right-oh," muttered Leatherhead, already obedient as he spoke.

Strange vellum

The address cleverly ascertained in advance by Chalksong turned out to belong to a building in a long row of dilapidated townhouses. The district was familiar to Pennyfeather. Many of the vagrant off-worlders found whatever solace and accommodation available to them in places half spectral, home to soulless memories and indifferent vermin. The balustrade supporting the spiral curve of the staircase was mostly complete. The rococo pattern of the threadbare carpet muttered in thin complaint the loss of better days.

The peeling paint on the walls was signed with the occasional scrawl of transient guests. It was not at all the place one would think to meet the Guardian. Several floors up, Pennyfeather began to wonder if the whole thing was an elaborate hoax. Chalksong was certainly capable of it. It was also possible, such treachery was not unknown, that he had been set up for assassination, though why anyone would go through such trouble to eliminate a minor civil servant was beyond calculation. No, he knew nothing and no one could conceivably covet his position.

It was within the penumbra of such fantasies that a door slowly swung open to reveal a chamber dressed in tapestries and fitted with gaudily carved furniture suited to the tastes of a Renaissance prince. Pennyfeather was surprised to find himself alone with Malchidion. If there were secretaries and guards, they were supremely out of sight. The Guardian settled heavily into a single chair that occupied the center of the room.

"Pennyfeather, is it? Good of you to make your way to see us on short notice." The voice was congenial ice. "But you will be wondering what service you may provide to your city?"

"I was surprised by the summons, Guardian."

"And no doubt the location of your audience. I have many such places. It is often advantageous to have them." Now that he was up close, the clerk discerned both native cunning and a kind of deep, mordant humor in his host. "I like to have my pomp and circumstance just so. It is a reminder, Pennyfeather, of the peculiar joke the universe is playing. We cannot help but order chaos."

"Might I ask —?"

"Why you are here?"

Malchidion drew Pennyfeather over to the small table upon which appeared a piece of vellum, a map of some region that might have pertained to an ancient realm in Elnaria. It was adorned in the high manner, depicted with flowers and plants never to be found in the world, with arcane symbols and tiny naked figures that sported amidst a forest of lettering. The inks had held up well for a document of such age. One could still discern the magentas, the umber, dragon's blood and indigo that indicated rivers, mountains, and long dead kingdoms.

"It is very beautiful," remarked Pennyfeather.

"Indeed. It is said to depict a region in the unknown *Chora*. But you have yet to see the most mystic property of the object. As a scholar, I suppose you are good at concentration?"

"It is generally helpful, Guardian."

"And have you read of diverse times and places in your studies?"

"There are many texts," said Pennyfeather.

"And yet perhaps there is just the one," remarked Malchidion. "Your Guardian asks you to select from your copious reading any place of interest. It may be fanciful or what we call real."

"I don't quite understand."

"You are not required to understand. Simply do, Pennyfeather."

Vaguely stressed and uncomprehending, the pin of Pennyfeather's imagination landed after brief and hurried flight, he could hardly have said why. Soon he gasped in wonder and fear, for the vellum had changed. Before him was a perfect map of Byzantium, so perfect that for a brief, horrifying moment, he felt himself transported within the ornate jewel of Orient Empire rife with intrigue and gorgeous artifact. He walked the golden streets, rubbed shoulders with their courtiers hoping none should question him.

And then, just as suddenly, he stood in the decayed and decadent chamber, shaking before the bemused gaze of Malchidion.

Stella aqua

From the terrace they listened to the happy rhythms of the kezmer music. Benedicta called it Hasidic jazz. In the distance, Sky observed a young woman in a blue dress and a black short jacket with a white collar. Her raven hair had been swept up into gleaming plaits. She was carrying a tall earthen pot which tapered like a bottle.

"Time," said the Elder, "is like a serpent. In order to move forward, as we think of it, we retreat inwards, within memory and the story we tell ourselves. It is from within recollection which is also a kind of art that we spring forth."

Sergeant Folkes, a retired soldier, had joined them. He liked to listen in on that sort of talk. The sergeant had a habit of absently rifling through old, yellowed letters from his estranged son. He'd pull them out just to feel the papers that bore witness to the existence of his progeny. Sky was sitting on his left, a faraway expression on her face.

"You're looking a fine young lady," averred the soldier.

Sky blushed at the compliment, for she understood that it was only recently that she had been universally acknowledged by the community as one of their own. The young woman with the pot was standing over a bare plot of land. Her eyes appeared closed, as if she were a somnambulist, her pretty lips a perfect little rose of peace. She tilted the pot, then, but to Sky's astonishment a sprinkling of shooting lights and stars poured forth.

"It seems to me that if we forget nothing, there is no art to memory." She had spoken unknowingly, like the sleeping girl watering the earth with stella aqua. They all looked at her with surprise.

"Yes," said Benedicta. "It's a kind of barbarism to forget nothing. Shame is a kind of tact that looks away."

This was not exactly what Sky had perhaps meant, if she meant anything by words culled more from deep feeling than explicit thought. Sky had unwittingly crossed a border into another time. She still did not understand it, but Benedicta had been there too, only older and in bewildering, dire circumstances. "What is four in the morning, two at noon, three in the gloaming of dusk?" The world of rationality devoid of imagination, univocal, solar, masculine, water not yet wine, sublunary, time as death spread out, death as time collapsed into a point. This was the Sphinx's riddle.

Oedipus thought that he had solved the riddle and escaped judgment. It was only later when he pronounced guilt on his own hubris by blinding himself. The riddle itself was doom. He did not escape.

Not a sphinx

The Elder and Sky walked silently together. Nothing had been said, but after their journey to the mountain and the night of the waves, the Elder seemed more open with her. They would seek each other out and somehow the girl's presence soothed the ache in his heart. He had spoken so little of his lost. Now Sky seemed to bear in part the burden of it.

Sky grew less evasive, too. She showed the orb ring off and confessed with shy confusion that sometimes it almost seemed to her as if she had become engaged. The Elder smiled and said "we long to live and love eternally." He looked as if he wanted to say more, but checked himself.

As they ascended a hill that led into an ancient part of the City with hanging gardens and walls covered in base relief sculpture, Sky suddenly froze and gasped. She pointed mutely in the direction of a winged beast with the head of an Assyrian king. The stone cutter's art responded to her awe with regal serenity. Recovering her voice, Sky asked what it was.

When the Elder informed her that it was a symbolic likeness of the Tetramorph, otherwise called Cherubim, all she would say for some time was "he's not a sphinx."

Their hearts are full of longing

"Most likely, should you leave this place, you will begin to doubt the witness of your senses. Or you shall cogitate some inexplicable mirroring of the mind, a fabulous parlor trick. Many such curiosities are gathering dust in small nooks and alcoves of the archives. The spiders array them with splendorous shrouds. Some member of your tribe has listed them by rough taxonomy. An amusing inventory. This, however, is different."

The relevant sentence in the Guardian's exposition was the subjunctive "should." This was not promising. Pennyfeather missed a considerable amount of the next few sentences. Malchidion had moved on to the unusual nature of the vellum.

"Tradesman, tanners, scholars of the esoteric and adepts of the occult arts have been consulted. It is not bovine or sheepskin, neither lizard, nor snake. It might be human, but no simple leather. Have you, by chance, heard of the Grail Atlas?"

Pennyfeather found his throat bone dry. He indicated, as smoothly as he could manage, his ignorance of the queried text.

"It is no matter," continued Malchidion, "but I have sometimes wondered if this is a page from that supposedly apocryphal volume."

Pennyfeather greatly wished to retreat into his quiet obscurity. He could not imagine what he had done to draw attention. "Well, I am told you are particularly gifted to recall what you see and hear," observed the Guardian by way of coming to a point.

The clerk shrugged. Morbid resignation had struck him and unloosed his tongue. "Scholars have a knack for it, I suppose."

"Above all, I want it straight. Your Guardian does not wish to hear pleasant tales."

"These are dangerous people?"

The Guardian sighed. Pennyfeather saw that beneath it all, Malchidion was tired. "Oh, yes. The worst kind. Their hearts are full of longing. Rumors are spreading among the Anshari. Folks claim to have seen the dead king. It bubbles up from time to time, but the tide is particularly strong. Again, there is talk of the Threshing, that ridiculous dream."

Porosity

The voices usually came to her at night. Sometimes, however, they would come anyway, risking the afternoon or early morning. Word images might meet her for breakfast with what could have been a joke at her expense. "And came forth like Venus from an ocean of heat waves, morning in his pockets and the buckets in his hands he emerged from the grey shed, tobacco and wind pursed together in song from his tight lips he gathered day and went out to cast wheat before swine." *Hmmph*, she thought. *I'm not a porker, I'll let you know.*

One morning, it was not even a voice, but a low, warm darkness interspersed with a scattering of red-golden, purple, and russet patches that covered the darkness like the coats of pixie folk. Sky slowly paused and read the messages woven in color and odors of harvest, decay, and festive liturgy, the tang of burnt umber and October mist rising from the black tar road.

And then a great rumbling stunned her. She froze, hesitant, before an elongated shiny maw and huge blank eyes. Petrified, sure it would destroy her, her heart beat with staccato rapidity. She wanted to run in a dozen directions. The very urgency of flight kept her pinned to the dark warmth.

The giant monster stopped and made an odd, bleating noise, a siren from dyspeptic bellows. Thankfully, the sound released her feet. She galloped first one way, then reversed and went back to green pastures. She sprang to the nearest wood tower, climbed up to a first floor balcony and watched the behemoth glide by with indifferent speed.

The god of pigs and the survivor of giants, she would have been surprised to learn, were etched elsewhere, attended in a text of living parchment.

All things seek the good

She'd catch him staring at her with a kind of perplexed wonder. When Sky answered back with a question in her eyes, he'd pretend not to have been studying her. This had been going on for some days when Sky felt she could no longer be put off.

"What?" she said, the single word compact with meaning.

It was impossible to evade such a direct demand for clarification, though this did not enforce a direct response. The Elder smiled and said that he had noticed Sky had a predilection for collecting odd bits of glass and paper, rocks and tiny plants. And suddenly she forgot all her boldness and felt exposed.

"Yes," she said shyly. "My menagerie."

"I do not mention it to embarrass you. Quite the opposite, Sparrow. You have affection for these little things?"

"I know that they are nothing, really, but I love them. I can't explain. When I see them, they speak to me. They can't actually speak, of course, but I feel as if they do. They call out to me to rescue them from the busy world that passes them by without . . . ."

"Without cherishing them."

"It's silly, I know."

"You are only saying that because you have been taught to be ashamed of a generous love. Beauty is useless, and yet it is the point of it all."

"But these little things —"

"Are beautiful, Sky. That is why you noticed them. Don't ever apologize for seeing more deeply than most. All things seek the good."

"I don't think you quite understand."

"I do understand. The Great Work is where harmonies of togetherness are formed. Some we can see or guess at, but much else is being accomplished whilst we struggle in perplexity. We have little sense of it, but love like yours intimates the joy hidden in our grief.

Do not doubt, Sparrow. A mysterious convergence is being effected in the course of things."

Providence

Mince stood in the apothecary shop looking quite squat and squinty eyed. Mr. Crispin looked up from his biscuits. He had been munching quite judiciously. Already, he had managed to shape one biscuit into something quite like the outline of Somaliland and he was presently engaged in a facsimile of the state of California, both fictional places he'd read about as a boy.

"Yes, can I help you?" he asked.

The short man grunted at him before reaching into the folds of his overcoat, from which he brought an elaborately brocaded silk purse. He wheezed and sputtered. He moved from the counter and looked out the window, his long nose pressed against the lowest pane. The man was quite a midget. Indeed, staring at his back, Mr. Crispin had to fight back the impression of a tail tripping out from behind the waistcoat.

"Mouse? Mouse!" he muttered to himself.

"I am looking for the proprietors of this establishment," intoned the midget in a high, nasal, peremptory voice, turning to glare dangerously at Mr. Crispin.

Mr. Crispin backed away slightly from the counter, an involuntary glance shot towards the exposed biscuits. After all, mice are not scrupulous. "The owner is not, I mean to say, Today — he is not in."

Mince twitched his nose in irritation and looked at Mr. Crispin as if he were emitting a foul odor. "He is not coming in at all then?" he asked, full of disbelief in the clerk.

"No. I'm afraid he can't be reached. His younger brother. The heart, they say. It was a great shock, you see?"

"Death is no excuse," frowned the squat man.

Mr. Crispin was suddenly angry. "I think it is, sir! I think it is!" he retorted, his pale face flushing pinkish.

Mince stared blankly at the clerk. After a blink or two, he appeared ready to answer him when he was overcome with a fit of wheezing. The midget produced a finely woven handkerchief and sneezed, his small mouth widening into a punctilious little 'o,' the whole movement punctuated by a long, dismal noise. "Nothing so like a mouse," thought Mr. Crispin as he absent-mindedly nibbled away Southern California.

After a prolonged silence, Mince made an elaborate pretense of ignoring the clerk's rebuke. With delicate care he handed a small business card to Mr. Crispin with an almost genial smile. It read:

M

PRIOR STREET

ACQUISITIONS

"I see," said Mr. Crispin, seeing not at all and attempting to sound as knowing as possible. "You are in acquisitions."

"I am," answered Mince, his eyes almost merry, round now and glistening like wet currants.

"And what is it, Mr., er, M, that you wish to acquire from Peridin and Sons?"

Mince coughed softly and looked away. Mr. Crispin felt himself to have committed some obscure *faux pas*. His pale cheeks turned scarlet as his visitor walked over once again to the window. A fog had entered the street, its cottony breath drifting gently against the glass and obscuring the view, which, in any event, was unremarkable. Still looking out the window in which there was nothing to see, Mince declared himself in a loud, authoritative voice.

"I do not need pear honey for the intestines. Nor do I wish for rose sage oil. I intend to leave something to be examined by the elder Mr. Peridin. Not the sons, you understand? It is an item of probable great value. I would not like to be you if some mishap were to befall it."

Mince spun quickly and faced Mr. Crispin with such a menacing demeanor that the clerk felt an urge to run from the room. A short, treacherous smile flitted across the face of the small man. These shifts in manner were quite unsettling. He opened the purse, and drew forth a pale lustrous thing that Mr. Crispin at first judged to be some kind of plate. After a soft cloth had been laid upon the counter, the visitor deposited the item gently, almost reverently. Then Mr. Crispin discovered that it was a rounded crystalline goblet, mostly milk white, but cut with dashes of crimson and golden swirls.

Words were spoken of which the attendant heard "cup of grief," "translation," and "Arimathea," but they came as disconnected bits that failed to conquer his elementary astonishment before the powerful aura of the stone.

"This is remarkable!" exclaimed Mr. Crispin.

Mince's eyes narrowed. "It must be kept secret. Very secret," he repeated, his glance darting quickly at the door.

Mr. Crispin primly boxed the precious thing. "I assure you, Mr. M. It shall be a matter known only to Mr. Peridin and I. But please, ahem, sir, what is it you want from Mr. Peridin?"

Mince fairly growled at Mr. Crispin. "I wish to know the provenance, of course. Is it genuine? The proprietor in years past has been helpful in matters of this sort. He is a man who knows."

Mince paused, and then added gravely, "he should keep better help."

"I'm sorry, Mr. M. I'm sure you're quite right. I am sure Mr. Peridin will help you with the providence."

"Provenance!" shouted the midget angrily. "It means where it comes from."

He turned and hurriedly left the shop, slamming the door behind him. Mr. Crispin sighed. His nerves were quite exercised. The clerk was just about to open the box, for he felt certain that were he to run his hand over the smooth, rounded surface that he would be calmed, when the door jerked open. Mince stood, half-in, half-out, his tiny hand held sagely against his long nose.

"Shhh. A secret," he said softly.

The door clinked shut and Mr. Crispin was alone again. Daring nothing, he carefully tied the box up with twine. On the top of the box, he wrote in big, block letters, 'PROVIDENCE.'

There is a warp in him

It was only after Pennyfeather had left the abandoned building, relieved and stunned at once, that Malchidion broke down into a long, extended fit of coughing. He had wanted to cough earlier, but had not permitted his body such a show of weakness. When the last echo of pulmonary vehemence had retreated into silence, the slow movement of a tapestry disclosed the presence of the crone.

She always brought with her the cold, moist scent of dark waters and ancient stone. The old woman appeared to be smiling. It was a rather ghastly visage that hardly fit her.

"Well, Uhraine, I hope you are satisfied."

"The boy is good stock. There is a warp in him. Hard to see, but useful to us."

"The memory of woman is prodigious for grudges."

Uhraine tapped the Guardian lightly. "Do not forget."

Malchidion laughed bitterly. "Are you deathless, old woman? Or is your secret that you died long ago?"

"My secret belongs to another. It is not mine to tell."

"Which means you do not know it."

"The answer is given when the answer is needed."

Malchidion gave vent to another fit of coughing, and then barked, "Enough of this! I am weary of such puzzles. We will see if this clerk is worthy of your guile."

A conversation

When the voices began, Sky was never sure if she was dreaming. Perhaps it was because she wore the orb ring. Neither did she know whether they knew she could hear them or if they were speaking to themselves or to an unknown god. Many of their concerns were the worries of ordinary living. A middle-aged woman felt herself no longer attractive. She was alone with her two children, could not pay the rent, and did not like her job. An elderly man suffered the leisure of last years. He did not care for card games or the tired jokes of his peers.

Other voices were far stranger. Sky could not avoid perplexity that sometimes became acute. She began to suspect that her presence was secretly felt, that she was not merely eavesdropping, but vaguely appealed to. A young creature, but also old, it came to her rich with paradox, walked along the remains of an ancient fortress. Dressed in a shimmering, unusual fabric, it was full of many images: a golden lamp stand, strange creatures of fire, and monstrous, quixotic beasts that seemed to prophesy.

There were decrepit bell towers, road paths taken over by jungle, golden eyes glistening in the night, but also, galaxies, starburst, and lovely chalk drawings made for a day. More recondite matters, too, came to her: ruminations upon what it meant to exist, of how random, tiny things can bring death or joy, and a questioning of how fragile and vulnerable the dearest are. There was a long sorrow of gray sea and the rhythm of half-recalled songs.

She was not certain it was human. "Do you see what I mean?" it asked. "There's no one else to tell."

Etheric intervention

The Etheric ambassador did not so much sit or stand as inhabit the region of the upper balcony, operating with a serene equipoise that seemed as if nothing extraordinary could ever startle. Long-robed, calm eyed, the Vendakar pursed its lips in the barest etch of a smile that retained a native equivocity. It might be the expression of a charming, carefree spirit or equally possible, haughty condescension towards the vulgar primitives who pranced about eager to please.

With languid grace beneath a sheath of fabric that shimmered like summer lightning, it hid from all the progress of its designs. At various times during the evening, a representative of Elnarian high society would approach with a vain attempt to take the measure of the Vendakar or perhaps simply to be seen so that they could gossip fabulous tales to their friends who were not present. Malchidion, of course, was not likely to step within the orbit of an unknown star, though a cadre of clerics lurked about taking notes.

Father Bunn nudged Sky from her reverie. "I do believe you are quite taken," he observed.

"I admit no such thing," she said without taking her eyes from the Vendakar. "I'm not even sure what species or gender is involved."

"Oh, don't let that trouble you," said the priest. "Etherics are not disposed to romance. It's almost as if they hardly notice desire in the way poor flesh suffers."

"I *am* fascinated, but it's not that at all. It's something else. I'm just interested," said Sky, not very satisfied with her words.

Just as she was feeling betrayed by an unwanted blush, goodness knows what it meant, a commotion arose at one of the lower tables. Two youths and a woman began shouting. One of the young men turned an angry face upwards and began yelling a litany of indecipherable grievances evidently intended for the Guardian's representatives. The woman threw herself in front of the boy and only then did Sky see the resemblance.

The boy had come to make some speech of rebellion, though probably he knew as little as Sky what anything was about. His mother and brother had followed, vainly wishing for the son and brother to return into obscurity. This was quickly followed by an inrush of even more violent fellows. A short scuffle ensued before the Vigiles arrived to put an end to it. Just as the incident appeared to have been quelled, there was the sound of breaking glass and a gasoline soaked burn bottle landed at the feet of the angry young man.

This, too, was professionally extinguished by the city watchmen. The entire episode might easily have been dismissed and forgotten, except that the woman had caught the brunt of the makeshift weapon. The younger son cried piteously, whilst the erstwhile rebel held his mother with desperate denial and nearly animal incomprehension.

A medic made his way through the gathering crowd only to shake his head in dismay. After that, some men came with a stretcher and carried her away.

"We should go," said Father Bunn, his brow fierce and sorrowing all at once. "They will take her to St. Rilians. Those boys will need someone to be there with them."

And though the priest knew the shortest way and they made haste, they were not first to the quiet room where the wounded woman had been taken. It was impossible, but the Vendakar was already in the act of leaving and just as strange, the woman looked remarkably well. Her body showed only a mild bruising rather than the mortal wounds they had already witnessed.

The Etheric paused, yes, Sky was certain of it, and for a long moment bestowed upon her that enigmatic regard that tantalized and almost haunted.

The patient herself was hardly more illuminating. "What did it say to you?" asked Father Bunn.

"Nothing in words," was all the woman could answer.

The full outfit

Benedicta had a feeling. She knew a lot about the girl, more than she was saying, and more than the Elder was letting on. No great thing happens apart from the long silence. Like the nine months in the womb, there is growth, development in the darkness, and all of time is a womb. Malice had thought to stop the girl, to keep her from her name, but even death is unable to make good that evil wish.

Anyway, Benedicta asked Sky to join her. There was a place she liked.

On the way to Benedicta's "hole in the wall," they came up against a crowd. There on the parapet, the one along the bridge double named for either an ancient governor's wife or alternatively and more popularly a saucy river nymph, a shouting voice was heard ascending to heights of wrath against the wealthy and the tax gatherers, not forgetting to include the many who occupied the seats of power.

At first, one could not see the source of prophetic ire, but there were odd, frequently obscene jokes thrown in and the folks laughed at these. Then sliding along the top of the barrier, a dwarf appeared with a feathered cap of leather and tall boots that had the affect of accentuating the brevity of his legs. Nonetheless, they were powerful. He would jump with nimble assurance, raise his fists to the sky, thunder at those below, stopping at times to engage in banter with a particular individual. It was a show of sorts.

Well, you can only take so much of that kind of thing. Sky looked to see if Benedicta approved of the prophet or not, but she wasn't saying. When they found their destination, it was the sort of place where you throw peanut shells on the floor as a sign of conviviality. The fella playing a lazy blues guitar gave them a friendly, casual glance from his perch on a small stage dropped down in the corner. He had on a black cowboy hat and sported a beard that would do a mountain man proud.

Benedicta ordered a beer. Sky opted to feign surprise. "I heard you were a nun," she said.

"What, you think that means I can't enjoy a good lager?"said Benedicta.

"No," said Sky. "Not that I thought about it much." The guitar began to strum Robert Johnson's "Crossroad Blues." "You're not wearing, what's it called?"

"A habit?"

"Yes, the full outfit. I guess that went out of fashion."

"It's a sign of consecration. You either have that or you don't," said Benedicta.

"I had a friend," said Sky. "He wasn't sure about the holy, but I think that's what he wanted. He said that's what we all want, we just don't know it."

Benedicta took a long gulp of the beer and stretched. "You're remembering more now. That's good. I had a friend, too," she said. "Maybe more than one."

"Are you confessing something?" laughed Sky.

"Well, not much," said Benedicta. "I used to write "dear Mr. Ingarten" who was occasionally dearest friend and once, I slipped up and wrote my darling. And then there was Hans."

The crunch of dry peanut shells and the fog of drifting tobacco smoke mixed with the lush murmur of other patrons unwinding. "Thing is," said Sky, "nothing ever came of it. It's like a missed opportunity, but I guess none of that matters if you're married to Jesus."

"Well, yes, there's that," admitted Benedicta. "Funny thing is Mr. Ingarten rather resented it. Men are an amusing lot."

"Not jealous?"

"No, nothing like that. He was already married by then. Still, he didn't like it."

The fella on stage was explaining that his mother always set a good example and his father always gave good advice, but all the same, the devil always made him think twice.

Gestalt recognition

Sky felt happy. She guarded this knowledge like a secret flame, folding her hands protectively over the little candle imperiled as it were by so many enemies of malice and circumstance, not to mention camels of indifference. She laughed again at the latter species derived from the cornucopia of Ratcatcher's gnomic observations. Father Bunn had translated whilst offering a scholar's gloss.

"It is a stubborn resistance," said her Maasai friend. "The sort of folk who carry an invisible hump of stupidity to carry them through, lest the desert tempt them to reconsider."

There is nothing wrong with being happy, she thought. Everyone desires to be happy. "Even Benedicta", she whispered to herself, not quite knowing why.

The Elder sensed something in her. He did not question, just looked at Sky with mild, appraising glance. Sky blushed and went out for a walk.

Rabbi Naftali greeted her with pleasure. He asked after the health of the Elder and wondered whether she was finding the City to her liking. "It is satisfactory," she answered, the glow of her happiness betraying her despite attempted neutrality.

"Have you met anyone special?"

"Not that I'm aware of, but sometimes you don't know," she said lightly.

And so it was, one stop after another filled with seemingly trivial amiability that pleased her beyond measure. The spirit of effervescence led her to a tiny square in the quarter where the Muslims dwelt. The ancient stone citadel that housed the Guardian's centurions rose above them. Some boys and old men were chatting by a well. They turned their eyes briefly upon her, but were evidently too engaged in their own affairs to censure the unveiled infidel.

A greyhound pranced about invoking good will. Then, it was as if one had walked into a gestalt drawing where the same figures demonstrate two entirely different realities. There was the watering place and the usual fellas and the sweet canine and there was also the strange embroidered robe of the Vendakar who turned to her with the faintest gesture of recognition.

Warning

Towards the end of her walk, Sky was surprised to recognize the little dwarf that had so raged at the fishmongers and the tax collectors. She hesitated and tried to think how to pass by without enraging him. The dwarf spied her alright, but he did not shout. He began to talk in a flow of language that was ambiguously directed into the ambient air, though possibly aimed.

"It's not that I have any illusions about changing your mind. You're perfectly free to think what you like. Nor do I have designs upon you. Let's just say that it's a pastime of mine. Some folks play poker, others read or travel. If you're not interested, I'm not keeping you. There's something rather inveterate about spirit or intellect – whether the mind is real or not I leave to the metaphysicians. You can't help thinking. You feel as if you are aware, isn't that so?"

He stopped then and rested his eyes upon her, so that Sky found herself shaking her head in assent, though she hardly knew what he was about.

Satisfied, the dwarf returned to his oration. "And I can't help wondering, you know, about the relentless cruelty. There's a lot of that. You can't miss it. Maybe you can miss it for a while if you're lucky and keep your head down. I can't help feeling there's cowardice involved there, though. I try not to judge."

Here, he stopped again and shrugged his shoulders. A brief, sad moment of introspection was but a lull, however. He soon resumed and now his voice was rising and Sky feared he would erupt into a full-fledged lamentation. In fact his voice quickly lowered and by the end he was speaking nearly in a whisper and glancing about as if he feared unseen observers.

"Thing is, all that pain and rank injustice, how can it be tolerated? We have to because endurance is our fate, but it's still intolerable. There are those who reject the gift. Unable to say amen, they curse. The son of the dragon, for one. Long has it been since praise entered his soul. I probably shouldn't have brought it up, except that I've seen them circling about, eyeing you. That lot is always on the prowl, but perhaps this is different. I thought it only decent to warn you."

"Thank you," said Sky, wondering who he could mean. It had been ages since the gray man had even bothered to haunt her dreams.

"Not at all," said the dwarf who bowed slightly in her direction. He then began to dance and sang a polyglot song whose drift appeared to announce the rapid decline of sentient life and the coming victory of gourds and creeping vines over the double-tongued who wantonly lie and lavishly oppress the poor.

Non-standard logic

When an Etheric spoke conversation was bound to be unusual. The voice was calm, flowing; though singular, suggesting the chant of many waters. Afterwards, Sky recollected the words and barely suppressed plurivocity (was it?) became more pronounced, as if in memory the chorus broke through a merely tacit boundary.

The words, too, were eccentric which did not surprise her. Yet she seemed to understand an import that clearly exceeded her capacities. It was a boon in earnest of what she would later endure. And so, in a charming, languid manner, the Vendakar advised her that there was a quality to motion not unremarked by the sages. Past, present, and future were spiritual realities that impinged through a dance that refused ordinary notions of causality and effect.

One was sure to be confounded by contradictions if the attempt was made to comprehend by rationality limited to standard logic. Nothing real comes before motion. Action is always from the first the establishment of habit, though how this could be at the outset puzzled Sky. One might try to think of action as a series of discreet, still moments, but this was an illicit condescension, a fixed, morbid fiction for a single living gesture.

The quest of the act resists capture, eludes the effort to confine it as predictable repetition, a quantified identity. All that metaphysics was an answer to Sky's initial wonder at the healing of the rebel's mother. The Etheric implied that it was possible to reach out beyond the grid-like chronotope which was necessarily local and that flesh was capable of bearing the Uncreated Light. And here, paradoxically, a flash of darkness. Not an image, nor a concept, but a feeling for infinity that was neither the indefinite nor the uncircumscribed aggregate of everything.

Like the thrall of waiting at the top of the rollercoaster before the plunge into a vertiginous drop, Sky sensed the beckoning of reality both desirable and terrifying. We are not hard, nor durable, nor machine-like. Rather, the emptiness (or perhaps also plenitude?) bore us in love. From the night, we are drawn. The creature is by way of fractures, the kindness of wounds, fractal wholeness. One must cross – and here, Sky could not quite translate -- *abyssal ways or hallows* in order to discover well-being.

Ansharu advice

The priest and the Ansharu asked her out. She was becoming a popular girl.

"What's with all the spooks?" she asked.

"Narghunel, lucidem boornish elgibar," said Ratcatcher.

"Yes, quite," agreed Father Bunn. Allowing for a beat or two so that Sky smoldered at the lack of translation, he added, "The shadow's false light pretends at mystery."

"That's pretty," admitted the girl.

"A shabby game played out with contrived ciphers aimed at constructed depths that are nothing more than our own banalities dressed up in the mystique of blood and politics."

"Ah, spooks are little boys and naughty gals caught up in pulp thrillers."

"It's a way to pass the time," drawled a fella in a fedora slant across his narrow face.

"Time's a funny thing," said Sky in a wounded wise fashion.

The fella pushed the hat higher on his forehead and looked at her with surprisingly guileless eyes. "Say, kid, do we know each other?"

"Not that I know of cowboy, but we might meet later on and play cards."

"Well, I'll say this. You learn quick, kid."

"Maybe I'm smart. Or maybe you're just slow."

The fella laughed and put the fedora back over his eyes.

"Bricknick ludem isha," said Ratcatcher.

Probably Sky didn't need the priest to translate that one, but he did for the fun of it. "He says never play games with a woman."

The black swan

Sky sat still and silent, her face turned away into the light of the sun. Faruiza perched amiably on her shoulder. Sky was remembering.

The day before, she had come upon a little boy in the park. He was huddled against a tree near the lake, disconsolate and fighting back tears. The boy was not famished and skeletal like the children in the Underground. He sported a plaid cap and his golden locks fell abundantly into eyes the color of whale song.

She looked about and nowhere could discover a governess or mama to attend to his sad little face. Then Sky had run over to him and when he gazed into her eyes there was surprise and then almost immediately shame. He dropped his head and refused to answer her questions, but nestled against her bosom and sobbed. After this, he pushed her away and stood a few feet before her. With resolute severity, he forced himself to look at her.

"It is my fault," he cried bitterly. "My fault. And nothing can be done about it."

"You're upset. When one is very sad making, things often seem much worse than they really are."

The boy frowned at her. He was so full with emotion, so at a loss for words.

"Once, I saw a fella make a tiny little ice cream cone for a squirrel. The squirrel took the cone from him and held it very demurely and ate the treat," said Sky.

The boy nearly forgot himself in pondering this image. "It must have been a pet," he said.

"Yes, I imagine so. People often think of them as vermin, but that's because they are dim and have stones for hearts."

"I have a dog named Jewels."

"What's that? I think you've been hiding it from me."

"Hiding what?"

"Those rosy cheeks and that perfect, impish smile."

The boy laughed softly. Then his sadness returned in a quieter mood. "When something bad happens, it's bad forever," he said.

As if in agreement with this somber reflection, a giant black swan appeared floating near the rim of the lake. Sky did not reply. Everyone believed what the boy said to be true.

"I shall die and never be whole!" cried the boy.

Then he ran to the edge of the water and threw his arms roughly about the neck of the swan. Even as she called after him, the boy was rapidly carried away from her, soon dwindling to a mere dot of memory.

Fairuza cooed softly into her ear.

"Yes, Faruiza," she said. "I know who he is."

Sky's prayer

The horizon was darkening. The first stars known to Elnaria began to peep out at Sky. She passed by a small arched bridge and heard the gentle swish of the waters of the canal. Sky gave a sort of prayer of regard towards the sleeping flowers in a garden bathed in soft moonlight. The lanterns of an ancient building lit up a gleaming parapet high above the garden. Then her heart caught and quickened. She had begun to think she had only dreamed him.

The impossible one crossed over, his cloak and tunic clothed in night, his burning eyes and silver hair gentled by a winsome smile. And words came to her, audible in her heart.

"You think I can return to the divine Father without all of my brethren, all that is human and every simple created thing -- animals, plants, stone, dust?"

The pilgrim Kheen

The pilgrim Kheen had the short beard and open face of a minor sectarian used to mild and congenial congress with an enclave of the like-minded. He might have been a young Mennonite temporarily separated from the brethren whilst traversing the solitude of the woods. And yet none of this would explain the idiosyncratic accoutrement of his garb.

His wide-brimmed hat opened out into a length of gauzy cloth that billowed with the swiftness of his movement. A thick serge material dyed a blue-gray hue that was once the signatory of a Dutch order of nuns formed the tightly buttoned neck and long sleeves of his tunic. Yet surely what would have caused an on-looker to doubt his vision was the way a construction of wooden armor was integrated into the fabric architecture. For the head looked out from within the enclosed space of a cabinet, the wooden doors of which were swung open to reveal the face of the traveler.

Beneath this, strips of wooden planking appeared in disparate places, sometimes as the inner lining of the cape, in other locations as an outer exterior that incongruously merged with the enveloping cloth. Further, small hooks and metal clasps had been embedded in this wooden carapace that allowed for the hanging of various items such as a cup and a tiny oval portrait. A tight leather band was affixed in such a way that a wooden flower pot containing a single pink rose was nestled against the heart of the pilgrim.

As for a staff, he bore a tall silver pole that concluded in a delicate fan of trapezoidal panels that swung about with the receptive momentum of a wind-mill.

Kheen followed a meandering path, stopping to rest upon an outcropping of moss-covered rock. Whether it had been waiting for him there or was, in fact, an inquiline lodger slipped from the eccentric accommodations of his traveling outfit, a stubbornly insistent mouse stood up and pattered meaningfully around the recumbent pilgrim in a harried, asymmetric *pas de deux*.

"Alright, Mince," said the pilgrim. "Do stop your timorous dance. I have discovered no indication of the celestial mercury, but quicksilver may elude our eyes. Maybe the elixir of the Kingdom has entered this realm. If it is the chalice of the Anointed, we'll know soon enough. Strange that we must risk leaving it in the hands of men, but only they reveal the truth that nonetheless they do not understand."

In the distance, an eagle circled the horizon. It cried out to all those below, but whether of woe or glory was anyone's guess.

Uhraine's visitor

Uhraine's chamber was austere by preference, consisting of bare stone walls, a simple wooden chair, and an iron kettle over a small hearth fire. The cupboard contained the few necessities she could not reproach herself for.

Strangely, Uhraine rarely felt old. There was that place in her heart that did not know age. But this day, a voice babbled venomously of the years and the fear she had thought mastered leapt up and bit her. It was just then that she noticed the Man standing in the doorway. The Man was watching her with a bemused smile on his face.

"When you were a child, I used to carry you in my arms," he said.

"Go away!" railed Uhraine. "I was never a child."

Chapter Four

The Cauldrons of Hephaestus

Merchant's ennui

R obinson Peacock looked over the appraisals from the Company. Wimber, Shackleton, & Bey had promoted and insured many an adventure over the generations. They were, nearly, diversified sufficiently against any catastrophe. The price of wheat had gone down more than he had expected, but they'd done well with tin and whale oil was always a solid commodity. The country folk still used it for kerosene and men's pomade and women's perfume were ready markets.

Peacock could feel the weight of the letter from Lady Winterbourne in his pocket. It was a provocative missive. As representative of the Company, he was often called upon to play many roles – diplomat, counselor, even spy. A merchant's star could rise to significant heights. Flavius George had even hinted at inviting him to the summer villa where his reclusive daughters were said to abide in unrivaled beauty.

By all accounts, his mood should have been, if not ebullient, reasonably bright, yet he remained subject to the unsettled, vague anxiety that had dogged him since the evening last. It had begun at the bridge where the dwarf, Elmerlin, had regaled them with a mix of fury and bawdy jokes. Ordinarily, he enjoyed these shows, but in the course of peering over the crowd, Elmerlin had fixed his eyes on Peacock, a trick to mesmerize the audience, no doubt. Nonetheless, the merchant was troubled.

And then, he had occasion to greet the young widow of Vorhaas. She had such an austere grace in her manner, and of course, it caused him to remember the sad and strange occasion of her husband's demise. *I cannot be the only one who knows, he thought to himself. But suppose I am the only one?* He shook the ledgers again. Ah, the yen for comet dust was on the upswing. He'd have to get in touch with his contact in the celestial service.

Deco and the Fates

"And how is the Snappety Beast?" asked Narina, glancing with merry eyes at her sister Aurora, though someone who knew her well would have discerned a real anxiety hiding like a meek creature under cover of her sportive manner. Aurora saw this in her younger sibling, but as she was rather pleased the favorite was currently under some sort of cloud, the exact nature of which had eluded her specific inquiries, the middle sister merely shrugged and went on with her needlework.

"He is cold and beastly, what else?" answered Diana, the eldest, who was this morning feeling mostly indifferent to Narina, but disliking her papa quite grandly.

"Oh, I'll be sure to tell him," smiled Rory.

"Make sure that you do," said Diana.

Narina moved softly to the window and peeked out. "Do you think it will rain? I have a dismal feeling it is going to pour and pour."

"Surely not," demurred Diana, joining her at the window.

Cook offered the hopeful suggestion that so long as no one hung out the wash, it would not rain. This was a truism from her rural childhood. Then she added, "But perhaps the sky is different away from the city?"

"You are a goose," snorted Diana. "Why should the sky be any different here or anywhere?"

"Oh, the light is quite altered once one gets far enough from the city," declared Aurora. "The stars at night are like purest diamonds scattered across the horizon."

Diana was not in the mood for contradiction, though Rory couldn't help being contrary. She changed the subject. "Deco came home late last night. I suppose he is sleeping in if he hasn't already gone off."

"He isn't sleeping," said Deco. "And how are my most agreeable sisters?"

"Next time, perhaps papa will take *all* of us to the summer house," pouted Narina in a trailing voice that threatened to turn into the full force of a mope.

"Was there very much to see?" asked Diana in a delicate voice.

"Not so very much. The emus are in fine feather. I did talk with her, if that's what you mean. Still refuses to see the point of anything, I'm afraid."

"You'll stay awhile?"

"Better not. I've left a letter."

"Deco, can't you just speak to him?"

"Yes, but you know how it is? Society frowns on sons challenging the paterfamilias to a duel."

"I'm sure you'd win," said Rory in a slow drawl that might have been a joke or genuine conjecture.

"Not at all. Papa would pay someone to shoot me in the back."

Narina looked at him with pleading eyes. "But Deco! I wanted to show you my arctic fox."

Deco kissed her, and then laughed. "Does your rooster know about this?"

Welcome to my parlor

Abiathar Fairgood had substantial holdings in transportation, agriculture, and mining. His distant cousin, Lady Winterbourne, occupied a stately home in Regency Park where a line of tall poplars decorated the boulevard that led to her estate. Peacock had done business with Fairgood, and found him somewhat of a

Puritan, eschewing tobacco and drink, but otherwise a responsible and practical man.

The merchant heretofore had no occasion to meet with Lady Winterbourne. All he knew of her was by reputation as she was said to share her relative's piety. A servant led him through the foyer to the front parlor which was furnished somewhat more grandiosely than he would have suspected. The household goods were after the tastes of several generations back, so the luxury was perhaps an inherited one now preserved by thrift. A small collection of religious sermons was open upon the reading table. Lady Winterbourne caught the merchant casually perusing the text when she entered.

"I am told that particular volume is rare and has value to certain experts in mystical lore," she announced in an arch tone that surprised him.

Certainly, she was prim with a straight back, dressed soberly in a simple cap that might have adorned any middle-aged maiden aunt, yet her eyes seemed lively. Robinson Peacock bowed and handed her his card.

"Wimber, Shackleton, & Bey at your service," he said sounding more portentous than he intended.

"Well now, Mr. Peacock, we shall see if you are able to match your fine plumage with the deed. We shall see, indeed," she said.

The Snappety Beast

It did not rain, but the air was misty and indecisive. As early as might be considered polite, a house maid entered with a card from

Prince N. Of course, the city was rife with princes where every rising merchant's son suddenly discovered a vein of unremarked royalty in the family inheritance. Prince N., however, was securely old money. He was genial, rather handsome, and good at cards. Cards bored Narina, but like all young girls she responded to a young man accustomed to winning. Alas, Prince N. would be refused an audience. The house rarely entertained guests.

Flavius George sat ensconced in pillows. Since arriving in the city, his beard had been dyed bright indigo and he had added a number of gold rings to his already burdened fingers. If he did not look ridiculous, it was because fashion temporarily shielded the offending victim from the absurdity of his position and because his daughters had the good sense not to laugh in the face of their capricious papa.

An open letter upon which Narina could discern the seal of her brother had been tossed haphazardly onto the raft of pillows. Deco, too, was a topic not to be broached, so she stood quite unprotected whilst the ancient servant of her father eyed her maliciously from a corner of the room and pretended to construe a ledger by chewing the nib of his pen. When the silence had become large and uncomfortable, Flavius George smiled softly to himself.

"Brumby," he said, as if he were greeting a long lost friend. He then continued talking, glancing with a kind eye at his daughter as if Narina were a much younger child and her loving papa were telling her a story to kiss evening into sleep. "When I was a boy, my father came home one day with a small paper house, exquisitely made, which turned out to be a cage. A cricket lived within. 'For luck,' he said. I was very proud of my little friend. He chirruped so nicely and was sure to bring good fortune, as well. Yes, I named him Brumby. I don't know why anymore. Have you found that shipment of cinnamon yet, Gulguluk?"

The servant startled to hear his name. He had been placing invisible mental pins into the third daughter of his majestic prince. Nevertheless, he answered serenely with a studied mix of vigilance and slight boredom.

"There is much corn, my master. Olive oil in abundance and the perfumed oils taken from the singing whales captured in the depths. Dried apricots and raisins burst through the bindings of their sacks and barley lies lascivious for the brewer's yeast. The cinnamon, however, remains unaccounted and a vagabond, though we shall persist until the missing scamp is rendered docile and tallied in the ranks of my master's lowly servants."

Flavius George did not appear to heed this aria to his rich storehouses.

"One day," he began again, "I was unhappy in a game of chance with my fellows. Marbles, I believe. I was compelled to give up a favorite aggie. Then the sound of my little friend's chatter began to seem mocking to me. The night was warm and I could not rest, but tossed and turned and Brumby whispered his enchanting promise of good luck. I was really quite annoyed, you know. So I took him from his beautiful palace of paper and thrust the liar into the agreeable maw of my mother's mynah bird. I must say I felt very much better."

Narina paled before her papa. "That is a perfectly dreadful story," she said at last.

"Oh, is it? Well, it isn't true, you know. But imagine if it were. An unpleasant tale and true, that is terribly unhappy. We must avoid such things in future. We really must."

The meaning of what is not said

The conversation afterwards was rather anticlimactic, though oddly stressful. Lady Winterbourne brought up various topics related to morality, aesthetics, and history touching upon subjects as disparate as the mating habits of giraffes, Galileo's theory of motion, and the works of Hermes Trismegistus. It was evident that she was remarkably well-read. The family fortune had allowed her this much provision.

Periodically, Lady Winterbourne would ask a question both obscure and seemingly without issue. Peacock did his best to keep up and to emulate genuine interest, though this was made hard to accomplish both by his indifference to the matters raised and by the incoherency of the apparently random sequence of Lady Winterbourne's curiosity.

"And do you know the story of Félix Ravaisson's proposed restoration of the Venus de Milo?" she asked. She seemed genuinely disappointed when the merchant failed to register the slightest awareness. "I have heard there is a fellow, somewhat dubious I confess, who could inform you of the details."

At the end of it, Peacock was no further enlightened as to what precisely he was supposed to procure for the satisfaction of Fairgood's cousin. Before his departure, he was provided an address, handwritten in an eccentric, elegant hand. No name was given, but he surmised a kind of title. It may be the Elder would offer him illumination.

The hierophant and the counting house man

Sky kept the intrigue of the Vendakar in a special place, a curio no one else should know about. She felt, somehow, that she had entered a path that might lead to answers the others either didn't know or weren't prepared to tell her. She wanted to be alone with this feeling, to luxuriate in it as in a warm bath. Whether the Elder was aware of her new pleasure or not, he desired her company.

One evening, a ragtag collection of cabs, motorbikes, and landau carriages congregated before a large apartment occupying several floors of a building on Kaplan Street. Sky was enchanted by the entrance. The door to the house led immediately onto a hallway painted a light pastel mint green. The wainscoting had been covered by an undulating fabric of soft ivory detailed with a roseate pattern of intricate design that was like Arabic script transformed into vegetal life. Delicate lamps with diminutive translucent shades shaped like pale flowers reached like gentle hands from their wall sconces to light the passage.

Yet this faerie world approach was but the setting for the inner door, a master work of thin columns of brightly stained wood and glass traced with opaque flowers. These vertical panels flowed seamlessly into an upper arch of bright green, navy, and azure glass. Laughter and the rambunctious babble of a dozen conversations reached the newcomer as one stepped from the lovely portal into a madcap display.

A middle-aged woman called Madame Dahlia was a tolerant hostess, overseeing the event with an apparent indifference that touched the hem of benign neglect. The mix of people who congregated in rooms and hallways demonstrated a democratic, if eccentric taste. Sky recognized familiar tavern faces dotted amongst bohemian artists, scholars, and more august figures that appeared both conscious of their dignity and anxious not to be made a fool. It was an overwhelming crush of eclectic humanity.

The Elder had brought with him his ancient staff. He'd found it lying behind an icon board and some whim of nostalgia had caused him to bring it along at the last minute. So now he appeared rather quixotically like a shepherd or storybook patriarch. Sky followed closely in the wake of his advancing steps, and breathed a sigh of relief when they discovered an inner chamber that appeared to have been magically set aside for quieter conversation.

Nonetheless, this room also was occupied by diverse figures. Students, clerks, a few merchants and working class folk formed an unlikely aggregate. Seated at a center table was Edward Caius, thirty years Questor, dressed in a long toga of purple damask with wide fur-lined ducal sleeves. Despite the exaggerated sartorial rhetoric of his office, his face was thinly blooded and austere. Evidently, he had been engaged in a rather one-sided dialogue with a ruddy faced fellow who kept identifying himself as a counting house man.

The hierophant spoke with the mild condescension of a superior used to dealing with the unfortunate fact that most men are dullards and few possess the energy or native talent to ascend the heights of mystagogic wisdom. "Understand that money in its aspiration is not a physical thing. If you like, money is abstract, symbolic, and concrete material all at once, but in its fullest development, it is universal, neutral, utterly liberated from material specificity."

"That's what I been trying to tell your honor," answered his hapless interlocutor. "It was a mistake to go off the gold standard. I know there are clever fellows who say it was holding us back, but I tell you it was the last bit of reality left in the game. It kept value tied to something real, you see?"

The doctor of the treasury nodded and did not sigh. Without acknowledging the objection, he went on with the refutation. "There is no doubt that men are fractious by nature. We live different lives, hold different beliefs, and ascribe differing values to various concepts and objects. The clash of our differences is apt to promote violence. What is needed, truly, is a mode of valuation *without* inherent value."

The sage paused to survey his audience with a magisterial gaze. When no one intervened to object to the sacred gnosis, he resumed the recitation of mysteries. "The mechanical rigidity and sameness of a substance venerated by tradition, jewels, for instance, is a clumsy tool. Money, ostensibly a trivial paper lacking any intrinsic power to entice—or better yet, a mere registry of number, an arithmetic tally lacking any material referent at all, becomes significant precisely because it is divorced from limited particularities.

Money is universally valid because it is not a thing at all, but an abstract representation. It is the mode by which people of differing walks of life and standards are able to interact, negotiate, and come to agreement. Money is indifferent to what one honors or dishonors, loves or hates. Without passion or value, money hides no secrets, can never disappoint."

The counting house man shrugged his shoulders and looked away. He could not fathom his defeat or even agree with it so far as he followed the oration, but he felt as if the weight of authority was furthered by an icy, ethereal abacus that saw right through his flesh to his naked bones.

A duel

The Elder bowed his head slightly to the Questor, and then bowed even more ostentatiously to the disconsolate fellow with hidebound ideas. This, of course, brought laughter and surprise. Taking a seat, he proceeded to pull out a knife, a chisel, and a small block of wood from one of the capacious pockets of his coat. Then he began to hum to himself and whittle.

Many people in the room took him for a clown and waited for an episode of buffoonery, whilst the more urbane were proactively embarrassed and wished to find an easy retreat from the putative entertainment. The Elder cleared his throat and addressed himself to the defeated. "Of course, the man without money, without the power to consume proffered goods is conveniently erased or determined an irresponsible idiot, a slave at best. Yet the fellow without a place to rest his head may very well be a king in disguise."

This rhetoric pulled them up short. The observers were now fastened to the drama. The Elder glanced about the room before continuing. "Have you ever walked about in a garden and been struck by the odd beauty of a simple red wheelbarrow? Or how the tart taste of an apple can bring back the memories of a dozen autumns? I was once impressed with the recurrence of patterns in the curve of a cello and of a woman's back. We sometimes miss these things because we are inattentive."

The counting house man did not know where the Elder was going, but he felt his heart beat a little faster. The small block of wood was turning into a thin column with a notched loop at the end.

"A champion," sneered the Questor from the plumage of his purple robe.

The Elder ignored him and continued to speak to the suddenly engaged audience. "Our language and our art, indeed, construct these meanings, but they are also gifts discovered rather than merely invented. The well-made thing emerges as a form that woos us, because truth is winsome and freedom is consent, not command."

The Elder pulled a few leather strips from a different pocket and began to string them through the loop of the newly made handle. The Questor shook his head in irritation.

"The whole economy of the world says otherwise," he stated blandly. "If it were not so, everyone would indulge these small childish fantasies. Just try to pay the mortgage with the fruit of such woolgathering." The hierophant stopped to survey his listeners. He noted with satisfaction general assent.

Then the Elder finished making some knots in the leather. He turned the miniature scourge towards the genius of money. Ovid translated by the Yorkshire vates came first to his lips. "Now comes the love of gain – a new god made out of the shadow of all the others. A god who peers grinning from the roots of the eye-teeth." And then he added another from that furious Frenchman, Bloy: "But how can a race of bureaucrats and janitors know what it means to enter the service of Splendor?"

A combination of gasps, applause, and sporadic laughter met this unexpected refusal to be cowed by the great man. Edward Caius Grant-Bromley secretly fumed to be grouped with clerks and menials. Yet he smiled in serpentine satisfaction.

"Are you going to whip me with your toy, old man?"

The Elder pondered. "Your tables have been turned over long ago. And your kind returned the favor a hundred fold. But even so —." Then the Elder paused and let his fury die. "You mistake the Good, its delicate courtesy and forbearance, its compassion, even for you, brother."

The savant of money did not like the epithet. Yet something in him was taken aback and he found he could not answer with his customary scorn. The Questor sighed in exasperation and made a gesture with his hands as if he were throwing invisible sand into his eyes.

"All the baffling and irritating aspects of the Man's endeavor achieve a pure line if one grasps that he lived out of a different economy. Everything that is common sense was vain, rotten, mean, and foolish by his own light," said the Elder.

This pedagogy embarrassed the Questor. He slunk back into his haughty superiority and shortly found an excuse to leave the room.

Prince of gypsies

Everyone breathed easier and loosened up once the dignitary had removed himself. A slow clapping from a darkened corner revealed itself to belong to a clerk who slowly emerged into the light. He was a youngish fellow, perhaps around twenty five, with a clever twist to his smile and carefully manicured hands.

"Well done, indeed," said Pennyfeather. "These pompous officials are not used to genuine opposition. They presume their premises and then logicize. Now he'll replay the conversation a hundred times trying to figure out how you bested him."

"I did nothing of the sort," said the Elder.

"Ah, but he didn't like that bit at the end," said the counting house man. "There was something in it his stomach couldn't take."

A young man, similar in age to the clerk, but dressed in a raffish, bohemian style joined them. With his dark, unruly locks and swarthy complexion, he might have been a prince of gypsies.

"It's because my uncle wanted to whip you himself. Trust me, I know him well. And when you forgave him and mastered your anger, he suddenly felt exposed."

"Manipulation is despair," pronounced the Elder.

The young man showed no inclination to pursue such gnomic provocations. The sages were always dropping little proverbs like that to puzzle the folk. "I *am* curious. When you began, did you know what you would do? That toy of yours is no joke close quarters."

"I did not know."

A young woman who looked not at all inhibited by dull virtue barged into their midst to hector the young man. "Deco, let's go!" she demanded.

"I'm staying," said the gypsy prince.

"I'm going!" answered the girl, giving a killing glance to Sky that managed to be both dismissive and jealous at once.

Unimpressed, Deco turned his back on her and rejoined the conversation. The clerk was discussing the meaning of money and whether or not it was, in fact, a just measure of worth. This somehow put the counting house man in mind of the gates of Chronos-Thoth and the Sha-Rule who were thought to be a kind of elevated record keepers assigned to facilitate cosmic justice.

"It's strange that you should mention that," said Deco. "My esteemed father has dealings with the servants of the Sha-Rule." The way he said esteemed was somewhat dubious. "And my youngest sister insists that she came face-to-face with the empress of the Sha-Rule, despite the fact that they are always masked. Narina was barely a toddler when she discovered the Empress speaking with our grandfather which was quite a trick, because he was dead by that time. Diana and Rory tease her to this day that she must have dreamt it, but I know my sister and I have always believed her."

Deco seemed to forget them in thinking of his favorite sibling. His features softened and Sky got a little dizzy. When he resumed, he spoke as if unaware that he had paused his tale. "My father said he was surprised about the doors."

"They say they are forged in angel fire," said the counting house man.

"A likely tale," said Pennyfeather. "Architecture is theater."

"For what audience?" Sky had blurted out her thought, and now she blushed to have them all looking at her. "If you see what I mean?"

"It's a good question," said Deco. "Not the public at large, but that's not really the point. My father expected massive doors constructed to protect us against the Expanse. But it wasn't like that at all. He said the servants of the Sha-rule told him it was a kind of portal to other times and places, but he took that to be a bit of fancy meant to keep him from seeing."

"Seeing what, lad?"

"That the doors were little more than a facade, nothing at all to keep the Chora Makra out."

"This City is exile," said the Elder. "We made it ourselves, this kingdom of shadows. The Questor is right about one thing. It's the only place his money has value."

The Elder explains about sex

The evening fled into early morning. The streets down which the
Elder, Sky, and the gypsy prince walked were lightly inhabited with
other stragglers of the night. Everyone was tired, but unwilling to
fall into sleep. Deco kept a wandering gait that was invisibly linked
to the old man and the girl. Every time it seemed that he had left
them, he'd suddenly reappear and amiably venture a new question.
The allure of Sky was part of it, but also, the Elder drew his interest.
There was something in his manner, something Flavius George
could not purchase or corner with cunning.

They came to a fountain and sat beside it, listening to its gentle
music. "I like this," said Sky. "It's a feeling I can hardly put a word
to and I know it won't last, yet it's real." Whether she meant her
secret about the Vendakar or not, even Sky did not know. They
all shared companionable silence while a young couple walked by
holding hands, lost to all else.

"The beloved flesh demands that we cherish, that we approach
with reverence," said the Elder. "But not without humor. Read
your Donne, young lovers."

Sky and Deco edged closer and the Elder continued. "My old
friend, Nikolai, used to say that the mystery of sex is revealed
only in love, though he was quick to point out that love lies on
another plane from that in which the human race lives and orders
its existence."

Deco gestured after the couple. "They seem to be doing something right."

"There is an ache to our desires," said the Elder. "Consider Ovid's *Metamorphoses*. It is astonishing that a civilization of soldiers and aqueducts should have produced such a poet. All of nature from his gods to humble creatures burn with beautiful anguish."

"But why must it be sad?" protested Sky.

It was not clear that the Elder heard her. "He felt the transcendence in our longing which cannot be disowned by the charming flesh. No surprise the vates, as much as St. John the Evangelist, ended an exile from empire." This bit of wisdom appeared to Deco as sleepy as the wayward morning. "The body bears many secrets," added the Elder with a glint in his eyes.

Deco smiled at this. "You cannot expect anyone with a soul to blink at that. You'll have to say more."

"There are stories, too many to tell," said the Elder. "Yet if one begins, they all come tumbling after. It is best to be wise, but ignorance is sometimes safer. To know a little, that is well known to bring danger."

They waited for a half dozen breaths while the Elder pondered. Deco looked over at Sky who offered no hint as to how to proceed. "Is he always like this?" whispered Deco. "I can't tell if he wants to tell us or not."

"That's just how he is," said Sky.

When the Elder decided to speak, it was a strange teaching he shared, seeming far from what they wanted to know. "The whole secret of Descartes' method is that it was designed to close off the world of faerie. Descartes employed a plain style. He wrote unadorned. That way, he proposed a manner of seeing. The new man claimed lucidity, and skepticism. Few understood the nature or consequences of a disenchantment spell. Regardless, it failed. The body is not so easily cast off and now that forlorn race makes sport unattended."

Without further explanation, the Elder began another tale. "It is necessary to listen with a musical ear. If you miss the beats, you don't know where to begin and end a movement, though truly the way of the Unnameable cannot be bound by a single melody. Think first of the arrival of the beloved as the Hebrews tell of it. Adam falls into a deep sleep, and from the depths, the answer to his heart thirst is found. Everything that happens after that, the divine presentation of Eve, the temptation itself, remains on a single plane.

It is of course a myth and not yet anything historical. How could it be, when the conditions for what men call ordinary time had not yet occurred? But here are the crucial words, the ending of that beat. After the sunderer, the *dia bolos*, had accomplished deception what resulted was a new kind of separation. *Then the eyes of both of them were opened.* Only now does deathward time encroach."

"But think. It is when a man's eyes are closed in prayer that wisdom often comes to him. Spectacle is distraction. Man and woman were distinguished, but lived in the harmony of a single being prior to mortal bondage. Eve was named in wonder, the high vision when both flourished in the dreamtime of Eden."

The human thing is a pleroma

"You've lost me somewhere," said Deco. "I get that they must have been wrong about love, but sex seems to have dropped out."

The Elder shrugged and then let more silence fall between them. He considered how best to tell it. When it seemed he had given up on speech, he spoke. "The entire mystery of the Virgin Mother is meant to hint at this great desire."

"We seem to be going backwards," said Deco.

The Elder laughed. "Let us just say that whether it is prized by Islamic warriors as a reward of heaven or treated as stigma by the jaded, virginity is thought as lack of sexual experience and a biological fact demonstrating a form of ignorance."

All this time, Sky was quiet. Something in the conversation stirred in her half-living memories of a friend on another world. She was almost crying now.

The Elder stopped and repented of his words. "My dear, I did not mean to upset you."

"It's not that," she said. "I'm only remembering. I can't say how, but I know you are right." And then with a half-hearted, but wholly winning laugh that glanced at the boy, she added, "Please continue. I'm sure that Deco is simply desperate to know."

The Elder assented, but he spoke more softly and with evident ambivalence. "The ancient Athenians believed that they did not come into being as others do. You will see this among some tribes as well, the belief that they were originally sprung up from the earth. There is a slight resemblance to the biblical creation myth. Aristophanes says the original human state was that of spherical beings. These creatures were akin to the cosmic divinities prior to the Olympian gods, though utterly ridiculous. They could not look into one another's eyes, or couple.

Because of their pride and ambition, Zeus cut them in half. Before that punishment, the spherical beings reproduced by planting seed in the ground. The separated ones died off, the generations created a mixed heritage. It was impossible to return to the original unity. The comic poet tells a hopeless tale, though the need of his spherical pairs is hardly erotic. It is closer to the affection we hold for our limbs or other body parts. No one wants to have their nose cut off, even if it is too large.

Nonetheless, the story has been assimilated at a different pitch. What is remembered is the separation of unities into longing halves. But take that only as an image for surely we *are* scattered and fragmented, however it happened. The important truth is that love demands what is not of this world. Sex is satisfied, then bored, wanting more, disgusted, inadequate, servant to imperatives that perpetuate the species, but love wants wholeness, wants happiness, wants the coincidence of opposites where satiation does not kill desire and desire is not lack.

This mysterious plenitude calls to us in every desire. The human thing is a pleroma that alone answers. And that is precisely the true meaning of the lost Virgin-Sophia. Let them laugh at that, if they will."

Rachel Cross

Into the study, when the men had gone to their beds, Rachel Cross would sometimes come on a night and ruminate. There would be empty glasses where they had drunk their port and the sweet, musky perfume of the ghosts of pipes smoked amidst muscular badinage — talk of politics and sport, God and woman. The particular order of conversation changed with the participants, but always, she knew, they came round to abstruse speculations on the divine economy and hushed, sly witticisms adverting to the curiously never exhausted theme of sex.

She liked to stand in the spaces that they had recently occupied and to run her hand over the bindings of books in languages she could never hope to decipher. There were books, of course, which she could read. There was the small library with a stock of novels and poets not too bawdy and a stack of old, faded issues of *The Rambler* left to her mother by a great uncle.

The study, however, in addition to titles by Greeks from Byzantium, a globe three feet in diameter, and the scribblings of Horace that had survived nine years in a drawer had an indefinable sense of mystery about it. She did not know if it contained volumes of pornographic illustrations or a map to secret treasure, but it called to her in an inviting, illicit whisper.

Sometimes, Miss Pinch would catch her there. Miss Pinch had long been in service and was looked upon less as a person in her own right, than as a kind of ministering spirit of the manor. While there was no official prohibition of this masculine sanctum to Rachel's presence, a feeling of embarrassment and resentment would come over her and she would invariably hurry out in a cold silence of flustered confusion.

She regretted glaring at Miss Pinch who had the kind of stern, ageless face that is never pretty, but is able to resist the most treacherous ravages of age for decades. The young woman, herself, had once been thought a great beauty, but it had proved a delicate, brief bloom and the reputation of stunning looks passed imperceptibly into the forgotten memory of the house.

Rachel thought of those days as if they were the long ago history of a princess in a foreign land. She could not but frown at the imperious and misguided pride of that young daughter to the king. She was not a frivolous person, even in her childhood, where frivolity may be excused, but she had not expected to be a beauty and when she suddenly found that she was, the flush of vanity had made her cruel and thoughtless with the affection of her suitors.

Over ten years had passed, since then. The flow of youth declaring undying love had made its way to the sea of lost opportunities. There were days she was bitter towards herself and the universe which had so unexpectedly bestowed on her such a deceptive and delicate beauty. Still, she had always loved her home and she admired her father, whom everyone thought a great man and she consoled herself that many marriages are difficult and the majority unhappy.

Her second favorite room was the conservatory, because of the large Welsh harp.

The Club of Useless Fellows

The professor was a tall man with a large head and leonine whiskers. He dressed in a linen seersucker suit in summer, woolen tweeds otherwise. From the heights of his angular frame, his eyes slightly unfocused, his mouth gripped by a permanent expression of wry humor, his conversation was spiced with quotes from Shakespeare and Cicero. The family fortune had allowed him to disdain the need to aggressively pursue money. He invested cautiously and prudently. The daughter was his only heir.

Doctor Cross may have preferred, perhaps, that she had married and provided a male to the line, but he was too often in the heights of philosophic speculation to worry over much with petty dynastic concerns. He had been a brilliant student, a veritable Jesus among the doctors. Though he did not have to take a degree, he did so. Likewise, he needn't have taught. He could have retired into the comfortable caverns of his home and led a life of leisure filled with avocations amenable to the dilettante. His moral strength of character, however, would not abide such a life. So he had taught and published and made a name for himself.

When Rachel went to visit her friends or to her box at the opera, she was invariably cornered by someone who would ask her not of herself, but of the current state and opinions of Doctor Cross. It was not meant, nor taken, as a slight. She rather glowed in gratification, for Rachel had learned to think of her father's work as somehow synonymous with herself – or, more accurately, as somehow of a piece, since they both were products of his being.

She was not rebellious by nature. She did not think of herself as "kept down." On the contrary, she thought herself tremendously, outrageously, free. Her social obligations were few and not onerous. There was nothing daring in her living, but she was pleased and mostly content and, if, at times, restlessness came over her, she knew that such moods must come to everyone and that if she waited, it would pass, which it always did.

It was her habit to make a brief, introductory appearance when her father had guests. Her mother did not care to officiate at the gatherings of intellectuals, always finding reason to visit a sister or cause to feel unwell. One day, her daughter found her in a back bedroom, her eyes red with tears. "I don't love him," she'd said, and the daughter felt a deep pit open up between them.

Nothing was said after that. Mrs. Cross spent a lot of time with her relatives, yet remained a semi-annual presence. It fell to the daughter to provide a brief glimpse of feminine solicitude. The loss of marital affection did not outwardly affect Professor Cross. He showed no signs of dismay and continued to regularly invite his more promising students along with a few colleagues to take part in discussions at his house.

"The Club of Useless Fellows" met on the second Thursday of every month. "Gentleman, this is Rachel," her father would say, and Rachel would smile and welcome them to the home and invariably they would drift as quickly as manners would allow into the study.

The Dream Book

When Rachel was in her princess phase, she had looked forward to seeing her father's visitors as so many mirrors in which to wonder at her transformation into a rose. Now, of course, that pleasure was lost to her and the young men appeared more callow and insipid as time went by. On a particular night, however, a Thursday of dark rain and thunder, a night of such horrendous downpour that most of the invited guests tacitly assumed the gathering had been cancelled, a strange young man appeared in the company of Dr. Bagehot.

Dr. Bagehot was the family physician, but he was also a friend with a surface knowledge of literature, and an unbounded fund of enthusiasm that tended to make him look rather foolish to people who did not know him well. Professor Cross, who was a good judge of character, valued him highly. The rapping at the door was somewhat too heavy for decorum, but the misery of wind and rain excused it. Dr. Bagehot led the way in, shaking his great coat and blustering like a large hound released from bondage in the cold kennel and anticipating the libertine pleasure of stretching out before the fireplace.

A wiry, bespectacled zoologist who had preceded him was glad enough not to be the only guest. He was evidently nervous, obsessively rubbing the rounded lenses of his glasses. In contrast, the young man in Dr. Bagehot's tow was very quiet and reserved, though with no hint of timidity. His cloak was gray homespun; a hood pulled high partially concealed his visage. There was something vaguely foreign in his looks that caused Rachel to pause over him, but she did not like to draw attention to herself, so she quickly turned to Miss Pinch. The travelers were provided with warm tea and towels while she fetched her father.

Her mother was home at the time and demanding that Rachel keep her occupied with a game of three handed cribbage. The pastime was made possible by drafting the chamber maid to play as well. As a result, Rachel saw little of her father's visitors. The man with the glasses, an Australian researcher or perhaps from New Zealand, evidently an expert on monotremes, read from a paper devoted to the duck-billed platypus and the echidna.

This led to a discussion on Goethe's views on form. She heard her father say that to understand Goethe's way of seeing one had to shift from a static to a mobile form. Then the foreign young man said something about reverence that seemed to embarrass the zoology professor. She would have liked to hear more, but the imperious maternal demand that she return to the card game ended her eavesdropping.

The physician's hearty laugh at some witticism appeared to drift through the empty hallways, oddly aimed at her chagrin. Dr. Bagehot she knew all too well. The young man, however, had stirred her curiosity. He was, most likely, another vapid youth with exotic packaging, but Rachel allowed herself to pretend that he might be truly interesting. In any event, the point was moot. The guests had been led to bed and they would, undoubtedly, leave by the usual passages of contingency which kept them from anything more than incidental contact with the daughter of the house.

At last released from her gaming obligations, Rachel sought the study. She tried to imagine what the rest of their conversation could have been like. Dr. Bagehot's loud, barking laugh she found easy to reproduce, as was her father's sonorous, slow voice, but she could make nothing of the young man, for she hadn't heard his voice with any clear distinction. She wondered, in fact, if she had truly heard him speak at all. She stood with one arm on the wing-back chair which habitually throned her father, looking absently at the dying flames of the fire. Her old borzoi, Sophia, lay dreaming before the hearth.

A worn leather book had been left on the seat. It did not appear to be one of her father's volumes. It was far too tattered, having lived a precarious existence. Upon closer inspection, the manuscript turned out to be a kind of notebook of blank vellum that had been inscribed in a neat, but very small hand. Numerous articles of tiny script were interspersed with a variety of drawings illustrating people in foreign costume and the flora and fauna of a distant land.

Rachel had some drawing and she recognized a skilled hand. She gently examined the pages in a kind of dream. Somehow, she could not say how, the images spoke to her. And then suddenly, she stopped, incredulous. Before her was a portrait, faded and weather worn. It was not quite accurate, younger and dressed in a fashion unknown to her, yet somehow true, truer than any mirror.

Amidst wondrous confusion, Rachel suddenly sensed she was being watched. She turned to vent her wrath upon Miss Pinch and stiffened. It was the young man.

"Please to forgive," he said. "I did not mean to disturb you. I left my book."

Rachel and the madman

Rachel could not take her eyes from him. He had discarded his cloak and his long windblown locks glistened in the flickering firelight. Momentarily, her imagination ran headlong into wildness. There was an odd luminescence, like a glow of moonlight that seemed to irradiate his flesh. But this was just a blink, however extraordinary. No, he was handsome, but certainly just an ordinary man. She could only understand her brief delusion as a continuation of her initial shock. She felt silly and blushed.

Silence reigned between them. Rachel sensed a desire on the young man's part to retrieve his volume and depart without further conversation. *"But I haven't, I haven't . . . had enough of you, yet,"* she thought. His complexion was dusky, with eyes that pierced like iron. He was, perhaps, eighteen or twenty. *What business have I to look at him like that?* She closed the book and carried it to him.

"It is a very interesting book. Are you one of my father's students?" she asked with a hastiness that brought an involuntary smile to his face.

"No. Dr. Bagehot was anxious for me to meet Professor Cross. He wanted him to see my book."

"Your book?" she asked in surprise. "Everyone always wants to see my father's books. Is it a special edition, then?" She had recovered herself and spoke with a bold forthrightness that might have been taken as even a trifle impertinent.

"No," he answered quietly. "Or yes, in a way."

He stood next to her and she could feel his breath softly on her shoulders as he turned the pages of the book.

"That's very nice," she said with approval. "Where is it?"

"From my home," he answered simply.

"And where is that?"

The young man who was not her father's student walked slowly over to the globe and spun it with a rueful, sad expression. Yes, she thought. That is him all over. He would not be himself with a great grin upon him. He is melancholy and that is his beauty. If he smiles, it is not japing, but a deep mirth of the soul.

"You must believe that I am not mad," he said at last with solemn gravity.

Rachel looked at him with as much seriousness as she could muster, though an imp was tugging at her heart. She wanted to laugh, though not to abuse him. She was filled with a tingling, warm hilarity. He looked at her a long moment to take her measure.

"It isn't on the map," he said at last. "My country is . . . mysterious. It is almost nowhere — or everywhere. I cannot explain."

Funny kind of madness

"There's something I've been meaning to tell you."

"Well, what's stopping you?"

"It isn't the sort of thing you can just say, Sparrow. Folks think you're crazy. It makes no sense."

Sky made an adorable face, just the right mix of precocious teasing and vulnerable hope. "Well, I already think you're mad."

The Elder laughed. "So long as we're clear on that. I wouldn't want to shock you."

They trudged along in silence then until Sky began to get angry. It was just like the Elder to

drop a hint like that and leave you waiting. "Don't worry about the shocking thing. You can tell me anything, okay?"

"Patience, my dear," said the Elder. They boarded a trolley and then stepped off before a corner edifice that sold dry goods and penny taffies. The man behind the counter was round with a little moustache and pudgy hands that looked as if they had just left off attending to the birth of confections. When he saw the Elder, he stood up straight.

"Going on a short trip. The usual, Otto."

"You're the boss, maestro."

"This is Miss Sky Odyssey who is going to accompany me."

"A pleasure, Miss."

Otto led them to a short corridor that gave way to a back staircase. After this, the Elder took charge, climbing several flights with a surprising burst of energy. At the top of a landing, they paused.

He tried to tell her what was coming, all the while knowing it is impossible. "Sky, I want to show you something. This *where* is mysterious. No one can find it on the map. The entrance is gift. This path we take is just for show, a convention so that you can talk about it later and tell folks, if they want to listen. But no one knows the way, because it is not a technique, but a grace, so cannot be prepared for, only received. Perhaps, one can prepare to be receptive, at least prepare not to be an obstruction."

"I've absolutely no idea what you're talking about," said Sky.

Instead of answering her, or possibly it was an answer in the indirect manner, the Elder continued his lecture. "History is full of particulars, those who enter upon the stage, the once and never more. The heart rages at that, though some seek to console, say it is illusion, *maya*. It is and it isn't. Nature knows nothing of the story. Brute generation, cycles, types – and then there are those who foresee Elysian Fields. They take memory straight and literal, transfer without addition or alteration. History is a dim copyist, a chronicler. Nature repeats without sorrow. Neither is right.

Your person is not the same as the fragile, finite self, shaped by time and circumstance, called forth by the smile of the mother, or someone, at any rate, some configuration of eyes and mouth, a face speaking. Yet the undeveloped infant knows in the emotional physical nexus called soul that to be thrust into being is also summons to a name.

Defining terms is useful. Let us say that the frequent application of soul and spirit as synonymous designations is not intended here. By spirit, a quality of the infinite is touched – some elemental source that often lies dormant in ordinary lived time, or at least, goes unremarked. It is because of spirit that consciousness is aware of limit, the sense of Not Yet, not enough. The world is not enough because of Spirit.

Most of your stories are deeply inadequate. They might be clever, even psychologically astute, and still miss the mark of the essential which founders on the paradox of the unique. The pleroma is not subject to finite antinomies."

Of course, Sky was not less baffled after all that. They stopped abruptly in front of a door. It was a common, plain door, so no one would think it had any claim to difference, even if it was the door to the one story that brought time's yearning to eternal joy. When they stepped through, however, Sky gasped in surprise. They were no longer in the interior of an old shoppe, but rather walking along a path in a green demesne that belonged to one of those large imposing manors that invariably attach to ancient bloodlines and wealth.

"The house belongs to old Troubinot who has got himself a young wife and saplings to carry on the name. The crone visits, along with her coterie of toadies and sages. We'll just drop in and say hello, so long as we are here."

The hidden country

"Think of the door as the cover of a story book. If you turned the page and it began to tell you about your ordinary day, you'd feel cheated, wouldn't you?" said the Elder.

Certainly, Sky was not cheated. The path to the manor house came to them filled with strange visions. First, there was a chubby fella, four-armed, with an elephant's head; Ganesha. His eyes looked out upon all with wise, enduring kindness. He blessed their beginning. Next, they came to a plain where the great warrior Gilgamesh wrestled his brother friend, Enkidu, dear to his heart. Not yet, the pain of loss, the questioning death.

Further along, Athos, Porthos, and Aramis pledged mutual aid, whilst Stephen Dedalus speculated God on vacation paring his fingernails. Not far from a maze of topiary, Artemis fled into her woods. Her divine face was oddly pale and sorrowing for the beautiful youth Hippolytus lay dying, a fate she could not cure, nor understand. In the distance, the valiant horn of Roland cried out its forlorn glory.

Antigone and Hamlet were a de facto couple. They ignored everyone and made a show of mourning. Throwing off negative sparks, they would punctuate brooding silence with mutual castigation, arguing which of them had been more wronged. Rapt in each other's gaze, they did not stop to ask the Elder and Sky to judge between them.

Soon, a commotion in dark clouds announced the advent of dueling aerialists: dragons perhaps, or cackling harpies. Yet too far away for decisive identification, Sky fancied pterodactyls in flight. Oblivious to the battle above them, David Hume and Doctor Johnson disputed the value of common sense. Machiavelli gazed at the newcomers with ambivalent scorn. He desperately wanted to inform them that cunning must use pleasure and pain to the measure of expediency, and that fear was always the surest bet to bring humankind to order — but clearly they were not princes, so he held his tongue.

It was only when the blooms of the garden dazzled in a painterly dance of color that Betty Boop arrived and asked if the old man wanted to buy some smokes. And then, just outside the servants' entrance, Emma Bovary strode forth clutching her bottle of poison. In the shadow of the main entrance, one last figure huddled. Mona Lisa smiled her enigmatic smile. She reached out her hand and lightly touched Sky as they passed. No need for words, she'd said everything in silence.

Already, a superior creature in livery was ushering them within. He turned a dour, grave face upon them even as the Elder explained. "Spiritual geography is not traversed in the plodding manner of linear time. Realms seemingly a vast distance apart are intimately entangled. It is but a feather of breath between them. Maybe you walk through many dimensions, blind to the hidden country that surrounds you, Sky. We are the book. There is so much more to us than you can imagine."

Play your card

The rather morbidly grim disapproval of the house servant failed to impress the Elder. Nor was he daunted as they were ushered through dark corridors and hazy rooms with windows covered in semi-opaque curtains that permitted light gray, diffused, or if brighter, still tinged with milky lavender.

At times, these drowsy fabrics were blown by irregular winds. The muted sounds of conversations, laughter, ribald or mocking, gnashing teeth, cries of delight, murmuring, didactic scold; a hundred variations of subtle human communication came to them after crossing untold deserts, desiccated and dried into a pale, pure essence.

And then they were abruptly led into just the sort of chamber one expected to find. Indeed, no one acted as if the rest of the edifice were a complex of shadows and dream. Ladies stood near the piano, whilst the young men moved about with a studied vigor, speaking with assumed candor and loudly voicing the ascendant opinions of the moment with enthusiasm.

Madame Troubinot was confused by the newcomers. Her still pretty face carried the impending anxiety of the matron she was to become, shy, retreating, always looking to her elderly spouse for guidance and wondering what she should do when he became a ghost. The lord of the manor sat before a table laden with papers. He was too busy in speech with Uhraine and the Questor to notice her silent entreaty.

The Elder was suddenly very quiet. The courtiers in the room tensed. The sound of child laughter came in with the light from the casement windows. Madame Troubinot's children were playing badminton on the green. The Lord of the Exchequer whispered into the ear of Uhraine. The ancient dowager of the City stared for a long moment, not at the Elder, but at the young woman who had accompanied him. Then she smiled, releasing the chamber from anxious expectation.

"I am informed you are a philosopher with interesting ideas," she said with humor that might be equally grace or subdued malice. "Well, traveler, you may play your card."

"In the morning, my sister's cat made play with a young blue bird," said the Elder. "Ewa rescued the fledgeling, placed it in a box to see if it might live, and chastised Emily for her wild and natural ways. In the afternoon, wild dogs caught and killed the cat, her beautiful pelt of black and white puzzle stilled and rent. Everyone cried, and you yawned, wench, for murder is your amoral, indifferent song. But I tell a different story, mother of death."

And then the Elder placed upon the table a card to make them boggle, though the sages only laughed. King, harlequin, the hanged man.

The devil of a place

"Musame, there is boy," said Mrs.Takashima as if it were an accusation. Deco stood at the door flashing a winning smile entirely lost upon one accustomed to the powerful charms of Mr. Takashima. Nonetheless, the girl seemed eager enough. Deco, for his part, had been delighted to hear that Sky was interested in the Underground.

The place he wanted to show her was something he had discovered while still a boy. His mates had dared him to enter the forbidden mazes. Of course, he'd gotten lost. By the time he found his way back, Flavius George had been advised of his son's foolishness. What a caning he got for that one! It made for a good story, though. For days, he spun a dozen tales of what he'd discovered to his peers who would never pluck courage to verify his reports. And yet, while he invented a great deal, those amusing fibs paled next to the experience he never did tell them. Later, when he was tempted to seek it out, to prove it had actually happened, the site proved elusive.

He forgot about it as boys often do, caught up in the fast moving events of youth. It was only recently, completely by chance, that he stumbled upon it again. And then, after some confusion and prolonged wandering that may have contributed to the unhappy result, he had taken a young woman to see it. Deco had felt the same numinous awe as the child he had been, but the paramour had merely stared with dutiful respect, repeating his words with unconvincing sincerity.

The path began in the boiler room of a defunct factory once dedicated to the manufacture of irons, kettles, and doorstops shaped like Scotty dogs. Near the back wall there was an iron plate which covered the entrance to a downward shaft that led onto ancient streets. The daylight traffic from above was muffled and the ghosts of the place untroubled by new lodgers. Deco lit his torch and followed a scrambling path which Sky managed without complaint.

They came to the ruins of an inn or perhaps a brothel judging from the uncouth graffiti. Deco turned to the left with more determination than certainty. Twenty minutes later he had slowed their pace. The easy patter of his voice faltered and his face unconsciously became that of a boy who can't get his sums to come right.

"It's the devil of a place," he admitted at last.

Sky was too good to scold and too smart to suggest retracing all the way back to the naughty inn. She would let Deco come to that conclusion himself. And he nearly did, when they were surprised by the sound of scurrying steps. At this, Deco handed a small revolver to Sky without asking if she had any knowledge of fire arms. He drew a bronze kopis for himself.

In such situations, even the shadows appear to move, but none emerged to claim ownership of the steps. "We could go back," suggested Deco gallantly.

"That's a Greek knife, isn't it?" said Sky. "My father owned one."

She paused, startled at the new memory. And then they decided to keep going. Soon, the pair was rewarded by a rough stairs that ended in a stone maze of passages that Deco recognized. The ground was uneven and marked by patches of moisture where condensation from the surface collected. Here, they stopped and listened. A distant sound of hushed voices and scurrying feet echoed through the empty spaces. It was evident whoever they had disturbed was uninterested in confrontation. Then Deco found the opening guarded by a token crossing of rusted iron poles and knew that they had reached the place after all.

He did not warn her. Deco wanted Sky to see it the way he had first come upon it. There, next to a brick column holding up the roof was the giant sculpted head, half sunk into the earth, so that only the curved nose, the crown, and the deeply cut eyes remained.

"Oh," said Sky, and her long silence was more eloquent than any words.

Somehow being with Sky, observing along with her, Deco found new insight. He noticed that it was precisely the lack of a mouth that gave to the eyes their gravity, their suffering wisdom. Even in the night or in the country, men carried the noises of the great town with them. Standing before the stone flesh, they suddenly felt as if the silence had grasped them so strongly that they might never speak again.

They masked the strange trepidation with a laughing run that took them to a corridor that ended in a cavernous chamber. And there in the shadows cast by Deco's torch were the children.

Fugitive memory

The soldiers were laughing and making faces at the infant, so that the child was delighted and returned their play with a smile of its own. Its mother was too petrified to cry out before the cavalry men. Then one of the warriors casually affixed a bayonet to his rifle. He waved it, gleaming, before the child, so that the light reflected the silvery surface of the blade.

The infant followed the brilliant ornament like a cat bemused by the fitful glimmer of a toy. Then another warrior with thick furs and animal pelts covering his body took the child from his mother and at last, the maternal scream began. The soldiers dandled the child and then began to hoist it into the air above them, shouting for joy and

*catching the little one, so that it became giddy with their excitement
and ignored the increasing terror of its mama.*

*All the while, the soldier with the bayonet held it vertical so that
the point kept careful vigilance with the sun.*

Wendy and the lost boy

Sky could barely hear Deco calling after her. Then she was walking
amidst the children who danced about her like lost boys in the
gravity tow of Wendy.

"Why are you hiding here?"

"We thought you were the Blue Hunter."

"Well, you see," said Sky.

"Yes."

"The Blue Hunter? Is it so bad as that?"

The children shook their heads vigorously. "He follows you
everywhere," cried a young girl. "He's going to eat us."

"You can't stay here," urged Sky. "You can come with my friend.
We'll take you to a place up top where no one will eat you."

But this idea seemed to terrify them. The children ran in all
directions, disappearing into a dozen hiding places. Deco and Sky
called out to no avail. One, perhaps, followed them. She saw the
boy shivering in the shadows. His skin was a token veil stretched
over the bones. From out of deep orbital sockets, the ghost of eyes
returned her gaze.

"I am not here to hurt you," she said.

"Why not?" whispered the boy. "It's what I want."

Warrior's boast

Sky approached him in tenderness. The boy looked up at her with a guarded smile, his eyes full of vipers. "A woman's heart is schooled to compassion – though I've known her quick to kill with harshness to make a man blink," he said with assurance and rancor. "I am older than you, Missy."

Sky stepped back. Deco joined her, his hand unconsciously reaching for the kopis. The child was goaded by their presence into a declaration, his skeletal chest ridiculously raised in remembered triumph. "I have ridden the high plains and conquered tens of thousands. I've carried the severed ears of my enemies in a bag and trampled their nobles to death with my dancing warrior's feet."

Then the boy crumpled into himself and looked about shivering with the dull vulnerability of a wounded animal. It was as if his outburst had taken the last reserves of his vital energy.

"Monster child," said Deco, "I am going to put my cape over you."

When he lifted the boy, he was as light as a stack of kindling.

"Take him to Benedicta, please," said Sky, her heart already guilty with relief at the thought of being done with the creature.

Minimum height

"No doubt, Mr. Peacock, our life here must seem dull compared to the busy world of commerce you and your kith inhabit. It must appear, how shall we say, a very small story in comparison?"

The merchant cleared his throat. Fortunately, he remembered something he had once read in a fortune cookie. "There are no small stories, Lady Winterbourne," he said. Whether she was satisfied with this response or not, she let it pass as sufficient. Peacock inwardly congratulated himself on his answer to a challenging initial gambit.

Why he should continue to repeat this inconsequential conversation to himself was something of a mystery Peacock could not solve. There was nothing erotically dangerous in the woman, far from it. Yet she had managed a touch, a subtle feint and then the blood. The brownstone was located in an older neighborhood, a still vigorous community filled mainly with Poles and Italians, though not far off there was an enclave of Hasidic Jews.

The first time he knocked at the door matching the designation written in the idiosyncratic hand of Lady Winterbourne, Peacock was met by a very tall priest of African descent whose tribal bearing belied a jovial English manner. An Ansharu wearing a top hat stood next to the cleric. While the merchant stood open mouthed and befuddled by the incongruous duo, the Ansharu greeted the newcomer with a burst of glossolalia.

"Ah, he says you are welcome to stay," explained the priest, "only as it is Wednesday, you shall have to play bridge. Know the rules, old boy?"

Peacock scrutinized the address and sadly concluded it was correct.

Several days later, the merchant tried again at a different hour. This time, a young woman and a large black and white dog met his inquiry.

"Oh, the Elder isn't here," she said. "Only do be a dear. There's a package at the dry goods store around the corner, could you get it?"

Peacock found himself unaccountably running the errand. He was developing a habit of talking to himself, the commentary a continuous sarcastic self-assessment of whether or not he was a fool.

Altogether, he hardly knew why he tried a third time. A distinguished older gentleman with the discernable air of a scholar and artisan answered the door. Peacock's relief, however, was brief. "Have you seen the angel of the earth?" asked the Elder.

The merchant stared back in blank incomprehension. "He's been about," prodded the Elder. "I have need of him."

"I presume he stands out in a crowd?" answered Peacock, fumbling for a thread of sanity.

To this, the Elder merely held his arm up to the general height advised as the minimum for a carnival ride. After he had his fill of mirth, the Elder shifted tone. It was evident he had been advised of Peacock's previous visits. "What is it you seek, merchant?"

The full ridiculousness of his position suddenly struck Peacock. "Lady Winterbourne gave me your address," he said miserably. "Something about the Venus de Milo, but I'm not sure what now."

"She is hooking you into an adventure," answered the Elder gravely.

"Yes, I'm afraid you're right."

The beauty that hides

"You asked about Ravaisson."

"I cannot be more specific. There must be something to it, but I've no clue, you see," said the merchant. It was rather embarrassing, but now that he had posed the required question, he suddenly felt something might come of it.

"A philosopher of repute in his day, and still worth knowing, Ravaisson chose not to get tied down to an academic life. One can hardly blame him there. The fellow had spent years as curator of antiquities at the Louvre. The Venus de Milo became an obsession in a very interesting way. He thought that the Venus was intended to be encountered from the side, you see. He removed wooden splints that had placed her plainly upright.

Ravaisson believed there was a "movement of torsion" that had been missed because of false assumptions. The upper part of the body should incline slightly forward, and impel to the left somewhat, her head even more so. From this attitude it becomes clear that the Venus is posed towards a missing other, and that her invisible limbs stretch out to an absent one.

"I am speaking as plainly as I can," said the Elder.

"I appreciate your candor," answered Peacock. "Please go on."

"There is not much more I can offer without overwhelming you. Ravaisson tried to explain himself by allusion to Virgil's *Aeneid*. The goddess Diana appears to the hero. The glory of that moment is secondary, however. As she turns from Aeneas, it is revealed that under the guise of the divine, it is the spirit of his mother that has come to him. In hiding herself, the beloved is revealed."

The Elder smiled. There was sadness and enigmatic whimsy in it. "There's more to the story. I'll tell you another time, perhaps."

They were silent together, and then Peacock rose from his seat with a satisfied air. "I trust then, Lady Winterbourne may be assured that her message was received."

The matrimonial angle

Peacock was cunning to a degree. It was an occupational requirement. Some merchants were careful, others bold. In that regards, Peacock tried to follow the golden mean and so far his inner sense had guided him well enough. The pursuits of scholars might appear abstruse and besides the point to most of his lot. There wasn't any money in it. Yet Peacock understood where his peers ordinarily did not that the well-rounded man was more likely to recognize and grasp opportunity.

So he did not disdain the Elder. On the contrary, the fellow was a center. Most folks were periphery or drifters or aggregate. The latter filled the needs of society. They could be useful, but often dull. Innovation and risk went together and where they converged, you'd find a center. Folks gravitated to centers, though when things went bad, they'd gather the torches.

Trajan, of course, found the whole thing hilarious. They met at the usual appointed hour within the cluttered walls of The Infant Dragon to discuss and boast and generally lie outrageously for the amusement of all. So, it was no surprise that Trajan took the matrimonial angle. "You can always have a saucy bit on the side, old man. Think of the investment possibilities."

It was, mostly, a joke. Peacock normally would have yawned and batted that back with lazy ease. His gut was nervous, though. He could only gulp down his ale and prod his pal further. "Yeah, yeah," he said.

"And then you might purchase your own cargo ship. Rig her good, name her The Prim Lass."

The lads were rolling all over the tables and Peacock could only nod and "yeah, yeah." It was a disaster.

"What's a matter, pal? You're green," said Trajan to even more guffaws.

Later, when it was just the two of them, they exchanged views on the Company. "Things are tight," said Trajan, suddenly serious. "We've got to watch it. Not sure what's up, but the board isn't fooling around. Snowdon came in light after the last expedition and now he's all by his lonesome, exiled to one of the border outposts."

"Too right," said Peacock. "There are worse things than marriage."

We are all contradictions

Rachel Cross could not hide her perplexity. The young man had come in the company of the doctor. Perhaps he was not so much a guest as a patient, though there did not appear to be anything lunatic about him. He stood before her with a kind of plea in his face that she respect his sanity and sincerity. "I suppose you've had a hard time of it," she said at last. "By the way, I'm afraid I was preoccupied when you arrived. I beg your pardon, but I have forgotten your name."

"Not at all." He bowed slightly with the old formal manner. "Please to forgive. I did not give it and Dr. Bagehot was too exuberant to be out of the rain for proper introductions. My name is Soren Blake."

"You are more interesting than my father's students, Mr. Blake."

He allowed a brief smile. "You are kind, Miss Cross. An exile is always interesting, perhaps, but never happy. Like Dante."

"I am sure that is often true."

"You know this yourself."

"What, am I an exile?"

"We are all exiles, Miss Cross. We are all contradictions."

"I'm afraid I don't understand you." His glance of gentle irony said otherwise. "Much," she added, sheepishly. "I sometimes think I don't know what I want,' she gasped out, wondering at herself for speaking so frankly.

A mirthful laugh entered his eyes. He was undeniably pleased with her. "Those who do not yearn will never discover."

"That sounds very profound."

"But you are not quite sure what it means?" Soren pointed to the sleeping Sophia whose hind legs gently moved. "You think she dreams of chasing a wolf? Perhaps she chases the wolf in order to dream."

"Do you talk like this to everyone?"

"Everyone who will listen."

"And do they? Listen, I mean."

He laughed outright. "Hardly ever. The Nocturnes are a stubborn race."

"Is that your people, the Nocturnes? Why are you smiling at me like that?"

Just as quickly, he was again serious and brooding. "A name is always a gift that we give to each other," he said. And then Soren Blake took his leave of her and she wondered if she would ever see him again.

A jest

The next morning had her doubting her senses even more. Her father remarked that Bagehot's friend was one of those inscrutable sorts, an enigmatic, green old man, still vigorous, but careful with his ideas. Rachel could not help laughing. "A twenty year old youth a green old man, indeed!"

When it became apparent that the professor was in earnest, she asked if there had perhaps been a mistake. Surely the good doctor also brought a young man with him? "No, the one guest only." When Rachel turned to Liza for confirmation, the chamber maid only gawked in mulish terror at being questioned.

Later in the day, the maid came to her in apologetic softness. "I didn't want to say, miss. It is all too strange."

"What do you mean, Liza?"

"Well, I saw quite clearly the boy Dr. Bagehot had with 'em."

"Boy, yes, so, not an old man. What could papa be thinking?"

The maid frowned. "Miss, when I say boy, I mean a little lad. Eight or nine years old. I brought him biscuits and milk."

It was unthinkable that the household had conspired to mock her with such a jest. Rachel penned a short note to be delivered to Dr. Bagehot. "Who was the fellow he brought in the middle of thunder and rain? What was his name, his age, please be direct." A day later, Miss Pinch handed her a short reply. It was so perfectly Bagehot. "Fellow was a nephew of someone I met at the club. No, no, that was someone else. A fine, interesting fellow, anyway. I cannot really recollect, but the Professor seemed pleased to see him, did he not?"

So much did the variable appearance of Soren Blake absorb her that it was only after nothing seemed to come of it that the image in the book came back to her with disarming insistence — how could it be that there should be a picture in that notebook she knew, but did not know? For surely, Rachel Cross had seen herself in Soren Blake's sketches from nowhere, that lovely ingénue lost forever in shadows of regret.

There is sorrow enough in one life

The Elder sighed at the sketch Sky had made. It was the girl who made herself small. He held it up before his face and Sky saw that his hand trembled.

"What happened to her?"

"If you stare too long into the abyss, the abyss looks back."

"Ohh, that's just one of your clever ways of putting a fella off. What does it mean, old man?"

"It's really not."

"Explain it then so that even a girl like Sky can understand it."

"I can't."

"Try anyway, please."

"Sparrow, there is sorrow enough in one life."

The Elder sank down onto a workbench and fell into silence. Then he gathered himself and spoke. "Some have sought to lessen the burden of evil. They claim it is dispersed in time and so no individual must endure the cumulative weight of it. Thus, they would banish the rage of conscience."

"Your friend didn't agree?"

"I didn't really understand her. She had gone beyond me."

"Were you mad about it?"

"I didn't think so, but I probably was . . . am. It doesn't make sense, but there it is." The Elder stared into the face of Sky's picture as if he would will the image into life. "There is another story. I was going to tell it the other night to you and Deco, but something in me refused. It is a strange tale of a dream of Wordsworth's. You can find it at the beginning of book five of *The Prelude*.

There, the vates confesses to a friend that he often worried that a great disaster might befall the world so that all the books containing human wisdom would be lost. His friend thought the poet rather extravagant in his neurosis, though admitted he had shared a similar thought. There must have been something in that era to bring out such fears. Human loneliness endures the unquiet feeling that everything dear and beautiful is destined for oblivion. And then the poet tells his dream.

Wordsworth finds himself wandering through endless barrens, dark and foreboding when he is suddenly joined by a Beduoin knight mounted on a camel. In one hand, the knight carries a stone and in another, a radiant shell. The knight tells him that the stone contains Euclid's geometry, but that the shell holds something much more to be treasured.

After this, Wordsworth is allowed to hear a prophecy of mystic tongues emanating from the shell foretelling a fateful deluge. As in dreams, the Beduoin, while remaining the knight, puts on another aspect. He now appears as Cervantes' beautiful fool, whilst simultaneously retaining a sense of his former presence. Wordsworth persists in following, but the urgency of mission causes the knight to evade him. It is a dark story."

"And I'm always afraid it's going to rain and worried about my misplaced umbrella!" admitted Sky.

"It's just that it reminded me of her. The stone knows much, but the shell is a book written by the spirit. Without the stone, the spirit should have nothing to elucidate, but without the shell, the stone has no reason to go on."

The keeper of the outpost

About three day's journey from the spur of an active line, Sergeant Folkes kept a small hunting lodge. This was not a matter of any significance. Lots of military had such places. They liked to putter about with guns and play in the woods. By happenstance, the cabin was located not too far from a tiny outpost of the Company. Chance and Providence are hard to distinguish. Different storytellers discern one or the other in the same event. So by chance or odd care, Peacock had come to know the Elder and the Elder knew the sergeant and the sergeant's lodge was nigh the outward looking face of Snowden's precipitous decline with Wimber, Shackleton, & Bey.

Peacock got word that Snowden was refusing to answer dispatches from the home office. Taking a bit of initiative, he asked his new friends if they might want to accompany him in his effort to contact his old comrade. The retired soldier waxed eloquent about the beauty of a nearby waterfall. He was secretly proud of his lodge and welcomed the opportunity to share hospitality in order to show it off. And so began the following adventure . . .

In the distance, the gold embroidered flag of Wimber, Shackleton & Bey wavered atop a shamble of makeshift buildings. Closer in, one saw long wooden poles topped by the skulls of various small creatures, mainly coyote and carrion birds. The windows of the compound were broken and patched with canvas or left naked to the wind.

Robinson Peacock shook his head. "This isn't like Snowdon," he said, which was risibly unnecessary, but everyone understood it was verbal expression of the shiver of dread.

No one answered their cries of salutation and concern. When they pushed into the living quarters, the air was moist, unnaturally cold, with a slightly bitter odor as of burnt almonds. Snowdon lay back in his chair, his straw blonde hair pushed rakishly across his pinkish forehead. A weed blackened and curled in necrotic decay stuck in the buttonhole of his lapel. Part of him appeared to be lolling carelessly, while a dark, umbratile aspect diverged from the abandoned figure, a crepuscular body sitting upright and alert.

"I've been waiting for you," declared the shadow Snowdon without looking at the newcomers. His voice was soft, barely above a whisper. "It's very lonely here. Hardly anything to do. Of course, I tried to stay busy."

The dark Snowdon half-turned. A wave of horror overtook them. There could be little doubt now that two beings somehow occupied the space where the body of Snowdon slouched in hapless morbidity. The shadow betrayed no glint of eyes or any other distinguishable feature. Nonetheless, one had the distinct feeling one was remarked, that perception was going on.

"I tried to tell this fellow —." A derisive note crawled into the low voice of Snowdon's darkness. It pitched its head slightly in the direction of his body. "A witless, polite dunce. No conversation at all. No aesthetic sense. Did a bit to fix the place up, you've seen."

The shadow paused and there was an appalling silence, nearly comic if it weren't so outrageous, in which it appeared that the monstrous, incredible figure was waiting for the visitors to congratulate it on decorative improvements. No one said anything, but the pseudo-Snowdon seemed unperturbed. Evidently it considered the muteness of its audience a measure of restrained agreement.

"Gentlemen, we are all gentlemen here, I presume? What I'd like to know is, well, many things, but what is it about these . . . bodies? Couldn't they have been designed so as not to stink? They must come from some grand Stinkmaker. Why can't shit smell like violets, for instance? Whose arrangements are responsible? Someone should look into it."

The shadow began to lose cohesion. In a final fit of giddiness, it slapped the still discernable lineaments of a thigh. "Ah, gentlemen. It is too good. And what about your little son, fine sir? Who would have thought he'd be so naughty? Yes. Yes. We like him very well."

At first, everyone was too stunned. The very words spoken did not seem to have meaning. Then shock gave way to anger. Sergeant Folkes, choked in rage, and would have rushed the insolent thing, but already it was dispersed into a sooty fog, the last droplets of which sputtered from the gaping mouth of Snowdon's corpse.

The devil has no back

The Elder had wanted a burial, but their nerves would not take it, so a fire had been hastily made. The rancid animal corpses and macabre totems cast smoky pillars of obeisance to the remains of Snowdon. They turned their backs upon the pyre and swiftly made their way from that place.

For a long while no one spoke. The party retraced the path to the foot of the waterfall, stopping at last in a quiet meadow whose innocence, if not powerful enough to expunge the visceral taint, provided sufficient feeling of solid goodness to enable them to rest.

"Vile, vile, vile," exclaimed Sergeant Folkes, his voice more a shriek of lament than human speech. Without explaining, they all felt that they had been brutalized, that a perverse power had violently despoiled their company and poisoned them. Their very bodies felt sick with shame.

Amidst brooding silence, the Elder prayed. After a while, the others muttered without knowing what they spoke or repressed sobs. "Listen," said the Elder. "The ancient word for mask is *lichina*. It is related to the old word, *larve*, which one catches a hint of in our larva. But even in Rome, larve meant a husk or shell. In other places, they are known as the *nagfalami*. The Choctaw will not even speak the name of Nalusa chito, but whatever you call it, the larve is vampiric and empty, without its own person.

What evil seeks is a living face that it may fasten upon and suck. At death, it may persist for a while, but note it has no depth, no form, no world. That is why among the folk, there is an expression, 'the devil has no back.'"

"So, you're saying these things take over people? That we might be walking around talking to some chum, and all the time it's this thing?" asked the merchant in a tone of dismay. An unspoken fear lunged at Sky like an adder's bite. She began to shake and then she fell to the ground in a dead faint.

Whilst the others crowded around her, Sergeant Folkes cried out, "I must find him. I must find my son!" The soldier ran out in sudden frenzy to be away, to search the seven seas and the astral belts. He knew it was a hopeless task. Once the burst of energy called forth by anguish and despair had subsided, the soldier sank down to the ground. Ten minutes later, he rejoined the camp. "How is the girl?" he asked in a husky voice.

Open sesame

Sky knew that there were people whose possessions were profligate to the point of collecting houses as some collect stamps. That Lord Raveh was such a fellow was hardly congruous with her impression of the man, who was anything but soft and indulgent. Nonetheless, Beorn had offered, quite casually, access to this particular residence as it had a nice library and a considerable view. "One sees far beyond the City into the distance of gray mists and purple hills."

Of course, she felt a fool the minute she had knocked. Sky was ready to run when the door opened to reveal the most hackneyed ancient retainer – dressed out in the usual livery with a severe look of disdain as if she were the unwanted present dragged in by the cat. Sky gulped and then tried to explain herself in a flurry of embarrassed half-sentences, all of which ended in the comic and happy conclusion of acceptance.

"Ah, Miss Odyssey," said the retainer in a cordial voice. The prince had not only made the invitation, he had smoothed the way.

Truant

"Where have you been hiding, Naya?"

Onahyu stood with arms akimbo, exactly as her mother, the first princess of the Southern Ram used to do when cross with her. Onahyu, hardly taller than a boy, regaled the prize student with the full flower of his office. He puffed at her with mock indignation, the crests of his wispy beard dancing at every breath. The arcana of the symbols etched intricately into the flesh of his wrinkled body traced out in purples, reds, green and black tattooing the sacred mysteries.

After the sage felt he had sufficiently performed dutiful chastisement, she saw his posture relax. A hint of humor flashed in his eyes. "Onahyu is truly quite shamed, Vanaya," he confided. "You cannot take advantage. The whole class knows that you are favored. When you skip, discipline is eroded. It is irresponsible. You must see that."

"I am sorry," said Vanaya, the spirit of play and boldness fleeing from her, though quick to return.

"I suppose you were in the Solarium?"

"I forgot. Time is different there. I met a friend."

"Yes, Naya. But you know these forms of contact are quite forbidden."

The maiden shrugged. It could not actually be wrong to seek wisdom. And there were so many doors. No one could open them all in a lifetime.

"Hurry along," said the priest. "At least pretend to be contrite."

Uncharted

The little library Beorn had told her about was revealed to be an immense collection that might have occupied an ordinary man's entire home. Slowly, almost beneath conscious awareness, Sky was approaching her destiny. The incident at the outpost had sparked an almost palpable awareness, something already touched in the Underground with Deco when she began to know more deeply the equivocities and darkness of the child Nocturnes. She herself was not incidental, not another random traveler, but an integral mission, the name of an action, some essential part of a mysterious justice, yet all that was more a feeling hardly tapped and not fully accepted.

She had come to the library with a sense that she might find answers amidst Lord Raveh's books, but she did not grasp the questions aright enough to point her inquiry. And then, something in her needed to step back and play. For an exquisite half hour, Sky merely danced about, letting her eyes feast on bindings embossed with gold, titles in a dozen languages and scripts, the very orthography appealing to her taste for the far flung.

At the end of one wing of the library, Sky discovered a set of tall, stately doors inset with frosted glass that led out onto an observation deck. A marble table laden with papers had been set near these doors. It had been a while. Apparently the staff was unwilling to disturb the arrangement of the objects. Thick dust covered a chart of lost kingdoms that was drawn across the table. Someone had placed an apple upon the edge to keep it from rolling up.

Sky swept this long shriveled sentinel away with disgust. The late sun coming through the glass bathed her in soft, warm light that lulled her. Sky was not content, but the edge of latent anxieties was blunted. She opened the doors and pulled a high backed chair from the library to a small wooden deck and made herself at home. In the distance, a green plain dotted with a herd of ruminant enacted a brief peace.

After a time of reverie, Sky sensed the voice of one she had come upon before. "I'm fine," she said to the silence. "Feeling much better."

"Tricks," said the unknown friend.

"Well, why shouldn't I? It can't be grief or adventures all the time, now can it?"

The silence offered no opinion upon the matter.

"If I had coffee, it would be nearly perfect," insisted Sky. "And where are you anyway?"

"In the Solarium," said Naya. "The door opposite has a better view."

"I like this one," said Sky.

"Onahyu says that the stars come down to us. Because our temple is the house of heaven, the land is bountiful."

"I suppose that's so," said Sky.

"It is not so," said Naya. "I cannot tell them. Their serenity is false and it is too small."

"And so the Empire teeters, defeated by a clever girl," declared Sky.

"What is coffee?" said the voice.

An invitation

On the way back from Prince Raveh's library in the second best house, Sky took stock. She had friends. The Takashimas had accepted her into their home almost as a daughter. The Elder increasingly took Sky into his confidence and cared for her. Yet in spite of provision made by fate or chance, she still felt a stranger in a strange land. How could Elnaria be anything else? The flash of memories that sometimes came brought only more questions.

Vexing uncertainties aside, Sky sensed a soul she knew without naming that needed her with painful intensity. And this might be true of every lost child. How to answer for all that? And then, drifting in the air before her, a most unusual request, iridescent, part crystalline flower, part celestial bird, unclear if it were product of technology or rare species, perhaps both, spoke not in words, but images, relaying a place in a secluded park, the directions implanted into her with the instinctive knowledge of swallows who faithfully return to Capistrano.

It seemed to Sky that everything that had happened to her had led to this moment. She could not help smiling. A small joy fluttered with soft, downy wings in her heart. Of course, she had no expectation of what she should find, but that the abode of the Etheric should be just this, a kind of living chamber of umber and purple rising from a placid lake like an architectural tulip filled her with a ridiculously proprietary admiration.

It was almost a lovely joke, yet with just that touch of perfect wit, as if the entire presentation were the end of a long, meandering though pleasant conversation with a particularly generous and courteous friend. Such courtesy is often discerned only in retrospect, for it effaces itself, unwilling to make the gifted blush to be the recipient of extraordinary care.

When Sky stepped to the edge of the lake, a glimmering path emerged just above the water and led to a door ivory, golden, nearly transparent, so that she could not quite recall the moment when she passed through the threshold and entered within. The chamber turned out to be more spacious than one expected from an exterior view. It seemed an impossible combination, very bright, but also soft, never glaring.

As with everything surrounding the Vendakar, it had an odd aesthetic, not without allure. A staircase led to several levels, some of which were little more than decks with curious furniture, whilst about midway a substantial living space built along the periphery allowed one to take in the substance of the edifice. At the top, an ornate cube seemed to gently rotate as if it were a tiny celestial rose arising from an astral stem rooted in the waters below.

No servant came to greet Sky, but this did not surprise her. Whatever communal forms the Vendakar may lay claim to, they appeared to those in other realms as habitually solitary. And yet, after walking about a bit, Sky became self-conscious. She called out to no avail. A slight misgiving, an embarrassing qualm shadowed her delight. In order to repudiate the unwelcome feeling, Sky ascended the staircase, looking about at every level for some indication of solicitude or at least direction. None came. In the end, she stood in uncertainty and puzzled before the levitating cube.

"I am here. I have come," she said, feeling she might cry at any moment.

It was great relief, but also astonishing, when the cube glimmered and then without rebuff, appeared to descend upon her like the dawn. Before she knew it, Sky was inside the cube. Not a dozen feet away perhaps, the Vendakar sat with its back to her, in the eccentric way that a Vendakar sat, almost standing, almost vigilant, but in repose.

Her relief, however, was brief. For repeated appeals did not muster movement in the Etheric. It remained oblivious to her presence. At length, Sky crept closer where it became apparent the Vendakar was either in a state of coma or something worse than somnolence. Indeed, she had no idea what death might be for an Etheric. Upon a small table, there was the inward side of a mask from which Sky could already trace the lineaments of an enigmatic smile.

Part of her wanted to flee, but the more forceful desire could not stop her from peering into the face of the ambassador at which she gasped in shocked wonder. There was no face! Neither was there void. The mask had occluded what seemed a living window into galaxies and star clusters. The longer Sky peered into the faceless face of the Vendakar, the more she had to fight back the guilty feeling of impertinence, but she could not stop staring.

Then Sky felt herself rock forward and a great anxiety entered her, as if she would lurch irretrievably into the celestial abyss. Bolting backwards with a scream, somehow she was no longer in the intimate chamber. No one impeded her flight. Sky kept running and did not stop until she had entered the familiar territory of the brownstone. The Takashimas and the Elder were kind and solicitous of her day, yet she was afraid of their comfort, afraid to try and explain. How could she explain?

"I am lost, lost," she thought.

Living parable

The Elder had not thought of a destination, but his wise feet found the path. When he showed up at the church, he told Father Bunn that he was the Inspector of Bats. The priest chuckled at the joke and handed him the keys to the door leading to the tiered belfry and the upper levels. From there, it was an easy negotiation to the rooftop. The pitch was gentle enough. All around him, clock towers, parapets, and domes dotted the horizon whilst smokestacks breathed out billowing trails like the foggy breath of dragons. In his heart, the Elder knew that he must act, but what to do? He ached for his Sparrow. It was not possible to reveal to Sky what can only be learned by the living and the dying and both of those were inextricably bound and often confused with each other.

The Elder was reminded of a story he used to tell the girl from beyond the stars. They had both felt its poignancy, but at the time he had not been able to discover anything other than nature's sadness and a kind of dark joy. In Southeast Asia resides a unique creature known as the Atlas moth, the largest of its kind. The wingspan of the female can approach the diameter of a dinner plate. Their beautiful wings of sunburst reds and dusky umbers taper into a golden edge at the wingtips that resemble, as the Chinese name for them indicates, the head of a snake. The cocoons of the species, a finely spun brown silk, were often turned into purses.

But the wisdom of this serpent was elusive. A very short life span marked the pathetic and strange destiny of the species. Having reached the apex of its maturity, the Atlas moth lived but for a brief week or two. In that time, it would hope to call in its urgency a mate in order to forge a link in the fragile chain of life. Yet their coupling embrace could only hide an invisible kiss, for the Atlas moth has no mouth. Though oddly beautiful and touching, the story seemed shadowed by the perverse. Or perhaps there was a hidden teaching: the courage and beauty of the martyr embedded in the silent tango of their attraction. He thought of the friend who had once written that "what we yearn for is inaccessible and intangible."

"For the living do not thrive by bread alone," he said aloud. "There is much that I would tell you, Sparrow, but the most important can hardly be said. There is a wisdom that is supreme Nothing, what in the Kabbalah is called *En sof.* How I would bring you to that silence where the unsayable speaks."

Key of reverie

"I have a journey to make," he told her, then answered cryptically all her questions. The Elder asked Sky to feed the cat and Feirefiz, the Landseer dog that stared after him with slow, compassionate eyes. Then he followed a crazy quilt path that went through tall iron gates seemingly locked and dilapidated buildings from which the hushed shadows listened intently.

At each stop, he plucked a chord from the lyre Joe Nighthorse had made for him, opening locks with a key of reverie. *"Pour ouir dans la chair pleurer le diamante,"* wrote Mallarmé. "To hear in its flesh the diamond crying." When at last he was confronted by a sentinel, he explained himself. The soldiers of that realm were hard to construe. Their language was archaic or perhaps far flung or future, the Sha-rule. The sentinel was joined by another figure swathed in black and the two had a brief conference.

Then he was blindfolded and led a twisted path, always clutching with tender concern the sacred instrument of his craft. He lurched along narrow steps and uneven ground, his guides silent as death. And when at last he thought he must stop or grow sick, someone was removing the thick fabric binding his eyes. The light was dark violet in the garden that let onto an ornate pagoda.

"Go, if you must," called out a woman's voice already trailing away. "Within is the Chamber of the Spider."

The chamber of the spider

The walls were opaque and delicate, made to slide to fit the needs of occasion. The Elder waited for his vision to adjust to the dimmed light. The Chinonmi sat in the middle of the room upon a simple mat of reeds. Its long, stilt-like legs, the color of ivory, bent inward, so that the delicate feet joined in a praying campanile before the soft and rolling belly. With closed eyes, its head perched erect upon the slender, swan-like neck, it was impossible to tell if it slept, was lost in private contemplation, or perhaps listened in the hush, secretly wary.

The Elder maintained his stillness. Then, it began to unbend its legs with a slow, deliberate motion. Two pair continued to rest upon the abdomen, but the other two began to swing and maneuver towards some intricate design. A soft clicking sound accompanied this motion. After some minutes of this, the Elder discerned a thread of spun silk originating from the protected region. The creature's feet exhibited the dexterity of human hands, the top pair laboring with pointed needles of bone, whilst the bottom waited ready to shear the new made artifice at the proper time.

The Chinonmi hummed gently, its face calm and content. A light pattering of rain tapped upon the roof timbers. The Elder sighed and drew out from the folds of his robe his vatic instrument. "Lyre, my lyre," he said, "let's make a song of it." And he sang then, of the warp and the weave, of the web of time and the eternal love that danced along the glistening evanescence and made enduring the shadows of the mutable.

He didn't know if it would work. In fact, he rather doubted it. His head began to swim and a dark pain, like the pain of an invisible poker bore with sharp anger into his brain.

Song of the Angel Lion

And how little you know of kings. You think we are here to gather your praises? You believe we lap up your fawning, desire your lick spittle, your weeping cries and false kisses? A king is not fattened on such surfeit. I shall tell you what a king is like, though you will not believe it.

First, you must understand, nay, that is too much to ask — you must recognize the quandary of a king. A king is a particular name, an aspect of the lover, so if you would grasp the hem of the royal robe, you must discern the figure of one who woos, which has its comic moments. And if you really want to know, the mystery of the king is the same as the mystery of the woman.

Yes, *that* you did not count on.

Song of the Angel Bull

I was in the natal land, I had been sent by Noe.

The sharp blade, the blood translation.

So I was there when he journeyed to the House of Bread, to the stable,

to the Theotokos. I was there to speak blessing, to tell him that in the gift, all is fore given. I   don't think he saw me, maybe out of the corner of his eye, while he was

staring in awe, kneeling before the maiden and the small flesh, that strange creature God.

Song of the Angel Eagle

I remember the path in autumn. I am one with the others, grazing, and running, we feed, alert. There is a brook, cool, I drink. I remember an elsewhere. I am tall. I look out upon the savannah. I cherish the watering hole, the oasis. There are the succulent leaves. Later, the two-footed, the stargazers, they will make jokes about the courtesy of the prince to his consort, some humor about the survival of the fittest. How dim, there is the dance, but war is their own, the spirit bondage. I remember the warm earth, the kind warmth, the sun covering the earth, the pungent mysteries, and the tales we told our young, together, the maze of the warren. I flit and feather, I buzz and creep, I jump, and wait, flee and capture, feed and am fed.

"We," said the eagle.

Song of the Empress of the Sha-Rule

"These words reach you, if they reach you, from beyond the cauldrons of Hephaestus," said the mistress of the Convent of the Virgin's Smile. "Nothing constructed can take the measure. You cannot make the cure. Coming from nothing, you fear. You think your loves are forgotten, that it is a miserable curse, this life, this famished hope to love. You are yet hardly a whisper on the way to real. Bereft of the plenitude, you do not understand what love has done for you, the death at the beginning."

Night episode

It was a joke among the lads that Peacock was naturally abstemious when it came to the fleshpots of Egypt. Whether this was a virtue or not could be debated as reserve was simply part of Peacock's psychology. So it was rather an extended prank cooked up by Trajan to surreptitiously string his comrade along until he should just by happenstance discover himself on a foray into the precincts of the Willow World.

Slight inebriation and desire not to upset the convivial evening led Peacock to the alley that seemed to have appeared magically out of an apparent dead end. In retrospect, it remained a mystery how he had crossed the frontier. A smattering of guffaws and ribald congratulation from his peers advised him that his astonishment was considered a fitting conclusion to the gag. Soon, however, those habituated to such fare found better forms of entertainment.

Trajan stayed behind briefly and suggested a particular establishment. Even in his dazed condition, Peacock's aversion to purely hedonistic entanglements proved stubbornly beyond persuasion. And then the merchant was left in wary solitude. He wandered about harassed from balconies and barked at by dubious fellows in threadbare suits promising enchantment behind the grandiose façade of rundown townhouses unconvincingly made bright in a veneer of fresh paint.

At last, growing faint and baffled as to how to escape the erotic underworld, Peacock found himself staring at a storefront occupied by young women dressed up in costumes evidently designed to cater to a variety of fetishistic tastes. How long he stood before this display he could not say, only that the beauty of one woman overwhelmed him.

Her face was neither salacious, nor a hard mask. The innocence of her expression shocked Peacock. He began to cry not out of desire, but because she seemed an angel so lovely and heedless of her abandon. She must have sensed his compassion and his difference. The girl was first angered at his stare. Then to get rid of him, she stepped down from her platform, came out and pointed roughly how he might escape those environs.

In the morning, the whole episode was hardly real. Later, he recognized her as the wife of Vorhaas.

Lack of orientation

It is unclear, perhaps, what was intended by the invisible gesture of Venus' hidden arms. Ravaisson surmised they were reaching out towards Mars. The masculine energy might be characterized as outward looking, seeking to conquer, to build, to draw from the wilds new goods in order to expand the generosity of civilized living. A decadent, forgetful society might later refuse to acknowledge the heroism of such a quest, dismiss its labor as wicked acquisition and colonial despotism whilst subsisting on the patrimony now fallen into disrepute.

If Venus subtly beckons to her consort, her peace is surely not so dull and thoughtless for her love must raise the meaning of what is actually a mutual effort.

Peacock could not embody or even imaginatively grasp certain elemental realities known to any soldier thrust into the immediacy of violence and blood doom. Yet the merchant knew the life of risk. No mere burgher growing fat on the labor of others, no matter what others surmised, he, too, understood the rhythms of dangerous outer realms and the protected home. He calculated the odds. A ship might wreck. You could lose everything. You'd still have life, if it was worth the candle. The gambler who failed might not see a path forwards. The Stoics said one could always end the role that had become unendurable. Merchants who lost often became Stoics.

The second meeting with Lady Winterbourne did not come off. She'd asked him to come by in order to discuss "certain urgent matters." The letter was scented, floral with a trace of vanilla. Was there not, perhaps, a hint of apology? Some feminine scruple had kept her from candor in the initial meeting. He'd hoped that he might at last gain clarity about what precisely the Company could do for her.

He'd taken a taxi. The cabbie remarked upon the clear night sky and warm air. Peacock drifted into hazy reminisce and dozed briefly. The cabbie's old horse went at a good clip and soon the hansom cab dropped him near a park he knew well enough. He wanted a brief stroll to gather his thoughts, but as he walked the usual route to her exclusive neighborhood dismay took hold of Peacock. He was no longer following familiar streets. Something bizarre had occurred. There was nothing in the land he recognized.

The skies above were equally alien. *These stars are not my own,* he thought. *I am lost in someone else's destiny.*

I take you for north

Certainly, Peacock tried retracing his steps. This was no good, as he could not pinpoint a moment of transition from the ordinary to the thoroughly unfamiliar. Once thrown into the completely novel, internal map points become useless. Had the issue been trivial, exasperation would have been normal. As it were, panic and the continual temptation to disbelief took hold of his heart.

After a while, he sat down upon the ground and held his head in his hands, groaning. Then his experience told him to pick a direction, any direction, and hold to it. One might get nowhere, might possibly be setting off towards an uncrossable emptiness, but to vacillate and twist and turn at whim was to lose any semblance of reason and the ghost of decision.

So he looked up to the forbidding star field and chose one by intuition saying "I take you for north. Be a friend star, and I shall follow to the end."

Regard

As he trudged through a patch of cold earth covered in tough, short grass, Peacock kept peering at the bright star. It was, of course, some *pathos* in the human condition that caused him to hope for care. There was no reason to suspect the distant light he had selected at random should be aware of his plight or that pity might be thrown his way, yet he found himself emotionally tethered to the random stellar object. He did not exactly pray to it, but he courted its regard. By hoping in the star, he was able to keep his feet moving.

Presently, Peacock discerned a fuzzy dark blotch on the horizon which clarified as he came near into a thicket of trees that introduced the beginnings of a forest. He began to follow what might have been a trail, a path at least that cut through the foliage and extended out towards the tree line. Most probably this was not a sign of artifice, but erosion due to the long habit of deer and other beasts – assuming he was still on a world that countenanced deer.

A warm feeling rose in his breast and tears welled up in his eyes as he glanced to the star in thanks. And then somewhere in the depths of the forest, he glimpsed a sharp radiant flash of violet. Keeping to the path, it would appear and disappear according to his progress and the specific aspect of angle and pitch that qualified his location. It stood like a distant, enigmatic tower. *I will make for that*, he thought, and his pace quickened.

White

The challenge became more bracing. The world Peacock had left was yet warm and surrounded by familiar life that only now he missed. Peacock labored in his steps, beginning to freeze as the temperature dropped precipitously. And then, was it delirium? He sensed along with the gelid touch of icy air not exactly music, but the impression of some alluring lyric that was nonetheless foreboding.

When he was favored with a glimpse of the purple light, the sensation of enchantment became more distinct and intense and the counterweight of anxious concern receded. Through a thicket of silver birches, Peacock heard a distinct voice emerge singing a song impossibly severe yet equally dulcet. It was not a song ever heard in human society.

Peacock took a step away from the path and climbed higher into the hills, hearkening to the sound, sinuous, sweet, and delicious with a subtle, arctic tang. No longer conscious of himself, he abandoned precaution, followed as rapidly as the broken landscape would allow. The music was near. He could hear its lush, crystalline echo across the rocks in the cold stream that splashed as he crossed.

The ground was covered in white powdery snow where he was watched by fox and ermine, each matched to the pristine brightness. Close now, he came to the sheltered waters where he saw her bathing, the singer of impossible song. He did not even stop to ponder what manner of being takes languorous ease in such frigid conditions. Her raven hair swept out against milky skin. Was she beautiful? Perhaps, but he could not think beyond the intake of breath in her presence which was sharp, stringent, painful and pleasurable all at once.

She turned her head slightly. Did she acknowledge his presence or was it serene, stark indifference?

And what became of her

It may seem odd, but though Miss Cross was intrigued by the coming of Soren Blake, she did not pursue the subject with her father, nor did she make independent inquiries. She continued to follow the serene, if perhaps, somewhat prosaic path of her regular existence with no outward sign to distinguish that anything of note had happened to bestir the placid equanimity of her soul.

A careful observer, however, might have noted a slight neurosis in her manner. She would find herself turning and casting a glance, now and again, at the sound of footfalls, the opening of doors. And yet it was very slight. She wondered herself at this reticence in her character. She wanted to ask after the young man. What had become of him? No one seemed to mention him. The silence was so complete that she began to wonder if she had imagined him. Perhaps he was part of Sophia's dream.

Then why, after all, didn't she speak? Was she afraid that she had truly been under a delusion? No, she did not really believe this. She decided, after much reflection, that she had become unused to adventure and both desired and feared it. So in the end, she did nothing, though such procrastination can only be indulged for so long before it either becomes desperate and provokes change or at length turns into vague regret, a fading ripple upon the pond.

Years later, when her father died she acquired a substantial inheritance, suddenly indulged a zeal for travel, gathered animals from far places, and finally retired to a fine old house on a tall green hill.

Covert aspect

The closer he came to stand within the shadow of the tower, the more Peacock's desire to reach it intensified. There was, indeed, an affinity of passion between the song of the arctic siren and the lure of the strange edifice. Peacock was enchanted by the vision of the ice maiden. He kept thinking about her face, its undeniable attraction that was nonetheless a frightening beauty, almost inhuman.

And yet, as he replayed the gesture of the movement of her head, the way her face turned towards him without quite acknowledging his presence, he thought she was familiar. She was, in fact, suggestive of Lady Winterbourne, only transfigured and changed, severity heightened and altered into that odd combination of alien eroticism — as if the mysterious transgression of boundaries that had impelled him upon his singular quest had opened up to him an aspect of her person normally shunted off from ordinary detection.

Were it not for the intensity of his desire to reach the tower, Peacock might have pondered further this quality of dimensional aspect. His wonder did not attain explicit questioning whether or not such metaphysical plasticity could properly pertain to persons as such.

The end of the dream

The land, if anything, grew more exotic. The forests gave way to long plains sugared with a down of snow. Then the waters came into abundance and Peacock had to pick his way through channels deep and narrowly gashing glacial mounds. He was surrounded by snow and strange, smoldering fires, as if subterranean volcanoes were venting through gaps in the ice.

Rising in the distance, the flash of light was no longer intermittent. A ribbon of purple seemed to reach into the very sky. His progress became hesitant. The path devoured his resolve with pitiless requests. It asked for the heat of his meager blood and in return led him to a shelf of ice from which he could no longer retreat or ascend. The silver wolves howled. Their sorrowful keening rode upon the whipping wind that lashed his abject body trapped against the frozen ledge.

The merchant felt the frigid cold sapping his last reserves. He could no longer remember what it felt like to be warm. He had been ashamed to tell his friends, well, fellows at any rate, that the whole reason he had become a merchant was that as a boy, he had watched the great ships depart for strange lands and had dreamed that one day he would bring back something absolutely without price, beautiful and unique. And now, it had come to this . . .

In the luminescence above the purple tower, dark eagles soared. From its sheer face, a portal opened from which an orb emerged. He watched as in a dream the globe's slow descent towards him. Either his perspective was skewed by the gigantic dimensions of the edifice or the bubble grew as it approached. When it was hovering just before him, the orb became translucent. It was a dream he did not believe. A woman stood at the center of the circle, untouched by the wilds.

"Did you think, Mr. Peacock, that we are so small a thing that we should be content within the confines of a Regency Park townhouse when there are worlds upon worlds to explore? The spirit is not so mean," snarled Lady Winterbourne.

Quotation References

p.3: Péguy quote is from Péguy, Charles. *Notes on Bergson and Descartes.* Trans. Bruce K. Ward. Eugene, Oregon: Cascade Books, 2019.

p. 10: The quote from "There in the Hollows of the Wind" is from Bonnefoy, Yves. *In the Shadow's Light.* Trans. John Naughton. Chicago: Univ. of Chicago Press, 1991.

pp. 34 – 35: The quote is from Murnane, Gerald. *Border Districts.* New York: Farrar, Straus, Giroux, 2017.

p. 37: The quote from John 21: 24 - 25 is from Hart, David Bentley. *The New Testament, a Translation.* New Haven: Yale Univ. Press, 2017.

p. 47: The quote is from the traditional Latin Mass.

p.54: The quote is certainly by Thomas Traherne, though the exact source is unclear.

p. 70: The line about the Sabbath is from Heschel, Abraham Joshua. *The Sabbath: its meaning for modern man.* New York: Farrar, Straus, and Giroux, 2005.

p. 71: The quote about the need to speak is from Rosenstock-Huessy, Eugen. *Practical Knowledge of the Soul*. Trans. Mark Huessy and Freya von Moltke. Eugene, Oregon: Wipf & Stock, 2015.

p. 78: Fragment of Herakleitos.

p. 88: Quotation from the Song of Songs 5:1 KJV. *The Holy Bible: Old and New Testaments in the King James Version*. Nashville: Thomas Nelson Publishers, 1976.

p.159: The line from Borges is from the essay "A New Refutation of Time" found in Borges, Jorge Luis. *Labyrinths: Selected Stories & Other Writings*. Ed. Donald A. Yates & James E. Irby. New York: New Directions Publishing Corporation, 1964.

p.162: The quoted line is from Von Hügel, Baron Friedrich. *Letters from Baron Friedrich Von Hügel to a Niece*. Ed. Gwendolen Greene. Chicago: Henry Regnery Company, 1955.

p.178: The line of poetry is from Lee, David. *The Porcine Canticles*. Port Townsend, WA: Copper Canyon Press, 2004.

p.200: Unknown source for the quote about return to the divine Father.

p. 216: The first quote is from Hughes, Ted. *Tales From Ovid*. New York: Farrar Straus Giroux, 1997. The Bloy quote is likely a paraphrase from memory, original source unknown.

p.269: The line is from a sonnet by Mallarmé, "Méry, sans trop d'aurore . . ." Translation and source is unknown.